# *Sarah Goldman*

To Janet

Wishing you
all the best

[illegible]

# *Sarah Goldman*

A novel by

**Réal Carpentier**

Published 2019

*Sarah Goldman*



Published by Réal Carpentier
First Printing 2019

ISBN 9781094718071

This book may be ordered through booksellers,

www.amazon.com, or by contacting:

Réal Carpentier
815 Sterling Rd.
Sterling, CT 06377
realcarpentier@gmail.com

*This novel is dedicated to my lovely wife and children, without whose support, Sarah Goldman would not have come to life.*

# Present Day

I DO MISS SARAH. I was a fifty-four-year-old Catholic man, and she was a twenty-five-year-old Jewish girl. I ponder this as I look at these walls that have very little, by way of color, and permit me even less of a sense of being home. It is hell and back from home when one lives in a small room with one window, one bed, and a small table that holds insignificant articles like outdated magazines and my reading glasses. The curtains in the window are at least light and see-through to allow in the day. Who cares about night? I have a few pictures hung up; mostly family both living and gone. The most important pictures, I keep in my wallet where no one can take them by mistake, or otherwise. I also keep a very important note in that wallet as well. It makes me feel like I'm still alive. She wrote me notes; many, but this one I kept.

My students used to call me Dr. Dina, as I insisted. I would never allow them to call me Raymond, or Ray. As long as I made sure they pronounced it DEE-nah, I was happy. Some eluded confusion altogether by calling me Dr. D. Nevertheless, I'm a retired psychology professor. My tenure was mostly at NYU, but I also taught at the University of Texas in Austin and a couple of universities abroad. I studied at the Universities of Chicago, and

Cambridge, along with non-matriculating course work here and there throughout the United States. Suffice it to say I knew, and still know, my profession.

I was also quite the musician, if I may say so. I'm not sure I could still play with the same agility as before because of the reduced reflexes that inevitably afflicts one who is along in age. But I must try again someday. Guitar was my forte, along with a few other instruments that caught my interest and presented some form of challenge. But I could sing to beat the band. It would be too easy to bestow compliments upon myself were I not so humble, but boy could I sing! I can still hold a note, but I'm afraid my age caught up with that as well. But enough about that.

I really mean to recount a very special time in my life that I will bring to my grave. It was about twenty years ago, if I recall correctly. I was teaching a fifteen-week semester psychology course for a class of psychologists-wanna-be at NYU; students who thought they could make a difference in people's lives just by getting a degree, and some who registered in the class just to feel intelligent and important. Still, I would give them the benefit of the doubt. Far be it from me to make judgments on the intentions of others. In any respect, during all my years of teaching, I had always been confident that what I taught was sound and compelling. Semesters came and went, as did the students. New student faces every semester kept me loving that job, as they always kept it interesting. There was one student, however, who stood above the rest and it turns out, made a difference in my life. She had an impact on me from the moment she entered my classroom. I should have expected something extraordinary from that moment, but you never know, so you don't give it a second thought. You simply let life throw you a curve unexpectedly and deal with the consequences; sometimes good, sometimes bad, and sometimes magical enough to change your life. I remember those days. They were good and not so good days, but now I miss her.

# Week 1

## ~Meeting Sarah~

IT was a Tuesday evening in January. There I was, entering the halls of the University of New York where I taught psychology. It was a pleasant day for the winter season, and this was the first day of the spring semester. The sky was overcast as any normal winter sky, but still fairly mild. A light jacket would suffice. I made my way to the classroom in a hurried fashion because, God knows, I have a propensity to be a little late at times, and I was. I peered through the window of my classroom door as I approached it and could see there were students already in place at their desks wondering what kind of professor would put them through the torture of a graduate school education. I finally reached the door and entered.

I looked their way and nodded, and they returned the sentiment as I walked to my desk. It was a class made up mainly of young women, with a few young men here and there. I wondered if those young men were there because they knew psychology attracts young women; a possibility which was and is most probable. There were still a few seats unoccupied, but like me, some are always a little late. I apologized for having them wait for me but made sure to warn them against complacency; class, after all, starts promptly at 6:00PM. I then proceeded to get my papers in order, take a quick attendance, and handed the syllabus out to the class.

"Are there any questions on the syllabus?" I asked. There were none, as the syllabus contained all the necessary information everyone at this grade level was used to. "Please note my contact info, as well as the assignments due, and grading for those assignments." I saw in their faces the normal anxiety a student gets when realizing all the work that had yet to be completed by the deadlines. "I'll be distributing the details of reports, their formats, and other pertinent information at our next session. Please have the listed textbook in your possession by then." If I didn't know better, I'd say they were already apprehensive about the course. So, I began.

"Welcome to Mind and Society; course number 502. If you are in the wrong class, please see your advisors now. I don't want any disruptions during class." No one moved, so I continued, "As you can see in your syllabi, Mind and Society covers a variety of topics, including social cognition and behavior, emotions, development, personality, and psychopathology. All these topics will be covered separately or together. Moreover, lectures will go into depth about topics I think are important, or interesting, or both."

I looked around and found no reaction; normal first day of class, I thought. I began a little review.

"All of you have had psychology courses in the recent past. Who can give me some names associated with the founding fathers of psychology?"

A young lady's hand went up after a spell.

"Yes, Miss…?"

"Leah Ferguson, sir." She replied.

"Go, Leah."

"Well, I think one of the names was Wundt?"

"Wilhelm Wundt, was the name; very good." I said. "Anyone else?"

Another brave soul raised her hand.

"Yes?"

"John Watson?" she asked.

"Are you asking, or telling me?"

She gave a little smile and answered, "Telling."

"Correct, Miss…?

"Kayra Huda." She replied with a thick Middle Eastern accent.

"Very good, Kayra. Anyone else?"

Everyone stared blankly at me as though they thought it would be a very long course. So, I had no choice but to bolster their fear lest they started thinking this was going to be a glorified quiz show. I began my lecture.

"Some of the names that come to mind are William James, Sigmund Freud, Carl Rogers, and many others who contributed to the evolution of psychology. But I'd like you to consider where the term psychology originated." I'm of the opinion that a good foundation of knowledge is critical to a good education. "The term psychology finds its origin in Germany by a theologian named Philip Melanchthon. It was probably coined in the mid sixteenth century as psychologia; the word logia, meaning 'the study of', and the word psykhe, meaning 'breath, spirit, or soul'. And so, the 'study of the soul' came to fruition, and soon after, 'the study of the mind', which is the real definition of psychology, was recorded in 1748."

They were all taking notes, I was happy to see. I knew from being a student myself for many years, when you hear a date you had better write it down. As I was about to continue, a young lady walked in the door to totally disrupt my momentum. Yes, I was annoyed.

"May I help you?" I asked.

"Sorry I'm late." she said, "I just had my schedule changed. I need this course to satisfy my degree audit. I won't graduate without it."

"Are you telling me that you belong in this class, young lady?"

"Yes." she replied, "I didn't want to miss a minute of your lecture. Oh, I'm sorry. Here's my schedule." She handed me her schedule, while fumbling and almost dropping her books. "I just had it changed." she said.

I took her schedule without moving my eyes from hers to let her know I was displeased by her interruptions. She had long brown hair flowing passed her shoulders. Her body was slim and shapely, and she was dressed in modest attire. Her brown eyes were big and bright; one might have thought she had a frightened look, since they were opened wide enough to expose much of the white around her iris. She wasn't wearing much makeup at all, as she seemed to be naturally pretty with her fair skin and facial features having almost perfect shape. These are the things I first noticed about her. Her other attributes I would notice later.

Finally, I took her schedule to my desk, wrote her name in the roster, turned and said, "Take a seat, er…" I glanced back at her schedule, "Sarah."

"Goldman." She said.

"Take a seat, Sarah Goldman, and here's your syllabus." I handed her schedule back to her as well. "There's a report due next Tuesday." I added.

"Thank you, sir." she replied, as she took her place at one of the vacant desks.

Her voice was that of a young girl who sounded hardly of age to be working on a graduate degree. I had yet to learn of her intellectual ability but stumbling in a classroom late while fumbling with her books and schedule, didn't give me much of an impression she was anything in the way of being intellectually gifted. I returned to my lecture, while making sure to look annoyed so no one assumed I was a pushover.

"Now, where was I...? I hate interruptions. Oh yes...the origin of the word psychology. It's important in that it was first coined in Germany in another form. That country's contributions to the world should never be overlooked."

At that, someone raised his hand quickly. He took the bait, I thought to myself. One thing I had learned after years of teaching is you can initiate a discussion by asking questions, which hardly ever works, or you can initiate it by making a statement that is inherently debatable. I pointed to him to speak.

"Finally, someone who recognizes the contributions of Germany. I'm glad to hear someone say that." he said.

"Your name is?"

"Sean Russell." he said.

"To what are you referring, Sean? Why do you say that?"

"The so-called holocaust." he replied. "The Nazis cleaned up and everybody thinks that was a bad thing."

I wasn't sure what to make of what he said, but I had suspicions. I was almost afraid to ask the next question. "Can you elaborate, Mr. Russell?"

"Just what I said, the Nazis cleaned up. Nothing happened that shouldn't have happened. There was nothing wrong with Hitler and his philosophy. He was just misunderstood."

I had grown accustomed to controlling my facial expressions, as I had heard it all in my years as an educator. I prided myself in being hard and stoic. However, I was taken aback by his statements. I should have ended the conversation there but was too shocked and curious as to why someone would have that mindset. "Misunderstood?" I asked.

"That's right, misunderstood." he replied.

"How so?"

"He wanted to eliminate the communists and take back what Germany lost during the First World War."

"What about all the millions of innocent people who were massacred?" I asked.

"Hey, that's war. That's what happens in war." he answered.

I looked around the class and saw a few students looking at one another in disbelief and disgust. I decided to not enable him any further. I had never met a neo Nazi before, but knew of their prejudice viewpoint. I didn't know if Sean was one of them but the way he talked definitely raised some red flags all over the place. On the other hand, I had also met many people who were not willing to forgive Germany for the atrocities perpetrated by the Nazis. Germany was a totally different country with a different political agenda, then they were during the early years leading up to the Second World War. Regardless of what had just been said, that subject matter seemed to spark some interest in these otherwise apathetic students. I took advantage of that by elaborating on it and linking it to a psychological discussion, as I continued the lecture.

"It's hard to deny that one of the most terrifying moments in history, was the holocaust during World War Two, which was at the heart of that same country." I said. "In that period of time, about 6 million Jews were persecuted by the Nazi regime, as you know. That being said, here's a question I'd like you to consider, relative to those turbulent times. How do you think the Jews were affected psychologically by what was happening to them during the holocaust?"

I looked at my roster as I called their names.

"James?"

"They were scared." he said.

"Yes, of course they were scared. They were terrified, but what was their fear? They were afraid of what?"

I saw the next name on the roster.

"Caitlin?"

"They were afraid to die." She said.

"Yes, they were afraid to die. It was a terrible fear of death. Can you imagine waiting and knowing that you would surely die because you belonged to a certain group of people? I mean, all our lives we fear being made fun of, being shunned, being rejected by peers because we may not meet someone else's standards of what a human being should be. How much worse were *their* fear, knowing they would die; and a horrible death at that?"

My response, slash question, seemed to generate some discussion. I was happy to learn I wouldn't be spending fifteen weeks looking at blank faces if these kinds of discussions continued. It's amazing how the walls seem to close in on you when time appears to stand still, while trying to engage a group of young adults. All the while I had an engaging discourse with my students, Sarah remained quiet. I decided to connect with them a little more.

"Do you think the Jews would have persecuted an entire group of people as the Nazis did, if they had been part of the Nazi regime?" I asked. "Let's see…Alexandra?"

"No, I don't think so."

"What makes you say no?"

"They were a more benevolent people."

My next question was obvious to me. "Are you suggesting there were no Nazis who were benevolent? What about loyalty to government? Wouldn't some of the Jews have gone along with the movement, if for no other reason but to save their own lives?"

I hoped it wasn't too strong of an inquiry on my part so as to shut down further responses. It wasn't. These young men and women were engaged in a fluid discussion until the end of the session, which was what I had hoped for when I first stepped into the room; even if I *was* late to class. Some responses were good, and some were more superficial in nature. Sean never budged from his biased view, which I expected from my experience. He seemed to be a hard-nosed individual whose upbringing might have included his getting everything and anything he ever wanted from mommy. He was a good-looking young man, but his arrogance removed some of the good looks he was obviously endowed with at birth. Funny how some people look good until they make known their character flaws. In my experience, people like Sean who were biased about one particular group, also had prejudices about other groups as well. No matter. In the end, everyone was engaged in the discussion; all except Sarah Goldman. She was happy to sit attentively and take it all in.

Finally, time had elapsed, and I proceeded to dismiss the class. Happy with my first session, I turned around, walked to my desk, sat, and checked my phone for any messages, as the group was exiting the room. With my head down, I had no notion Sarah hadn't left with the others. She was the only student in the room with me. She approached me and began to speak.

"Doctor Dina?"

I looked up to see her. Her stance was far from intimidating, but resolute. I didn't respond right away, which made her begin to play with her hair as a little girl would when caught doing something wrong.

"Yes, Sarah?" I asked.

"You were wrong, sir."

"Excuse me?"

"You were wrong about the Jews' fear of death."

At hearing that, I stood. She didn't budge.

"Well *that's* interesting. How so?"

"They weren't afraid to die."

"I see." I paused for a moment. "Are you suggesting there was no fear at all?"

"No."

"So, you're saying there was fear?"

"Yes."

"Then if not death, what did they fear?"

"They were afraid to lose their humanity, which usually happened eventually. They feared being reduced to cattle; being butchered and burned as though they had no worth as human beings."

It was the first time since joining the class she had any indication of an opinion.

"What about death?" I asked.

"Death was accepted because there was no way to stop it." She said.

"I see."

I was waiting for more.

She continued, "And your other question concerning their ability to do the same as the Nazis?"

"Yes?"

"The Jews would not have done the same thing."

"What makes you so sure?"

"The Jews believe in God. As such, they could not have gone against their conviction. It would have been as though they were killing themselves."

"You make some very profound statements." I said, "You seem to be almost intuitive with regards to that particular subject matter. Is it safe to assume that you're of Jewish descent?"

"Yes. My grandmother, Dalia, was the second to the youngest child to be captive during the war. She was also waiting to die, but she survived. So, I've had firsthand accounts of what it was like, and how people thought and felt."

"I'm sorry to hear that." I was sincere. "I'm also sorry you had to hear Sean talk the way he did."

"Oh, I'm sure he just wanted some attention. I'm sure he doesn't really believe all that."

"Still, allow me apologize for him."

"Thank you. You're very kind."

"But very wrong?" I asked, smiling at her.

She seemed more relaxed at that point; no longer curling her hair with her fingers.

"No, we're all trying to figure things out." she replied. "We live a life of asking questions and learning. We just need to make sure we learn the truth."

I couldn't help but dig deeper into her observation, if for no other reason but to play devil's advocate. This young stumbling woman, as I had seen her walking in, was not on par with my first impressions of her. Upon conversing with her, which was almost a debate of sorts, I came to the realization she was much more than the awkward vision I saw, upon her entrance into the room. I pressed on, knowing this was the most in-depth discussion I'd had in this class so far.

"But how do we discern what the truth really is? I mean, all our lives we're taught that we can achieve anything if we only have faith in ourselves and keep trying. As we get older, we come to recognize that that's clearly false. Don't you agree?"

She looked at me in reply as if to say 'gotcha'.

"Yes, I do agree that that's clearly false. But the opposite is clearly true; that if you don't have faith in yourself and don't keep trying, you'll never achieve anything."

We smiled at each other for a while; both waiting to see if our deliberation would turn into a battle of wits. I decided it shouldn't.

"You're a very perceptive woman, Sarah." I meant that explicitly. "I have to admit it'll be a pleasure having you in class this semester."

"Thank you. I'm looking forward to it." She spoke with sincerity and I thought I noted a hint of admiration.

"So, I'll see you next Tuesday, then?" I asked.

"Sooner if it's at all possible. I'd like to ask you to be my mentor for an empirical research I'm doing for another class. We were told to find a mentor, preferably within the faculty."

Here we go; more responsibility. I always thought it would be nice to go above and beyond the call of duty, but I had had it with mentoring. It never failed. Each semester was the same, 'Can you be my mentor?' or, 'I won't make the semester without your help.' At first it was a good thing, but it quickly got old. Some hardly put any effort into what they were doing, I might add.

"Why me?" I asked.

"Because my professor told me that you're the most knowledgeable on quantitative and qualitative research, and statistical formulas. I hope you have the time."

What can I say? I'm an old softy when it comes to this; just can't say no. So, I replied, "I always make the time for any of my students with such high prospects." What a lie, I thought.

She giggled and said, "Great! I need to come up with an introduction and methodology first. Can I stop by your office this weekend?"

"Let's meet in the library on Friday at noon."

I've always been of the prudent opinion that a teacher should never be alone with a student if they can help it. I explained specifically where to meet, and she agreed. With that, she wished me a good evening and went on her way. I sat back down at my desk for a while just pondering all we talked about; how she seemed like such a naïve little girl, but suddenly became willing to test how far we could debate. I'm not so egocentric as to believe she wouldn't have won such a debate, but then again, I can certainly hold my own. One can only speculate about incidental outcomes such as these, but it's always fun to imagine.

I looked about the classroom and saw how empty it was, but also knew the potential pedagogical power within its walls. I stopped to consider, as I do at every start of each semester, how I could be the driving force behind that power. I also thought about the rest of the class and the answers they provided, which were the catalyst for much discussion in our three-hour time slot. How wonderful it is to be open, I thought, and willing to inquire about such things; to learn and teach. God knows I experience my share of learning as much as they. These young men and women would someday be great psychologists, engineers, technicians, counselors, or whatever they wished to be. If only they had faith in themselves and kept trying? I didn't really believe that for one minute. As I said, one can only speculate about incidental outcomes such as these, but it's always fun to imagine.

## ~The First Session~

The rest of the week, up until our first mentoring session, was uneventful; the normal drudgery of correcting assignments, creating lesson plans, making sure my deadlines were met according to a tight schedule. Fifteen weeks seem long when you're in class, but they really aren't; especially when you have snow days, Spring break, midterms, and finals. Effectively, we only had twelve weeks of class time. At least the weather was fine for a winter season, so snow days seemed unlikely.

We met as planned in the Elmer Holmes Bobst Library on Washington Square that Friday at noon. I loved that library; all twelve stories of it. It was massive with plenty of space for leisure reading, computer centers, seminar rooms, periodicals and newspapers, dissertation writers' rooms, you name it. I surprised myself by not being late and waited for her at the designated area. It was a bit cold that particular day, but I didn't mind waiting. When she arrived, she looked different from the way she looked in class. Maybe it was due to not being in a rush and having to disrupt the class after it had started, for which I forgave her. Or maybe it was the way people look when they're outside in the sunlight, as opposed to being corralled up in a room under rows of fluorescent lights. Regardless, I thought she looked more at ease with me and, frankly, more radiant. We shook hands and she apologized for being late. I told her it was quite alright, but we both knew better.

We didn't say much on our way to our destination, where I hoped our mentoring session would not be a waste of time. I've had students who said they were willing to learn, only to find out they weren't. I hoped this time was the real thing and she was willing to put the effort into the work she was responsible for. My life was too busy for anything else. We settled on the lower level 1 computer center, for our initial meeting and gathered the information we needed to begin. We soon moved to the graduate study room located on the same level, where we began discussing details of her paper.

"The null hypothesis is the hypothesis the researcher tries to disprove." I explained.

"Okay and where should I put my variables?"

"Since it's experimental research, you can put both the dependent and independent variables in your hypothesis."

Funny how you recall these little details, as insignificant as they are in the scheme of life. They say you retain ninety percent of what you teach others. It doesn't surprise me, then, that I could still recall all this information. I had taught it enough years. In any event, the session went smoothly, and she seemed to grasp the core concepts of the subject matter. There were plenty of times when we got off topic, to be sure, but we got some work done. We worked for about ninety minutes and called it a day. It's amazing how your body tells you when you've had enough of something. Besides seeing blurry and experiencing a lack of concentration, you simply get uncomfortable sitting in the same seat and position. We both started feeling those same symptoms and decided to quit.

We were both a little hungry, so we made our way to the snack lounge near the stairwell at that same floor level. It was a little loud in that area, but not so overwhelming. It could have been a little quieter for my taste, as well as a little less congested with people I didn't want to be around. But it is what it is, and one has to bear the moments we don't necessarily enjoy. There, we continued with small talk and trivialities. I noticed she seemed to smile more, and her body language was more relaxed. I don't mind taking some credit for that. I hoped she would bring that kind of casual composure back to class with her, next Tuesday.

We ate a little. She ordered first, after making sure they had what she liked. Hers was a kosher diet, and her order was specific. She was adamant about not straying from her cultural upbringing; inquiring if they served things like matzah, brisket, or knish. She finally settled on something, and I simply ordered a couple of hot wieners with the works.

After enough eating and conversing, we decided to part ways with the understanding that we would continue with her mentoring sessions. I thought the first session was a successful one and wasn't disappointed with her responsible attitude. I must say it was unexpected and an encouraging change from what I'd been privy to in my not-too-distant past. When all was said and done, I reminded her of the report due Tuesday, and she thanked me again, as we left the library.

On my way home I had the radio on, listening to classic rock. I wasn't and still am not one to listen to contemporary music, with all of its fake samples and loops. At the news break, the meteorologist announced a

Nor'easter heading our way, which would arrive within the next few days. Great, I thought sarcastically, winter's here. Up to that particular week, it was quite a mild winter; almost feeling like the seasons had not changed at all. It felt like autumn was still in the air, waiting for that obligatory solstice to happen.

When I got home, I performed my regular routine; hung up my coat, went to the bathroom, and things of that nature. I lived alone, so needless to say, I made my own food and ran my own errands. I didn't have anyone to share my life with except my two boys, whom I didn't see much. One had a family of his own up in Vermont. He had a very pregnant wife who wanted to live near her folks. The other was trying to make a go of his acting career in LA. I missed them both and would have given anything to see them more often, or in the case of my actor son, see him at all.

Later that afternoon, I started getting my work together for the coming week of class. Looking in various places for misplaced papers, books, notepads, and writing implements, I noticed a small piece of paper tucked in my school bag. I knew it wasn't anything of mine, since I don't own any purple notepads. I picked it up and read it. It was a note from Sarah that simply read, 'Thank you' with her initials written below. She undoubtedly snuck it in at the snack lounge when I wasn't looking. I immediately thought of how nice that was. I like how some people, mostly women from my experience, seem to have the good sense to do nice things like that. I would never in a million years have thought of leaving a thank you note to someone, lest they might consider me a changed individual from my aloofness; a personal attribute, I was proud to be gifted with. Maybe, that's what makes people who they are. You expect things like that from some people and expect the opposite from others. I felt a little guilt when I threw the note away, but really, what would I do with it? I would acknowledge it next time I saw her. That thought made me feel a little less guilty. I have no doubt a woman like Sarah would probably have cherished it for years; kept it in some little trinket box that had sentimental value because it was passed down to her from her great grandmother or something. Sometimes I wish I had those sentiments.

# ~Church~

I usually went to church on Saturday afternoons to avoid rushing on Sundays. After all, Sunday is a day of rest. So, I kept my regular routine of visiting Saint Joseph's Church in Greenwich Village for the Saturday vigil. I tried to practice my catholic faith even if I was not perfect and made my share of mistakes, which are imperfections I still struggle with. The pastor talked with me many times in the past about joining the choir, but I'd have none of that. Don't get me wrong, the choir was excellent. I just thought my voice wasn't needed. They sounded great without me. I always had a problem with taking part in something, when it didn't matter if I showed up or not. I know it's the wrong attitude, but that's the way I've always felt. I also know what everyone says about attitudes like that; 'if everyone thought that way, there'd be no choir at all'. I always dismissed those as just words to make you feel guilty, because not everyone has the same attitude. The fact there was a choir, was proof of that. However, if everyone *did* have that attitude, there would be no choir, and I could become the sole singer whose presence would suddenly matter. Anyway, during a moment of prayer and reflection, I prayed for a successful school term. I also prayed that the coming Nor'easter wouldn't be too bad.

# Week 2

## ~Snow Day~

THE Nor'easter was bad. It was a blizzard that started around midday on Monday and didn't end until midday on Tuesday. I spent most of that time reading and writing, while watching the storm from my window. It was a beautiful sight. The flakes took me to a place that was familiar and forever ingrained in the recesses of my mind. I was seven years old and looking at the falling snow, out of one of our very dirty and grimy windows. I didn't mind pressing my nose against it, dirty as it was. What seven-year-old even cares about such things? There wasn't much traffic on the road, but once in a while, a car would try desperately to make it up the hill that was visible from our house just a few yards away. There were also pedestrians and kids playing near the road with their sleds. Even at age seven, I knew that was foolish but wanted to be out there with them regardless. I can still feel the draft from the uneven and partly damaged window sash and hear the squealing of the car wheels as they labored tirelessly to gain traction on the snowy road. The snowflakes appeared blue and were being tossed around by the wind, which sounded like a hungry howling wolf anticipating a long famine in the wake of a long and wintry season. There was a chill in the air causing goosebumps to grow on my arms, as the night would eventually overtake the feeling of play and give way to the sensation of sleepiness. But until that time, I enjoyed the view and the sounds of winter. Suddenly, there was a very long car horn blaring, followed by a dull thud type of sound. Upon hearing the commotion, my parents ran to the window to see what had happened. Next, my father ran out the door to render assistance to the victim of the accident who was lying in the road unresponsive from the impact with the vehicle. I watched through that window as my father tried hard to help. I could hardly see, as the snow was falling and drifting with the wind and made the scenery look like a white canvas waiting to be the instrument of its artist's new creation. After quite a while, I heard sirens and saw more commotion, as my father returned with the news that the person in the road appeared to be dead. I had witnessed the whole thing; the accident, my father trying to save a life, and finally the exhausted look on my father's face that spoke of a feeling of helplessness and despair. I would remember that day for the rest of my life, as I was brought back to that very moment during the Nor'easter. But I tried hard to put it in the back of my mind, partly because I had work to do but mostly because I wanted that thought to go away.

We had an accumulation of more than fifteen inches, after all was said and done. NYU, as well as all other local schools were under the same blanket of snow, which prompted an announcement that all day and evening classes would be cancelled for Tuesday. If my son Joey had been around, he would have joked about how I never work. That's what he used to say whenever I had some time off from school. He would kid around with me, saying I was always home because of snow days, holidays, vacation days, personal days, this day, and that day. God, I miss him.

On Tuesday, after the storm and cleaning off the snow from the driveway, I had a little time to myself since classes were cancelled. I'm sure many people appreciated their time off as well, after having survived Thanksgiving and Christmas. I was hoping for some inspiration for my next project. So, I decided to look over one of my empirical research papers entitled, "Development and Validation of Psychotherapy and its Working Alliance." I had published it in APA's Journal of Counseling Psychology a few years back. Exciting, right? My family was more than impressed when I got it published. Likewise, I would be lying if I said I wasn't as well. As I read it, however, I started questioning whether anyone else had read it or even cared about the data and the core concepts of the study. I couldn't help but wonder if publishing it, or even writing it wasn't a waste of time.

Time for me, was an enigma. At fifty-four years old, I often looked back on some moment in my life and pondered this whole notion of wasting time. I would think back about five years and wonder what I might have done differently to have a more meaningful time or improve the quality of my life. Then I'd start thinking about five years from then. Would I ask the same question? Would I think I wasted five years of my life? I often mulled over what I could do to make sure those questions were met with a positive response. What is it that defines good quality of life, I thought? Is it by contributing to improving society as a whole? Or is it simply to make your own happiness a priority? If it's happiness that matters, what if you're happy just sitting there doing nothing but watching TV for a length of time? Is that a waste? What if composing music is your thing; music that goes nowhere and doesn't get recognized as anything worth listening to even if it's great? Are addicts happy? They're certainly indulging in behavior that satisfies them, albeit with bad consequences. But they live for the moment and that's okay with them. After five years of addiction, I wonder if they would think they wasted all that time. Or would someone be happier doing good for mankind? Were the saints and martyrs happy with their lives? Or did they hope for a better life someday that never came? People say to enjoy each moment of life. I found that hard to do, especially when some moments were not worth enjoying. So what's a person to do to make sure they live life to their full potential? I don't know. I guess it's up to each individual. My advice would be to laugh a lot; I mean the real belly laughs that bring on an almost uncontrollable urge to pee. As for me, I wrote empirical research papers that no one read, and I sometimes questioned the purpose and value of their publication. These days, I'm okay with having written and published them.

As I was reading my publication, my mind wandered like that as it would when I was in high school struggling to get through the required reading books no one liked. I wasn't sure if I zoned out because the paper was boring, or if I needed a break. Nevertheless, I kept reading and wandering.

I thought about my new classes, and the students. They were the normal students you'd expect from a psychology course; the preppies, the nerds, the ones who didn't want to be there. Whoever and whatever they were, I seemed to connect with them. I started thinking about the elusive magic that results in a teacher connecting with students. No one can define it. You either have it or you don't. I think part of the equation is to find something you might have in common. Whatever the equation might be, once you can connect with them, you own them, and they trust you. Thereafter, they don't mind learning whatever you can throw at them.

It was during this day-dreaming sequence that my phone received a notification indicating I just got an email. I looked and was surprised to find it was from Sarah. She undoubtedly made good use of the syllabus I had given her. I would have liked to think she referenced it for more than to get my email address; for instance, to get acquainted with the reports and projects, for which she would eventually be responsible. Nevertheless, she was wondering if we would still have our session on Friday, since class was cancelled on that Tuesday. I replied and told her it was probably a good idea to do so. We made plans for Friday at noon of that week; same place. At least it wouldn't be a wasted week for me, I told her. After our plan was settled, I decided to put away my paper. Enough time was wasted, I thought. Inspiration would have to come at a later time when my heart was in it. It was time to get down to the most important business at hand. I turned up the heat in the house, made myself a bag of popcorn, and sat down with my feet up watching old reruns of Seinfeld and Gilligan's Island for hours. I laughed until I peed.

# ~Joey Calls~

My musicianship was put to good use. On Thursday of that week, I took my guitar to a local senior center and entertained the residents. I played quite often in nursing homes. It was the most satisfying aspect of my musical work I had ever experienced. To say I was using my talent for the greater good, would be an understatement. The residents loved it. It made a difference in their lonely lives. At least that's what they said, and I had no reason to doubt it. They made it known to me but they didn't have to, because I could see it in their faces. Those places were all the same. It didn't matter if they were called nursing homes, health care centers, or living centers. They were all the same. Upon entering the facility, you could smell something unrecognizable. It wasn't a pleasant smell, nor was it an objectionable one. It simply revealed a uniqueness of the place that reflected the circumstances and manner of the residents. If you could smell loneliness, I guess it's possible it might have the same smell. The walls with their insipid colors, had pleasant picture frames that gave the hallways a false sense of happiness in most cases. The staff always tried to make the activities room a little cheerier than their bedroom, but it didn't seem to help. The residents all had the same old sad faces; that is, until I started playing and singing. I played songs they recognized; songs they grew up with, and songs they could sing along with. They sang with all the I-remember-when-I-was-a-kid enthusiasm they could muster from their weakened state. It was beautiful and rewarding from my personal perspective because they loved it. I could see it in their faces.

Anyway, I had a great time entertaining them and they seemed to enjoy my being there as well. I used to try to look at them while I played, that is, when I was playing a song that didn't require too much concentration. The look on their faces said it all. They were happy to have me play for them and they seemed to live in the moment. I wondered about all of the things they had seen in their lifetime; all the pain, joy, laughter, fear, feelings of helplessness, and all the emotions that we all have in common. I wondered if time had hardened their hearts, or if some of them reluctantly surrendered in defeat after years and years of trying to attain happiness, to no avail. All these things, I wondered. But the most important thought at the time was knowing they were happy I was there to be their outlet for a little while. After the gig, I received many compliments as I packed up to leave. What greater reward was there?

Later that evening would have been matter-of-course, were it not for a phone call I received from Joey.

"Hi dad." the voice from the other end of the phone said, wistfully.

"Hey Joey, how are you?" I replied.

"I'm fine. Just wanted to call and see how you're making out with the storm."

"It wasn't too bad clearing it out with the snow blower, but classes were cancelled just after the second week of the semester. Can you believe it?" Just then my attention turned to his wellbeing after hearing the tone of his voice. "Are you okay? You sound a little down or something."

I was genuinely concerned. I didn't really want to waste time with small talk with my own son. If there was a problem, I wanted to know about it.

"Yeah, everything's fine. I guess I just miss you, that's all." he replied.

"I miss you too; and Derek too."

Did he really say, 'that's all?' Missing a family member is not trivial. If I knew him well, and I did, I'd say he didn't want to make a big deal of it. But I knew homesick when I heard it. St. Johnsbury, being forty-five minutes from the Canadian border, is a long way from New York in the winter. I also didn't mean to mention his brother Derek, since they hadn't spoken in a couple of years. Derek left for L.A. in pursuit of unlikely happiness despite my objection. He and Joey had it out before leaving because of an incident that happened with Joey's wife. I didn't think they would ever reconcile. I was right.

"So, no work again, huh?" he quipped.

He completely ignored the mention of his brother.

"That's right." I replied. "You chose the wrong profession. Education is where it's at."

"No kidding. You guys take snow days in the summer."

That was a good one, and almost true. I laughed, which made both of us try to top it with something funnier. That usually never works. After a few failed attempts at being funny, I decided to change the subject.

"When are you coming over with the family?"

"We'll have some time around April, hopefully. Francine has some vacation time coming and we're going to try to schedule it with mine."

"How is she doing with the pregnancy? She must be in a hurry to hatch."

"Yeah, she's finding it tough to take care of the baby with another one on the way, but it's all good."

"Good, I'm starting to miss you guys. How's the weather up there?" I was hearing myself engage in small talk without realizing it.

"Typical for up north."

"Listen, I really hope everything is fine. You'd let me know if anything was wrong, right?"

"Everything's good, dad. Just wanted to check in on you, that's all."

"Thank you. I'm fine."

As was usually inevitable, he brought up the subject he usually mentions when I hear from him.

"You should call mom, dad." he said.

"I don't think so. She's pretty well decided about things."

"Just call her up and explain things. It wouldn't hurt to explain things."

"Well, maybe." I replied, knowing I wouldn't.

"You shouldn't be alone, Dad."

I felt his concern; even over three hundred miles away. But getting back together with my ex-wife was not an option, even if it was hard for Joey to accept.

"Well I appreciate that. How's the baby?" I said, trying to change the subject again.

"Diaper rash cleared up, and we're finally getting some sleep again."

"That's good. I know it's tough when they're young, but it gets better."

"I hope so."

We talked for about ten minutes on a variety of subjects including his job, her job, and prospects for advancement. No one had gotten the flu so far, so that was good. He made sure I was feeling fine and asked about my classes so far. After we were satisfied everyone was doing relatively well, it was time to end the conversation.

"Alright dad, gotta go." he said.

"Okay, Joey. Love you."

"Love you too."

"Bye."

"Bye." he said, then hung up.

After hearing the click on the other end, I hung up too. If anything sounded like small talk, it was our parting words. I guess even trivial-sounding talk is as sincere and important as it can be. Nevertheless, I was happy to hear from him. It made my day. If only I could have heard from Derek too. I hoped he was doing well.

## ~Natania~

Friday morning was as mild a day, as the Friday before. I didn't want to eat breakfast at home, so I got ready for the day and left to eat at a local diner. I stopped to get the morning paper and made my way to the Hu Kitchen in Union Square. Looking at the menu, I couldn't help but wonder if people thought NYU professors made so much money as to be able to pay eight dollars for a bowl of oatmeal. I finally settled for some pancakes and coffee.

I read the paper as I ate. There were the normal headlines that made you depressed if you thought about them too much. The actual news articles weren't as bad as the headlines themselves, most of the time. One headline in particular caught my eye. It read, *High School Teacher on Administrative Leave.* It seems this teacher was caught touching one of his students inappropriately. Reading the article made me cringe. I thought how devastating it must be to flush your career down the toilet just because you're too weak to refrain from doing something unethical, if not illegal. I was glad it wasn't me. At any rate, what would have been really devastating, would have been to meet up with some of my former students I didn't care for. Fortunately, that didn't happen. I sat there for a while reading the paper, and before I knew it, it was time to meet Sarah.

We met at the same location as the week before, made pleasantries, and proceeded to the spot we had found the previous Friday. Her clothes were still modest, and her hair was worn differently, but I didn't know what was different about it. I was astute enough to know that certain people noticed details, and some could only see the big picture. I was the latter, and still am. However, I was not astute enough to know what was different about her hair.

I acknowledged the thank you note I had found in my bag and said she was welcome. She looked at me perplexed and asked what note I was talking about. We sat there, silent. She stared at me waiting for an answer, as I was trying to figure out who might have left a note if it wasn't Sarah. That's when I saw her lips curl into a smile, which made me feel like a fool. I was taken in by a student of mine, who just a few years before was an adolescent, impatient about graduating high school. That broke the ice for the second session.

This meeting was a lot more relaxed than the first. We, of course, engaged in the obligatory small talk that makes me want to crawl away. The only thing worse than small talk is when someone exclaims that a particular situation is awkward. Nothing makes you feel more awkward than when someone vocalizes it. Fortunately, neither of us said such a thing. We discussed her paper and covered most of what needed to be covered; the abstract, the introduction, methods, results, discussion, references, and so on. We also covered details on pagination, spacing, tables and figures, and most particulars of APA formatting. We would eventually get into a more important discourse, though; our families and life in general. I didn't normally talk about such things with just anyone, much less one of my students. But somehow when we talked, it was okay to get personal. I don't know why; I just know it happened that way. Like I said, I don't pay attention to details much. I guess it helped a little when she dropped all her books on the floor. There's nothing like a good laugh to get the ball rolling. We even got some dirty looks for being too loud, which made me feel like a little kid getting away with something I shouldn't be doing. I helped her pick them up, of course, and would have felt bad for her had she not laughed at herself. It was a decisive moment that changed our relationship.

After the work was done, we made our way to the snack lounge, as we did before. She ordered and I just had a coffee, having had breakfast not long before. We sat at a table we found in a section that was not too congested. She seemed to be much like I am when it comes to crowds; not interested in hearing too much noise or hearing some pretentious loud person who has an orgasm from hearing themselves talk. We sat and began small talk at first, but then our conversation evolved into something that would find us divulging some personal information about ourselves. I'm not sure how it happened. Those things just happen on their own. I think she might have seen a picture of my sons in my wallet or something. Before I knew it, I was talking about my family, which led her to talk about *her* personal experiences.

"These are my two sons." I said, as I showed her pictures.

"Nice family. Are they from around here?"

"No, one is up North with his family, and the other is out West with friends."

I didn't know how many friends Derek had in L.A., but I had to say something about him. I hoped he *had* friends.

"Cool," she replied, "and you?"

"Me?"

"How did you become such an important figure at NYU?" She no longer spoke as a younger student of mine, but rather as a colleague; someone my age, perhaps.

"I guess I was always fascinated with the way people are." I said. "People are strange. If you don't end up studying them to reach some personal growth, you end up hating them."

That made her laugh, which was not my goal. I was absolutely serious. When I saw her laugh, however, I laughed too. I had to go along with such a witty remark I hadn't intended to make. Yet, I think the way she laughed was what made *me* laugh. Sometimes someone will laugh not because something is funny, but rather to acknowledge a situation as being fun. Moreover, she seemed to laugh with her eyes. Even when the laughter subsided, her eyes were smiling. She continued eating, while we talked.

"What else do you like to do, Dr. Dina?" she asked.

"I'm a musician."

She seemed excited at the prospect. The one thing I noticed about people is they get excited about certain things. If you say you're a musician, eyebrows go up followed by, 'Really?' Same thing happens when you tell someone you're a professor. She didn't disappoint.

"Really?" she asked excitedly.

"Yes, really." I said with a smile.

"What do you play?"

"Mostly guitar."

"Do you play anywhere in public?"

"I do some gigs at senior centers a lot."

"Cool."

"I played a gig yesterday, in fact, at Our Lady of Pompeii Senior Center right here on Carmine Street."

"Really? How'd it go?" she asked.

"It was great!"

I told her some generalities about what it's like to play these places; how you don't get the same type of reaction as you get when playing a nightclub or restaurant. I explained that the entertainer at those centers shouldn't expect to hear roaring applause or get standing ovations.

"The residents appreciate and love the music even more than those people who frequent other establishments." I said. "You see it in their eyes." Much like I saw laughter in Sarah's eyes, I thought to myself.

"That's so nice."

"And you, Sarah?"

"Me?"

"What do *you* do with your time?"

"Not much; just study and work."

"What kind of work?"

"I tutor." she said. "I'm tutoring someone with special needs right now. Her name is Natania. She struggles with writing, so I help her out a couple times a week."

"Oh, nice. How did you get started with that?"

"One of my professors knew I was looking for some work. She suggested I look into SCO Family of Services. So, I did and got a job as a tutor."

"Congratulations. You like it?"

"Yeah, but it's depressing sometimes." she said, as she started curling her hair with her finger.

"How do you mean?"

Having finished eating, she pushed her plate aside and began explaining. "Well, Natania is in her mid-forties. She's attending BMCC here in Manhattan. I guess her counselor or advisor from SCO suggested she go to a community college and work towards getting a good job. I was assigned to her because of my writing skills." She paused and stared at her plate for a moment; not really looking at it, but rather seemed to be pondering something. After a moment, she continued. "Anyway, I got a hold of one of her previous papers she had to write for a class. She wanted me to read it. It was a paper she had to write on life-changing moments. Needless to say, she wrote about things in her life that should be kept out of a class assignment. She doesn't know any better. When I read it, I learned all about her."

I gave a look of acknowledgement, as she seemed to hesitate. She then decided to share what she had learned about Natania, which is not the most ethical thing to do if one wanted to get technical. However, I guess some things are more important than being ethical at a given time. She continued to confide.

"She's been a special needs person all her life; since she was a kid. She was in special classes at a young age, and all that. The kids in regular classes always made fun of her and the other special kids. They didn't just make fun of her, they picked on her and hurt her. She's had to deal with that all her life. Her mother died when she was very young, and she didn't know her father. She wrote about her two sisters who seem to live a normal life. They take care of Natania as much as they can. I guess they're the ones who got her into family services."

"Seems a sad life." I added.

"It certainly does."

"How is she doing with the course work?"

"Not good at all." She continued, "I basically write the paper for her. She just waits there with her fingers ready at the keyboard and waits for me to tell her what to write."

"So, she's not learning a thing?"

"No, she's not. I tried the other day to pull some knowledge out of her, but she just looked and waited for me to tell her the next move. I went over the scenarios of this particular section of the paper. I went over details. I explained and compared a couple of possibilities she should consider next for the paper. She seemed to understand all I was saying, so I told her to go ahead and write it. She couldn't. She didn't know what to write."

"So, she's not going to get anything out of her education." I said, stating a fact rather than asking a question.

"No, she's not. I don't know why someone would have suggested she go to school if they knew it would be a misuse of time and resources. Her education is coming from state subsidies, I bet. It seems a loss.

"So, you think her education is a waste?"

"It seems it." She was deliberate with what she said next. "Is it ethical for someone to guide another person in a particular direction, knowing full well that that person won't be successful? It seems cruel."

I replied with a question of my own. "But would it be ethical to not guide someone towards self-improvement because one believes they'll never be successful? Isn't that presupposing failure?"

"I guess it *would* presuppose failure. But what about the poor person who'll eventually discover that they failed? Don't we have the moral responsibility to protect those people like Natania; especially if they can't protect themselves?"

I decided to agree with her, while keeping the philosophical consideration open-ended. "I believe we do, but some would argue that what it comes down to is who is going to benefit from a situation like that. The school will benefit because they're getting their tuition. You are getting paid money, which you need. The SCO is receiving state funds."

"At the expense of unsuspecting people." she said sternly.

"Yes." I replied. "People will get hurt and others will benefit." She looked at me in disbelief. I continued. "So, what do we do about it?"

"Is it ethical for these institutions to make money by going along with something so seemingly wrong? Is it ethical for me to continue tutoring, knowing that maybe I shouldn't?" she asked.

I didn't answer that. I simply repeated my question. "So, what do we do about it?"

She paused a moment, then shook her head and softly said, "I don't know."

I wasn't sure if she shook her head because she didn't know or because she was disgusted with the whole conversation. One thing was sure, Sarah cared about Natania, and that was a nice thought for me to realize.

"Do you sometimes think it must be terrible to live a life like that?" I questioned.

"All the time."

"I wonder." I said.

"What do you mean?"

I explained with all the compassion I could find within me. "She doesn't know the situation she's in because of her mental state. She's most likely happy. We get upset at the system because we know better. In many ways, she's better off than we are. She's not trying to attain the happiness we know is beyond her reach."

She looked at me and quietly said, "I know."

With that, we both remained silent for a moment and her eyes were shinier than they usually were. I could tell it wouldn't take much more to make her cry. I suddenly felt very bad and made sure the conversation came to a screeching halt. Her tutoring sessions with Natania would be more difficult than ever from then on, I was sure. I told her that educators at any level, whether they're teaching graduate classes or tutoring, were doing something absolutely noble. The world is a better place because of them. I said this even at the risk of sounding self-serving. It didn't appear to help, but she agreed with me and didn't seem to hold any resentment towards me for engaging her in such a profound and emotional conversation. We talked a little more, but about nothing substantial.

After a while, I told her I had to go and run some errands, which was a total lie. So, we began to get ready to leave and go our separate ways. I walked her to the door, and we again shook hands to say goodbye. We made plans for next Friday; same place, same time. She asked me if we could exchange phone numbers so if anything came up and had to change plans, we could text each other. I found that to be a good idea, as texting is more convenient and faster than communicating via email. I normally wouldn't agree to this, but seeing we were meeting weekly, it seemed reasonable. We exchanged numbers and went on our way.

On the way home, I thought about our conversation in the snack lounge. I hoped I didn't go too far, then wondered why I even cared. She was, after all, just another student of mine, I thought. I soon dismissed that notion because I knew she was more than that. At the very least, I regarded her as my intellectual equal. But I wondered if there was something more. I leaned over and opened my bag to find what I thought I would find; a little purple note that said thank you, with her initials below it. I couldn't eat for the rest of that day. Maybe it was the food I ate at the Hu Kitchen, or maybe it was something more that made me lose my appetite. Regardless of what it was, I wasn't hungry.

That evening, I took a little time to get my work done for the coming week. I was hoping we wouldn't get hit with another blizzard causing classes to be cancelled for a second week in a row. It turns out there were no major storms on the horizon, and I was able to plan ahead without having to worry about that. I made sure to include some of the materials we had missed on our stormy Tuesday. I hoped next week's class would be as fruitful as the first. Sometimes classes lose momentum when you have to skip a week. When that happens, students can come back to class as if we'd had a few weeks' vacation; back to square one, having to reintroduce material. We would have to see, I thought. After my work was finished, although it was still very early, I went to bed. It took me forever to get to sleep.

On the following day, I kept my regular routine of going to church. I said hello to the people I acknowledged at every mass, then found my usual pew. I immediately knelt, bowed my head, and prayed for Natania.

# Week 3

## ~Perceptions and the Report~

"WHICH is farther west, San Diego California or Reno Nevada?" I asked the class.

Most said San Diego, one or two said Reno, and some tried hard to stay out of the line of fire.

I continued, "We think of California as being West of Nevada, so our first inkling would be to say that San Diego is farther West. But that's wrong. There's a section of California that is just South of Nevada. Looking at a map, clearly indicates Reno to be farther West." I waited a moment to let it sink in, then continued. "My point should be taken as; perception or mental maps are not always right. We could be led astray if we can't think beyond our current perception of the way things are. If you're not diligent enough, I could probably convince you to join a new religion by putting together a neat presentation complete with slides, charts, and figures." I saw doubt in some faces and agreement in others. "That's why it's critical to question what we hear, what we see, or even what we know." I pressed on, "We can also infer wrongly about information, with which we associate. If I gave you these two statements; nothing is better than a piece of warm pie; a few crumbs of bread are better than nothing. When we hear these two statements, we could wrongly conclude that a few crumbs are better than warm pie." Some were engaged in what I was saying and some clearly didn't care. For what it was worth, I made my point. "Folks, we've become a nation willing to accept anything thrown at us in the media; whether it be T.V., the paper, the internet, or what have you. If you get nothing out of this class, at least take *this* with you; question the validity of what you hear and see. Don't follow the crowd. They may lead you over the proverbial cliff."

A young lady raised her hand.

"Yes?" I asked.

"What if you don't have access to the data? What do we do then? How do we verify the validity?"

I rubbed my chin as some might do if they need a moment to think. "Some things remain theories. Not everything can be put into an equation and get an answer. You can't verify everything, but learn to trust your common sense. If you're not sure of something, admit it. Don't try to sound intelligent by recycling information you've heard, but not sure of. Be honest with yourself. What transpires in this class, or any class for that matter, is not something students walk away with as a better person. It is simply a moment in time that allows a step towards a better understanding of one's self." I made sure they understood that before they left. "Eventually, these little steps may make a difference, but it's up to the individual's ability to change, and think about themselves and the world around them."

That was my rant for the week for this class. It's always nice to have a captive audience when doing so. I made sure they knew it pertained to the major topics of the class, lest someone questioned *its* validity which they had every right to question, by the way. Before I enlightened them with this fine lecture, however, I made sure to collect their reports that were due on our stormy Tuesday. I told them they had a week's reprieve and there should be no reason for late or missing papers. No one disappointed me.

This particular session seemed very short for a three-hour class, considering all the materials I had to cover because of the storm. All too soon, the class was over, and I had no choice but to dismiss everyone. Sarah stayed a while to confirm our next session. We talked a little and made sure the arrangements were clear.

"So, Friday?" she asked.

"Friday, it is."

"Wonderful lecture, tonight, Dr. Dina."

"Thank you." I repeated what I thought during the lecture. "It's always nice to have a captive audience to listen to you." She chuckled, as I switched the conversation back to our impending meeting. "Just as a reminder, make sure to go over your abstract and method for that paper."

"I will."

"In the meantime, I'll be looking over the report you handed

in this Evening."

"I hope you like it. What I mean is, I hope it's what you wanted." She didn't seem too concerned. Her facial expression displayed the confidence of a hawk diving into a chicken run for dinner.

"We'll see. I'm sure it'll be fine." I replied.

"I was inspired by our discussion Friday." she said, "You'll see it in the paper."

"Were you? I didn't know if I pushed the envelope a little too much."

"No, you didn't. Sometimes you have to push to truly reflect."

"I agree."

After a few more pleasantries, she was ready to leave. "See you Friday." she said.

"See you then. And I saw your other note. You're welcome, anytime."

She smiled, waved, and left.

I sat at my desk with all these reports in front of me. How could I give myself so much work, I thought? Why can't I be one of those teachers who lets students get away with murder and not have to do any work, correcting? I knew the answer to that, so I picked them up and began reading. The subject matter of the reports I had them write, pertained to the class theme of mind and society. More specifically, I wanted them to write something relevant, but hopefully something they experienced. I wasn't too impressed with the first couple I had read, so I flipped through them all to find Sarah's. I began reading it.

It was well written with the proper elements of a good paper in place; a good introduction with thesis, key-point paragraphs, and a conclusion that was linked to her thesis. She followed the APA format, which not everyone did. Even the conventions of grammar, spelling, punctuation, and so on, were quite accurate with a couple of oversights here and there. I could tell why she was chosen to help Natania with writing. She wrote about her experience with one boy she tutored a few months back. He was in the sixth grade; not under the care of SCO, but a private client. His parents asked her if she wouldn't mind tutoring for math. She took the job, since he was only in the early grades and math was not so much of a challenge for those grades. She didn't describe the process of tutoring, which I was happy about. That would have missed the point of the paper, totally. Her point, rather, was a strong suggestion that parents should take part in their child's education as much as they can. It seems the parents of this boy she was tutoring for math, were more than capable of helping him out themselves. His mother was an accounting professor at Columbia University, and his father was a certified public accountant. Why were they not there to help their own son, she asked in her paper? Why couldn't they take the time for him, and why would they allow some stranger to come in and help him with his work? She was obviously concerned with right and wrong; accountability and irresponsibility. It made me happy to read that. It spoke of her strong character. I gave it an A+. She deserved it.

After grading it, I collected my things together and got ready to go home. It wasn't a bad semester all in all, but the other classes I had on Wednesdays, weren't as interesting as the one I had just dismissed. I was tired but once home, I would eventually find the energy to go through the other papers. My life was a well-timed, well-tuned, well-synchronized, automated machine with a deliberate purpose. I sometimes wondered what that purpose was.

## ~Change in Plans~

Before I left the school for the evening, I checked my phone messages; nothing there. I went back to my office and checked my voicemail; nothing there either. So, there was nothing left to do but leave. On my way out, I saw the bulletin board that was affixed right near the exit. I usually didn't pay attention to it because it contained mostly announcements for the students; Christian alliance, LGBTQ meetings, and that sort of thing. For some reason, I glanced at it that evening and saw an announcement of a conference for educators in upstate New York for that Saturday. I read a little more about it and determined it would be a great opportunity to mingle with other educators at every level. I knew I had to leave on Friday the latest, even though I had just confirmed a session with Sarah. I decided if I could reschedule our mentoring session, I would go to the conference. I would at least email them to see if there was room, since this seemed short notice. I wrote down the contact information and left. It was beginning to snow a little but nothing to worry about. To be honest, I didn't mind the winter, but I was ready for the spring. The road was not slippery yet, but I could tell it would soon become slick enough to warrant cautious driving.

When I got home, I called Sarah. I didn't want to text her. If there were any uncertainties about rescheduling, I wanted to hear them in her voice. I didn't hear any.

"Hello?" I heard her say on the other end of the phone. Her voice sounded a little different. I assumed she was busy with something, or just relaxed to the point where her voice sounded like she had just woken up.

"Hi." I said, "It's Ray Dina."

"Oh, hi Dr. Dina." She sounded more like herself.

"I just called up to say that something's come up and I'll probably have to be out of town Friday. How about if we meet on Thursday instead?"

"Yeah, alright; that sounds good."

"I thought maybe we could have a working luncheon this time, at a different location." I suggested.

"Okay, where?"

"Are you familiar with Mocha Burger on LaGuardia Place?"

"Yeah, I go there often. I love the place."

"Great, then it's settled."

"Why there?" she asked.

"What do you mean?"

"It's a kosher diner. I hope you're not doing this just for me."

"No, of course not. I've been there many times before and I like the atmosphere."

"Oh, okay." she said.

With that, I suggested we meet right outside the entrance at noon and take it from there. She agreed, we wished each other goodnight, and hung up. I then proceeded to email the contact person for the conference, and hoped it wasn't too late. I always enjoyed being busy; taking on many projects at once. It made me prioritize and plan despite my propensity to avoid work at times. Mentoring, writing, reading, teaching, going to conferences, playing music, and anything else I could occupy my time with, was exhilarating and in many ways, kept me feeling young. I had become more aware of my age, of late, and didn't fancy the fact I was getting older. Eventually, I would slow down and not be able to do what I love to do. Keeping busy allowed me to concentrate on more important things than getting old. The process of getting things done was rewarding; not so much the accomplishment of work, but rather the process; the means to an end. That's what was important and keeping me young and alive.

## ~The Dream~

I went to bed early that night again. Again, I couldn't sleep. I put the T.V. on in my room, and since there was nothing worth watching, something that had become a fact of life in recent years, I started reading instead. I picked out a compilation of C. S. Lewis favorites, but the pages looked a little blurry and I found myself wandering again; another bad habit, I thought. Finally, after about thirty minutes of reading, I surrendered to another fact of life; when you're not in the mood to read, you shouldn't read. I settled on turning the light off and closing my eyes.

I thought about many things while lying there. I thought about Joey and Derek; two brothers who haven't spoken in a long time and would probably never speak again. I thought about Carolyn, the woman whom I had divorced after having been married to for years. I also thought about how vulnerable Sarah seemed to be. I thought of all these things sometimes separately, sometimes randomly, and sometimes relative to one another. After a while, my thoughts about them intertwined, meshed, and weaved until finally, I fell asleep.

That night I had a dream. It didn't fall under the category of a nightmare, but rather what seemed to be an eerie, and some might suggest, somewhat of a spine-chilling dream. I dreamt I was walking towards a house, not belong to me, but clearly familiar. It seemed abandoned. I went against my better instincts and approached it. What drew me to it was something shiny I saw on the front porch. As I drew nearer, I saw the shiny object glimmering in the sun, was a key. It fit into the front door keyhole perfectly and unlocked it with a click whose echo I could hear within the walls of the room beyond the door. I went in. As I walked around, I seemed to know my way from room to room. I also knew what each room looked like before I entered it. I finally entered a room that had a hole in the wall about the size of a basketball. This, I did not expect. The room contained the furniture, curtains, light fixtures, and everything else I foresaw before walking into it. However, the opening in the wall was a surprise I couldn't foresee. This aperture didn't expose the outside daylight, but rather darkness. I looked in but could see nothing but a black void. I was suddenly compelled to put my hand in it to see what I could feel. As I reached further and further, I could feel something unrecognizable to the touch but couldn't grab it. That made me reach deeper to feel it again and suddenly have it snatched beyond my reach again, as though someone were toying with me. I reached as far as I could, until I felt it no more. I kept my arm in there, up to my shoulder and felt around for something; anything. Then suddenly, I heard a loud bang behind me as though someone had hit the opposite wall with a sledgehammer. I suddenly woke up to feel my heart racing. In a daze, I looked at my phone to see the time. I had been asleep for a while, as it was almost four in the morning. I also saw a reply email to my inquiry about the conference. They had made a reservation for me. That reply brought me back to a sense of reality. Fully awake, I wondered about the dream. I was not and am not the kind of person who thinks every dream means something or is trying to tell you something from your unconscious. However, being in the profession I was in, it was almost a spontaneous reaction to analyze at least a little. I thought of what Freud would think about such a dream and dismissed the notion immediately. Although with a dream like that, it would be difficult to argue against his obvious analysis. But I wondered. Could I have been longing for something unknown in my conscious life that was beyond the scope of my reach or ability, I thought? What did the house represent, and why was it familiar to me? Even the rooms looked like what I envisioned before entering. The hole in the wall was obviously significant. Why was it there and why couldn't I see inside it? What was the bang? There were many possibilities. Too many for that time of the morning. Resolved to not think about it further, I got up and took a shower to get ready for the day; even if it was only four in the morning.

## ~Sarah's Grandmother~

That day was an ordinary day of lecturing a couple of other classes in the morning and afternoon, and getting some school work done. I hadn't motivated myself to correct the rest of the students' papers the night before, as I had thought. So, I had to push myself on Wednesday. It would have been a carefree day, were it not for that dream still in the back of my mind. It lingered in my mind as any nightmare might have. I always considered nightmares to be scary, even to the point of someone being frightened for the entire day after; children and adults alike. Even though the dream was not scary, it left a sense of reality in me as though it actually happened. Nevertheless, I had to get through the day, and I did. I felt, however, I wasn't at my best and probably seemed preoccupied to some of my students, if not all of them. I also wondered if I gave my full attention to reading and correcting the rest of the papers. At any rate, at least I had corrected Sarah's accurately; rendering my full diligence.

The next day, I met Sarah at the Mocha Burger for noon. I wasn't late but upon my arrival, I could see she was there waiting at the entrance. As I drove around for a parking spot, I could tell by the number of cars this was a popular place. I finally parked and walked up to meet Sarah. We didn't shake hands this time, as that is a normal custom for people who meet for the first or second time. Our meeting had become almost routine. We said hi, and proceeded in.

I had been there before but could never get over the decor. It was a varied mix of Western, old world

European, and modern New York City feel. On one side, was a wall with a rustic look. It contained a long bench that ran the length of the restaurant with tables of two all along it. On the other side, was a brick wall, where there were tables of four. The ceiling was adorned with modest light fixtures that hung over the tables. Overall, the atmosphere had a distinction all its own. The kosher menu and service were also commendable. After we ordered, she asked me how my week was.

"It was a strange week." I said. "I had a bad dream Tuesday night."

"Oh really? What was it?"

"If I tell you, will you analyze me and tell me if I have psychological complications?"

She laughed at that, like I had never seen her laugh. Perhaps I had never noticed her laugh before as I did then, or perhaps my senses were keener that evening, or perhaps it was the mood I was in. Regardless, I enjoyed seeing her have a good time. After joking around a little more, I told her the dream. As I told it, I could see the suspense in her eyes. It was sincere. She had the look she probably had when watching a psychological thriller. It was not hard to notice the anticipation in her eyes and the movement of her eyebrows reacting to the suspense of each moment of the dream I uttered.

After I was done, she thought for a while, then said, "I think I know what it means."

"What?"

"You want something you can't have."

"Oh really?" I replied. "Thank you, Dr. Goldman, for your dubious analysis."

"Dubious?"

"Yes. What is it that I want?"

"I don't know. You're the one who wants it."

We both laughed at that. In fact, we were both very much at ease throughout the working lunch. After ordering, we started working on her paper before the food came and continued as best we could while eating. We discussed formatting a little, as well as the results and references. We also talked about where to specifically place her variables. Altogether, it was a very practical and effective lunch; not to mention delicious.

When the waiter returned with the check, I gave it back to him with my card. Seeing I was picking up the tab, Sarah protested. I gave the waiter the signal to proceed with the checkout anyway, and he left towards the backroom to complete the transaction. I told her I insisted on paying, since it was my idea to come eat and work. After some resistance, she agreed but said she would pay for the next lunch. I thought maybe I started something, since we were now talking about our next lunches as opposed to our next mentoring sessions. The waiter soon returned with the slip, which I signed, and told us there was no hurry for us to leave. We thanked him, as he left us, and continued our conversation.

"Did you enjoy your lunch?" I asked.

"I did. How about you?"

"I did indeed."

"And we got some work done." she added.

"You know Sarah, for a young woman, you're very serious about your work. You know that?"

"That's because I have no life."

We both chuckled.

"Neither do I." I said.

"What do you mean? You *have* a life."

"Here I am with a twenty-five-year-old woman talking about methodology and variables."

I was afraid she wouldn't laugh at that. I meant it as a joke, even if it was the truth. I was relieved when she *did* laugh. I immediately thought of how refreshing it was to be with someone who had a sense of humor. In those days, people were always tip toeing on eggshells around each other, so as to not offend anybody, much like today.

"Sarah," I asked, "Would you mind telling me more about your grandmother?"

"Why?"

"It'd be a great opportunity to learn firsthand how it was during the holocaust."

Her expression changed to a serious one. I thought it was curious that the joke didn't offend her, but this might have. I hoped I was wrong.

"Oh, I don't know." she said.

"I hope that didn't offend you."

"Why would that offend me?"

"I don't mean to undermine the suffering she had to go through."

"Dr. Dina, you could never offend me." she replied. Then, she seemed to have a change of heart. "It's all good. We can talk about it. And you're not undermining anything. I just don't know why it affects me the way it does."

"You must love your grandmother very much."

"I do. I love her more than anything."

"It's great that there's such a bond between distant generations like that."

"I think so too."

"Tell me about her." I said, delicately.

"Okay, what would you like to know?"

"Well, for instance, was she deprived of food and water when she was captive?"

She spoke in a somber tone. "Yes, they all were. When they got to the camps, they were given a little piece of stale bread with raw potato. Sometimes they were given soup, but I'm not sure about that. I think that's what she said."

"That must have been hell."

"It must have been *complete* hell. Aside from not being fed properly, everyone saw people get killed. There were piles of dead bodies. There were body parts all over. After all these years, she still has nightmares about what she saw and went through."

"She was reminded regularly that that could be her fate." I added.

"Yes. Also, over and under a certain age, they were sent to the gas chambers. But there were things happening that were worse than death." She continued, "The Nazis used the Jews to perform medical experiments on. For instance, they would break their bones, let them heal, and then break them again. They repeated this over and over to see how they mended each time. But I'm sure I'm not telling you anything you don't already know."

"No, I want to hear it. I want to hear it all."

She went on, "They took off layers of skin, and somehow made lampshades with them. They also removed all their gold teeth. There were no mates. Men and women were separated."

"Did your grandmother have family with her?" I asked.

Her expression became more serious. I knew immediately I was treading shallow water, under which an emotional secret dwelt. She was very reluctant to answer, but after a while of pondering if she should or not, she finally did.

"Yes."

"What happened to them?"

"I don't know."

"She didn't tell you?"

I could tell she didn't want to talk about something specific.

"Please…" she pleaded, shaking her head in an attempt to keep the secret buried.

"Sarah, it's best to talk about it." I meant that. I wanted her to talk about it because I felt this must have been bothering her for a long time. Talking was the proper therapy for something so terrifying, I thought. "I have a feeling something happened to your grandmother that really devastated her." I said.

"Why do you think that?"

"I can hear it in your voice."

I knew full well there was more she didn't want to revisit.

"Why so interested?"

"Because I know it bothers you, and the best thing to do is talk about it."

She looked around the restaurant, then asked if we could go outside to talk.

"Of course." I replied.

We put our coats on and started walking to the door. Neither of us said a word on the way out; I guess because there was nothing to say, but what was on her mind. She would speak about it in her own good time, I thought. I was okay with that. Sometimes, silence is best. We made our way outside, where the temperature was chilly but not intolerable. Our breath was a visible condensation in the cold air, but our jackets kept us from being too cold. There was a bench about twenty-five feet from the door, which she made her way towards, and I followed. When we sat, I sat close enough to allow her to keep her voice down if she needed to. At times, she looked away from me as she spoke.

"My grandmother *did* have family with her. Her mother was there along with her little sister who was just an infant at the time." She choked up a bit but continued. "As I said earlier, under and over a certain age, the prisoners were sent to the gas chambers. One day…" She hesitated. I wanted to hold her hand, but I feared her reaction to that.

I simply said, "It's okay."

She continued, "One day, my grandmother was taken away from her mother and placed with other young people. Her mother, still holding her little sister, was sent to stand in a line. That line began walking away." Sarah's eyes began to water as they did during our discussion of Natania. She was silent for a while, then finished her story while struggling to get the words out. "My grandmother watched her mother and baby sister go to their deaths." Her voice became louder, and her tone became angrier. "Her mother looked back to see her one last time, and she was hit for disrupting the line; even with an infant in her arms."

Sarah began to cry as though a dam had finally broken after years and years of being pummeled and battered by a surf of raging, restless waters. I wanted to hold and comfort her, but I just looked at her and waited. I knew the emotion had to run its course. After what seemed forever, she composed herself again.

I started softly, "I'm sorry." That was all anyone could say.

"How can anyone be so cruel?" she asked.

"I know. I wish I knew what to say."

She looked at me and smiled, wiping her eyes and cheeks. "Well, I didn't mean to ruin your day."

"You didn't. I'm the one who made you talk. I'm sorry for that."

"It's something that happened, and I have to face the fact that she went through hell. In a way, it makes me appreciate the life *I* have."

"Yes," I said, "we should all count our blessings, as they say." After a moment, I asked her, "You okay?"

"Yes, thank you. You're very sweet." She looked at her phone to check the time, I gathered, then said, "I should be going."

"Okay, let me walk you to your car." I felt as if she shouldn't be alone for too long.

"No, I'll be alright. Thank you."

"You sure?"

"Yeah."

She gathered her papers and belongings, then we both got up. We smiled and shook hands. As we did, I thought I could almost see the relief in her eyes. There was also a sadness; the kind of sadness you feel when you can't change a past regret, when you can't undo something terrible that is so easy to do, when you've tried and tried at something beyond your reach and suddenly realize it may be time to give up. As we shook hands, I could almost read her thoughts. Soon, we bade each other goodnight and she started walking towards her car.

I called out, "Sarah." She stopped and turned to look at me. "Thank you for confiding in me." I said. "It means a lot."

She simply waved, turned, and walked to her car. I walked to mine as well, but I didn't get in right away. I watched as she left the parking lot, knowing she had released emotions that were bottled up inside her for many years. After she was gone, I got in my car and drove away. As I drove, I kept thinking about how bad it must have been for all the victims of the holocaust. We have a tendency to think about it as a moment in history, not really associating it with anyone we know, necessarily. I then had a new perspective. Not only did I know someone who had a close relation with a victim, but who felt deep emotional sadness that someone she loves was directly affected.

When I got home, I got packed and ready for the conference. I didn't feel like going anymore, but I attributed that to the emotional state I was in. I checked my bag carefully for another note she might have left but didn't find one. I had come to expect those little purple notes. Even if there had been a note in my bag, I would have been slightly disappointed if it hadn't been from a purple notepad. That was her signature way of appreciation, and I loved it. I started my lesson plans for the following week, as I would be busy all weekend. There was a chapter in the textbook devoted to the psychology of emotion. I thought it would be appropriate to lecture a little on that, since it's such a critical aspect of life; especially when I was feeling emotional myself. I find the lectures I feel strongly about, really flow without having to put too much effort into it. Lectures as such, seem to come to light so well. So, I decided emotions it would be, and worked on my lesson plans.

I wasn't done my lesson, when I received a phone call. It was my father. I thought it was strange for him to call me, as he didn't seem to have a reason. We made small talk for a while. I thought it was good that we didn't start talking about anything of a personal nature, as we often disagreed. However, as fate would have it, we ended up talking about something that happened in the past and it didn't end well. We argued for about ten minutes and finally hung up without saying goodbye. I was okay with that, as I had more important things to think about.

That evening, I laid in bed thinking about how Sarah was feeling. Was she upset at me because I pried into her private life? Was she upset at herself because she allowed herself to be vulnerable in the company of her mentor? I had many questions before I went to sleep. The answers would eventually become evident.

# ~Trip to Syracuse~

Next morning, I finished packing my things to get ready to leave. I had made a checklist so as to not forget anything, since I would be gone for the weekend. When I was satisfied everything was packed, it was time to eat a little and relax. I poured myself some cereal and checked my phone for messages. Part of me was hoping to see an email from the conference saying there was a mistake; there wasn't room for me after all. I saw no such email. I also wanted to text Sarah to see how she was doing but decided against it.

I left for Syracuse at around two o'clock, so I could check into the hotel around six. I thought driving was a better choice than flying, since it was a weekend and there were no storms in the horizon that would affect the North East. I drove for a while, then decided to stop for a coffee. I wanted to stay awake for the drive, as it would soon get dark. I stopped at a quaint little place just off the highway, which served sandwiches of all types and beverages. I ordered and found a nice little table for two on the far end wall. There, I rested a bit while drinking my coffee, which was probably the best coffee I had ever had. As I sat, I read the local paper I had gotten from a newspaper rack at the entrance. The politicians were at it again, the price of gas was going up, there was some commentator who had written about the gloom and doom of climate change; all bad news. Nothing worth reading about that might spark some optimism. Somethings will never change, I thought, and one should not expect them to but rather go on living life as if it's worth living, because it is. I had had enough, finally. I folded the paper and put it to one side so I could think about good things in my life. That's when I realized the good things in my life were few. Oh, there were a few things I was blessed with, but to say I was complete and without void, would have been a stretch. After about fifteen minutes, I finished the coffee and decided it was time to get back on the road. I visited the restroom to refresh myself and made my way out, thanking the server as I passed her. She replied in kind.

On my way out of the mom and pop diner parking lot, I noticed a billboard advertising a real estate agent named, Carl Feinberg. *Number one in the county,* it said. How embarrassed I would be to have my face displayed on a billboard, I thought. Then, something caught my eye on the bottom right hand corner of the billboard. I couldn't believe it. I couldn't believe how people could be so callous and hateful. I thought I might have been seeing something other than what it was, but it was all too real. There, below the letters that spelled the word county, was a hand painted swastika that was plain as day.

"Why?" I asked myself out loud in anger. It was a rhetorical question, since I already knew the answer. It would take a lot, I thought, to restore my faith in humanity after seeing this. Trying not to think about it any longer, I kept driving until I reached my destination. But it turns out, I would think about it for a long time.

The hotel I made reservations for, was simple, clean, and modest. I was never one for fancy hotel suites. I was satisfied with a place to sleep and shower, much like I am now.

I attended the conference on Saturday as planned. It was quite a turn out, as there were people from all over New York State. I sat there looking around and listening to the presenters. One by one, they spoke of education reform, the progress we've made over the years, and how our schools need to be the best in the world. There were the usual political advocates trying to push their agenda. There were the superintendents of schools making sure they agreed with school committee members, to get the proper funding for their districts. There were the hypocrites, I thought, and I was one of them by virtue of being there instead of providing music for the elderly or doing something else more productive. I suddenly felt alone and wanted to leave. As soon as they provided a break for us, I left and went back to the hotel. I had had it. I thought taking a shower was more important than being in a room full of self-serving politicians.

After my shower, I noticed there was a notification on my phone. I hoped it was a text from Sarah, but it wasn't. It was from Joey. It simply said he was trying to call me, but I wouldn't pick up; could I call him as soon as possible? I called right away and learned the bad news. As he spoke, I let myself fall sitting on the bed, and listened intensely. After we hung up, I immediately gathered my things, checked out, and left for home.

# Week 4

## ~Emotions~

ONE might say I wasn't fit to be good company after hearing the news from Joey. I tried to avoid others, especially those who knew me, lest they interpreted my aloofness as indifference to them. I was going through a difficult time, suddenly, and knew it would pass. However, I didn't want to have to explain it to anyone. I wasn't and am not the type to open up to anybody, much less at such a time. I hoped I could get through Tuesday night's class alright, but some emotions are just too strong. It was a rough weekend all in all, having gone to that conference, then back and forth to the hospital. Still, were it not for the incident, I probably would have left Syracuse early anyway.

I found myself exhausted and not in the mood to teach on Tuesday night, but life goes on and so do responsibilities. Even if you want to crawl away and not deal with those responsibilities. Nevertheless, I was determined to present my lecture by rote and not be affected by preoccupations.

Tuesday night's class started well despite how I was feeling. I could very well have stayed home and not felt any guilt about ignoring my responsibilities to my students. We talked about up and coming assignments they had questions on. We discussed their previous reports and how they were graded, weighted, and so on. I also showed a video on the behaviors associated with Attention Deficit Hyperactivity Disorder. We then had a healthy exchange on whether ADHD was over-diagnosed, or if it even exists. Some believed in it wholeheartedly. Sean Russell, my neo-Nazi, thought it was a conspiracy against the nation's student population, perpetrated by the pharmaceutical companies and the government for the sake of the almighty dollar. I wasn't surprised to hear him say that. As he spoke, I got angry as I recalled the swastika I had seen on the billboard days before. As for me, I couldn't have cared less about ADHD at that moment in time. Although, I did have some apprehension about the possible long-term effects of the medicines used to alleviate the symptoms. Sarah was quiet throughout. About half way through the class, I began my lecture on the psychology of emotions and their effect on human behavior.

"The psychology of emotion is not only intriguing, but also elusive. You can understand exactly why someone is emotional, but it's almost impossible to define. Is there a link between emotion and practical reasoning?" I waited but got no response; just blank stares. I continued with examples, "If you've just won the lottery; no one can put you in a bad mood. You've just lost a loved one; nothing anyone says can make you feel better. Have a positive attitude, you're told. The glass is half full, not half empty. Does a positive attitude help? Do negative thoughts have the opposite effect?" I asked.

I could have gotten more of a response from a goldfish floating upside down in a septic tank. Needless to say, I was getting annoyed, having put so much work in this lesson; compounded by the previous restless weekend I had to live through. I looked around and everyone seemed disjointed. Sarah seemed to be studying me. I was suddenly inspired by our talk of Sarah's grandmother, during which we agreed we should count our blessings.

I continued, "I trust everyone read the chapter for this week. Let me get more general and ask you this. Does counting your good fortunes and aspirations really have a positive impact on your life? What do you think?"

I called on Kayra, "Kayra, what do you think, and according to the text, do we have enough data to support a valid answer?"

Kayra simply said, "Yes, it has a positive impact."

I asked again, "Do we have the data to support a yes answer, or is that your opinion?"

She gave me a look that told me she didn't read the chapter.

"Anyone else?" I asked. I called on someone else, "Julia?"

"No." she answered.

"No, we don't have the data, or no it doesn't have an impact on your life?" I asked, trying to get more out of her. I got nothing in return. I started to lose my patience. "Come on," I said angrily, "Where are my psychologists?"

Sarah raised her hand. I called on her and finally got an answer from someone. Sarah began to speak. "There hasn't been much experimental research on whether counting your favorable circumstances really helps elevate someone's mood, or whether gratitude has a positive impact on our lives." She added, "Although I'm sure that the practice of counting one's blessings is considered a worthwhile practice."

"Yes! Correct!" I shouted to the rest of the class, "That's all I'm looking for!"

I furiously and deliberately paraphrased her answer to them, "There has been very little experimental work that correlates gratitude with positive emotions." I continued, "Now, how come no one knew that? What am I teaching here, a bunch of seventh graders? We're a quarter of the way through the semester and you're still giving me yes, no answers? If you don't want to be here, get out!" I blared, pointing to the door.

They sat there looking at me in wonder. They had just seen a side of me they didn't know existed. I waited and looked at them but didn't dare look at Sarah. I suddenly felt embarrassed for losing my temper over something that again, has very little significance in the big picture of life. It was a moment of silence that was awkward, as though I had exposed myself to be their enemy. Although it wasn't time yet, I elected to call it a night. I didn't want any more outbursts on my part and risk alienating these students who were at times, very much engaged. However, I was still upset at their passivity with regard to the discussion I tried to generate. I tried to compose myself the best I could. I finally broke the silence, "I want you to read chapters eight through ten by next Tuesday. We'll discuss those topics then."

Having said that, I dismissed the class early. I went back to my desk with my back to the students, pretending to be busy with something important, as they were leaving quietly. I didn't want to make eye contact, much less speak to any of them. After they left, I wasn't a bit surprised to hear Sarah's voice. I really didn't want to talk to anybody, but I knew that would be impossible. She spoke gently.

"Dr. Dina?"

I turned to look at her. She had a worried look in her eyes. I tried to sound like nothing happened.

"Very good, Sarah. It was a very good answer. That's what I was looking for."

"Thank you." she said.

"No, thank *you*. You saved me from a class full of seventh graders."

That response was meant to get a chuckle. It didn't work.

"You've helped me with my empirical paper enough, the least I could do is return the favor. I must say it was an interesting lecture, though."

I knew what she meant by that, but I was hoping to guide her in another direction.

"Yes," I said, "human emotions have yet to be explored further."

"That's not what I meant. You don't seem yourself, if I may say so. I don't mean any disrespect."

"No, of course not. And you're right, I'm not myself today. I'm sorry I blew up at the class. I pride myself in my ability for self-control."

"You're human."

"Some would argue that."

She finally smiled, and it made me feel better.

"May I ask what's wrong?" she asked.

"Nothing, but thank you for asking."

"It's quite obvious there's something, sir. Since day one, I've never seen you lose your temper like that."

"Well, it's a bad day, Sarah."

"I'd like to know what's wrong." she persisted.

I made up some excuse, and thought if my students can do it, so can I. "My laptop crapped out today. I had so much stuff on there, too." I was hoping that would be a sufficient answer. I should have known better.

"Your laptop?" she asked.

"Yeah, I don't know what's wrong with it. I'm afraid I've lost a lot of work."

"I see." She waited a while just looking at me. She had that look everyone's mother has when she knows you're lying. Then she added, "So now can you tell me what the real problem is?"

"I just did; my laptop." I insisted.

There's something real you experience when you're getting found out. It's a feeling. You can't help but feel like a little kid who's done something wrong and wants to conceal it at all cost. I don't know if it's the look you get from someone, or just your conscience getting the better of you, but I do know that feeling exists. It certainly existed at that moment with Sarah; a young lady who was my student, and yet a force to be reckoned with.

"Laptops break, and you move on. Your laptop is not the problem." She sounded sure of herself. "I know there's a problem and it's not as simple as a laptop being broken. Please tell me. I want to know."

There was no escaping the truth. In a way, I thought it was good I had someone to confront me. So, I told her what was wrong, and hoped I would be strong enough to maintain my composure.

"My father is dying." I said.

"Oh no, I'm so sorry. What happened?"

"He had a stroke this last Saturday. He's in critical care and is not expected to survive. He's not responsive. I went to see him throughout the last few days to talk to him, but he couldn't respond. He didn't even know I was there. His eyes were closed, and he didn't seem to hear." I suddenly felt as though I was talking to a loved one. "I love him, Sarah."

"Oh my God, of course you do; and he loves you too."

"You don't understand. We had an argument Friday night on the phone. I hung up on him. I never got a chance to talk to him again to apologize. The funny thing is I don't even remember why I got so mad at him."

"I'm sure he realized it was just a heated moment, and what was said wasn't to be taken to heart. People say things they don't mean when they're upset. That's all it was. You were both upset, and things were said."

"No, Sarah. Things were said that shouldn't have been said. Things were uncovered that should have been kept locked up. I wish I could take it all back. I wish I could talk to him again and explain how foolish I was and how sorry I am, but I can't. I think it's too late."

"I wish I knew what to say. I can't imagine how you must feel."

"Thank you, Sarah."

"I'm sure he thought nothing of it; the argument, I mean."

I could hear the desperate hope in her voice. She was genuinely feeling as bad as I was, it seemed. Her empathy was liberating, and I wanted to confide in her all the more.

"Do you want to know the last thing I told him; the last thing he'll ever hear from me?" I asked, trying to contain myself. I felt as though if I were able to tell her, it would somehow bring closure.

"Dr. Dina, please don't do this to yourself." she replied.

I could tell she knew what to expect. I continued despite her request to not beat myself up any longer. I simply couldn't help myself. I felt I had to tell someone. So, I confessed to Sarah with great difficulty. "I told him how much I was ashamed of him."

At that, she simply said, "Oh my God." and reached out to hug me. I didn't resist. She hugged me tight, and I did the same. We stood together for a while; long enough for me to start crying.

There's something about being in someone's arms at a time of grief. You can maintain control forever, but when someone holds you, it somehow brings everything out. That's when you lose control and let the other person take care of you. I cried on her shoulder. All the while I cried, she was sighing as if to say she understood how I felt. I could smell the fragrance of her hair, feel the softness of her touch, and hear the compassion in her voice. What she imparted to me was in such contrast to what I had been feeling all weekend, that the two emotions made me lose all sense of control. I drew myself from the comfort of her arms and took a gentle hold of her shoulders. Closing my eyes, I brought her closer and kissed her. It was a soft kiss, but I immediately pulled away and began to apologize. All the while I was speaking, she just looked into my eyes.

"I'm sorry." I said, feeling greater remorse than I had felt moments earlier. "I don't know what came over me. Please don't take it the wrong way. I would never…"

Before I could finish my rambling apologies, she softly said, "It's okay."

Then, she put her arms around my neck, drew me closer, and kissed me with all the passion I had secretly imagined. She didn't resist, as I pulled her closer and tighter.

## ~The Aftermath~

We stood there looking in each other's eyes for the longest time saying nothing. It was as though we could read each other's minds and had mixed emotions from what we were thinking. It was so wrong yet felt so natural and liberating. All the time I focused on her gaze, I tried to read her true emotions. She kissed back. This, I knew for sure. There was no mistake. The more I thought about her reciprocating, the happier I became. I eventually smiled at her and she smiled back. There was no question. She felt the same as I did at that wonderful moment of passion. Only, I still wasn't sure if it was a moment of passion or just mixed feelings; perhaps a desperate act initiated by my sense of despair and confusion because of my father's condition. Whatever it was, it had happened for better or for worse. I was able and willing to deal with whatever happened next. For better or for worse? My God, that sounded too much like the marriage vows and promise Carolyn and I had made to each other, but neither of us kept. But everything happens for a reason and I would have to have faith in my actions, in myself, and now in Sarah Goldman.

We still held each other closely, as I wondered what would happen next. I'm certain she wondered the same. This was not an awkward moment by any means, but somehow, we would have to get passed the moment and face reality again of who we were to each other; teacher and student who were generations apart. As I began wiping the tears from my face with my hand, she immediately reached for the tissues on my desk and began to wipe them for me. She wiped them with such gentle motion, as to almost caress my face; a moment I would never forget. I thanked her. Then, coming back to my senses of what had happened, I broke the ice.

"We need to talk." I said.

She raised her eyebrows. "You think so?"

She began to smile. Before I knew it, we were both laughing; not one of those belly laughs, but more of a hesitant laugh one has when one needs to break the ice in the face of a tentative situation. I wasn't sure why we laughed at our newly found relationship, but I knew absurdity was not the reason. Neither of us thought it was absurd. It was serious. Our giddy moment might have been the result of the tension of emotions we had just experienced by my loss of patience with the class, or it might have been a number of things. The reason didn't really matter, however. We had something more important to deal with.

"So…" I said.

"So…"

"So, what do we do now?"

"We talk about it."

"I know it seemed a bit spontaneous..."

She interrupted. "Was it?"

Her eyes were brilliant from the combination of residue of tears and the way the light reflected from them.

I responded, "I guess if I were to psychoanalyze myself, I'd have to admit that it's been on my mind for a while."

"Same here." she replied, to my surprise.

It never dawned on me that she might have feelings for me. I guess I knew how *I* felt, but now realized I had been in denial. Or, at the very least, didn't want to act on those feelings. The incident with my father was still on my mind, however, and it must have shown in my face. My mind was racing.

"Are you okay? I mean, are you feeling better about things?" she asked.

I knew she meant my father. I answered, "Yes, I'm fine. Sometimes, you have to come to terms with certain tragedies. You can't hold yourself responsible for things you have no control over."

"That's true, but it's easy to reason like that. It's another thing altogether to realize it."

"I'm fine." I assured her.

"Good. I'm glad."

"So, what do we do about us?" I asked.

"I'd like to talk about it."

That response told me she didn't want to ignore what happened and wanted to discuss if and how it could work, as much as I did. I have to admit; I wanted our relationship to work even if it was wrong. Since it was still early in the evening, we decided to go have dinner and talk it out. I got my things together, shut the room lights, and walked her to her car. We made plans to meet at 2nd Ave Deli on East 33rd Street, where we could eat light, as neither of us were really hungry. At least we could sit and talk. We got to her car, and before she got in, I took her arm and gently turned her towards me. At first, her look was one of concern, as though she didn't know what would happen next. That expression soon changed, as we looked at each other and smiled. Then, we kissed again.

We arrived at the restaurant at the same time and went in together. We tried to sit at a table away from others, but that was hardly possible. We settled for something that was relatively private. She had her books with her, so as to not give the wrong impression if we met someone we knew. We weren't very hungry, so she ordered spinach knish and I had a salad. We hardly touched any of it throughout our discussion. After sitting a while and just looking at each other and others around us, I initiated the conversation.

"I just want to put your mind at ease and tell you upfront that I'm not married. I've been divorced for a few years."

She replied, "Well I'm sorry to hear that, and yet I'm not. I'd hate to be a homewrecker."

"You're not, Sarah. Trust me."

"I do trust you."

"And I'd like you to call me Ray from now on."

"I prefer Raymond," she replied. "But I promise I won't in class."

"Raymond is perfect." I said, smiling.

"Can I ask what happened with your wife?"

"Carolyn and I simply drifted apart." I said. "We had two boys together and everything was fine. As the boys were growing up, they became a priority over our marriage."

"I'm sure it's difficult to avoid that."

"It is. Children take over your life whether you're married or not. There were great times, though; the

Easter egg hunts, throwing the Frisbee around, wrestling on the floor..."

"You really love them, don't you?"

"Well, there were some bad times too; the tough love disciplines, and the endless nights helping with their homework; all these things. Good or bad, they took up most of our lives and we hardly had time for each other."

"That's too bad." she said.

"Well, it's more common than you might think. If couples don't take time out for themselves, they become estranged, almost. They grow apart, and their marriage is no longer as important as it once was. Something else takes over."

"That's what caused the divorce?"

"Well that was one of the major contributors, among other things. With almost every situation, there are a lot of variables. In this particular case, any one of those variables might have triggered the decision to split up, and eventually follow through with a divorce."

I heard myself sounding like a professor, and hoped it wasn't a turn off.

"It's too bad that it happens that way sometimes." she said.

"I know." I decided to change the subject to more important matters. "What about us; our age difference?" I asked.

"What about it?"

"Well, you could be my daughter."

"Age is just a number. I'm not your daughter, so don't worry." She continued, "We don't know what the future holds. We shouldn't jump the gun and worry about what doesn't exist yet, or ever will."

That sounded logical enough for me. I must admit, I didn't want to think about anything gloomy. It was nice to just think about what feels right for a change. There were ramifications we would have to discuss later. But for now, we just wanted to focus on the present and how happy we were just talking to each other. We didn't talk about anything negative for a while; no divorce, no dying fathers, no reports, no classes; just good things. We simply enjoyed each other's company. We laughed a bit and talked a bit. Before we knew it, our appetite returned. We were both eating and enjoying our time together. I felt young again.

Finally, it was getting very late and we were both ready to leave. I walked with her in the parking lot to her car. When she was safely in the car I began to walk away, but almost immediately heard her calling my name again. I thought something was wrong. I turned and saw her signal me to come back to her. When I did, she drew me closer and kissed me again.

"Happy Valentine's Day, Raymond." she said.

I must have had a surprised look on my face because she started laughing. I knew Valentine's Day was on February 14th every year but had lost all track of time and day.

"I completely forgot." I said with a smile. "Well, Happy Valentine's Day." I replied.

"Will you be alright?" she asked.

"Yes I'm fine. Thank you for being there. I feel much better."

"You sure?"

"Yes. It was a rough Valentine's Day, but one of the best Valentine's Nights I've had in a long time."

I really meant it, and I could tell by her look she believed it. That made her smile. At that, we said goodnight, I walked to my car, got in and drove. About half way home, it dawned on me to check my coat pockets for the familiar purple note. She hadn't disappointed me. There it was, in the recesses of my coat pocket, the little purple note saying I was a good kisser. I smiled and chuckled while I drove home happier than I had been in a long time.

## ~Derek~

It was almost midnight when I got home. I had had a great time with Sarah, but the surroundings of home made me think about my father again. I also thought about Joey and Derek. How were they, with the news? Did Derek even know? I wondered if they were really affected as I was. They were grandsons of his, after all. My father was hardly immediate family to them. I was sure they weren't as devastated as I was, which made me feel worse. I selfishly wanted everyone to feel the way I did, if for no other reason than to honor a decent man who raised a good family. I wanted to call them both, but it was quite late. My anxious concern would have to wait until morning.

I took a shower and went to bed. After lying there in the dark, wide awake for a while, I decided to turn the light on and check my phone messages. I saw a message from Joey who was concerned about me. I replied that I was alright, which was the truth. I was also happy to see a message from Sarah. It simply said 'goodnight'. I replied with a goodnight of my own. I turned the light off again, and contentedly lay back down waiting for sleep to come. I didn't sleep well that night. I didn't have any bad dreams, but it was one of those light sleeps; in and out. I was aware of and heard every little creek and sound a house makes in the middle of the night. My house suddenly seemed like the house in the dream. When I was half asleep, my mind would race like a speed train. I even felt like I was moving for some unknown reason; moving fast like one of those crash test dummies they put in cars to study what kind of injuries would be inflicted by a crash. I wondered if my father was suffering with pain, if Sarah would feel the same by morning, if Derek knew about the news, and why the hospital called Joey instead of me. Was it because my father wanted my family to know but didn't want anything to do with *me*? When I wasn't half asleep, I was totally awake. I felt the adrenaline flowing. I couldn't imagine sitting up and reading or watching T.V. because I couldn't concentrate on anything other than what was happening in my life at the moment. It wasn't a good night, and I couldn't wait until morning when I would call Derek. Why does it take a tragedy in the family to get in touch after so long, I thought? They say sometimes hardship will bring people together. So, I wondered if Joey and Derek would reconcile their differences and become brothers again. Yet, I tried not to think of that. It's useless worrying about something you can't control or change. Morning would finally come, but not soon enough. I lay awake watching the outside window. I saw the black night turn into daylight. It was a gradual change that took forever; like watching and waiting for water to boil, or paint to dry. I kept looking at the time to make it go faster, but that didn't work.

While waiting for morning light, my mind wandered and took me back to the old days. Derek was young then and quite restless. The expectation of his being a good boy at school, was synonymous with the Ford Edsel being the ultimate car of the future. He wouldn't get in trouble, necessarily, because he knew how far to take his antics. Most restless and disobedient kids would break the rules, but not Derek. He would *bend* the rules; bend them about eighty-nine degrees, just before breaking them, and then backing off. So, he hardly got in trouble because he didn't break the rules but bent them enough to get the other kids in trouble; the ones who were involved. That was Derek; usually coming out innocent while the others took the rap. In retrospect, it seems to me he had a condition known as Gifted and Talented; hardly ever diagnosed. He was very capable in school but had a tendency to disturb the class because of boredom. T and G students weren't recognized for who they were in those days. Some of them came off as just being problem kids, even though they were brilliant and could excel beyond the rest of the class. Even today, he would probably be misdiagnosed as having ADHD, OCD, ODD, or some similar condition.

Both my sons were always very close when they were kids. As they grew older, they drifted apart and had their own interests. Joey was more practical, and in many ways, more mature. He pursued his education and wound up with a good job in marketing, which had him travelling the North East. I never really had concern for Joey, but Derek became disquieting. Derek was the carefree, live-for-today kind of guy. He really had no ambition to speak of, except to have as much fun as possible. I attributed that to be the result of educators allowing him to fall through the cracks during his school years. He ended up going from job to job that didn't amount to much. Most of the time, he would just borrow money from whomever would lend any. Both boys had their own friends, who didn't care for the friends of the other.

He grew up to be quite a handsome young man with big brown eyes the girls usually commented on. His build was tall and slender with upper body muscles you could notice even with his shirt on. He also sported a dark beard that made him look a little mysterious. Yes, Derek had all of the attributes needed to be considered a chick magnet by some of his friends. In my opinion, and many others, he could certainly hold his own against any of the Hollywood heartthrobs of the time. His antics continued into adulthood, however; only worse and more creative. It was hard for him to stay out of trouble. His problems were mostly related to women and drinking, which cost him a couple teeth once in a fight he had with a jealous boyfriend. He also had a tendency to drive fast on the road and wound up with a few speeding tickets he avoided paying. So, he had a few court dates as well. But still, he never went to jail.

In his early twenties, he made a serious decision to become an actor. He had always been interested in watching movies and going out to see a play. He would critique what he saw as though he knew the craft better than the actors themselves. But at a certain age, he got serious about it and talked often about moving out west, where the opportunities were. I was against the notion, since his odds of making it were no better than anyone else's, and *those* odds were never very good. I was more in favor of his learning some kind of trade, so as to not have to go through too much academics. He wouldn't hear of it. In his mind, he would become famous and make it rich. Despite my uneasiness about his moving out, he finally decided to do so. He was twenty-three when he moved. Carolyn wanted some kind of going away party for him, even if we were against it. So, we set it up and got a bunch of party things and food. The party wasn't anything special. We didn't rent a hall and things like that. We wanted to keep it fairly low key, while at the same time, making sure he knew we supported his decision to leave. We didn't like it, but we supported it. We had invited Derek's friends, some family members, and of course Joey's fiancée, Francine. From the start of the festivities Derek was loud, and some would say, obnoxious. He had been drinking most of the day and it showed. I told Carolyn and Joey to just bear it, so we went about celebrating and wishing him well with his future prospects. Later that evening, most of us were in the living room. We were eating, drinking, and having a good time. Music and voices were blaring. Suddenly we heard a ruckus that sounded like someone wrestling, as well as breakables falling to the floor in one of the bedrooms upstairs. I ran to the stairs, as did everyone else, to suddenly see Derek and Joey fighting. It wasn't easy to break up, but with the help of Derek's friends, we finally did. Derek was bleeding from the nose, while Joey had a welt on his left eye. Also, in the room, was Joey's fiancée, who was sitting on the bed crying. Her sweater was torn, and her hair was disheveled. It turns out Derek tried to force himself on her. She had come out of the upstairs bathroom, all the while he was waiting for her. As she came out, he grabbed her and forced her into the nearest bedroom, where he attacked her on the bed against her will. Fortunately, Joey was on his way upstairs to see her, when he heard the commotion.

After the fight was broken up, Derek stormed out; staggering, and mumbling something no one heard. He took the front door and we never saw him again. Over time, and only on special occasions, he would get in touch with me from L.A. to say hi. It's a good thing he did, otherwise I would never have gotten his number. However, he never reached out to his brother to apologize. Joey finally married Francine but never bothered to invite Derek. Who could blame him, really?

## ~The Phone Calls~

After a long night of reminiscing and waiting for morning, it was daybreak and late enough for me to call Derek without having to worry about depriving him of any sleep. Even if he was still sleeping, I could tell him it was late enough to get up.

I went to the bathroom and got ready for the day, as I had a couple of day classes later. When I got out, I made coffee and sat down in the living room looking at my phone. It took me a while to find his number, as I hardly ever called it. At last I found it, and in a New York minute, started dialing.

As I heard the ringtone, I began to think whether it was a good idea to call. What if he was busy with some rehearsal or something, I thought? There's no way he would be able to answer without disrupting things on the set; assuming he was busy on a set, that is. If that was the case, I'd probably hear some kind of recording telling me to leave a message, which I wasn't prepared to do. What would I say? 'Hey, did you hear about your grandfather?' That wouldn't have been appropriate, even if Derek was the type to leave such a message himself. As I was thinking about what to say in his voicemail, I heard someone pick up on the other end, and a voice said hello.

"Hi Derek, it's Dad."

"Oh, hey." Then he paused a bit. "What's up?"

"How are you?"

"Okay. How about you?"

Here was that small talk again. It's incredible how often people use small talk to get around the conversations they want to avoid.

"Hey, did you happen to get a message from Joey recently?" I asked, as if I didn't know the answer to that.

"No, why would I get a message from *him*?"

"It's your grandpa, Derek. He had a stroke last Saturday."

"Oh wow, I didn't know that. Is he alright?"

I could tell in his voice he wasn't moved much. If I could have seen his face, it would have been even more obvious, I'm sure. Especially if he had tried to fake his expression to seem like he cared. He was never very good at hiding his true feelings. Then I figured, why *should* he care? It's not like he's been a part of the family in recent years or anything. The last time he had seen my father was when he was in a drunken stupor a few years back during a New Year's Eve party. I remember my father being appalled at how obnoxious and inconsiderate Derek was, which I took to be a reflection on me.

"No, he's not alright." I replied. "He's in the critical care unit. He's not responsive and doesn't even realize anyone's in the room with him."

"Oh, wow. That sucks." was his response.

I knew I should maybe change the subject at that moment. Why waste time talking about someone he doesn't care about, much less come for a visit to see him? I thought I would at least catch up with how things were with him. I was at a point where I wouldn't even mind some small talk with my son.

"How have you been?" I asked. "Are you working?"

"Yeah. I wait on tables every once in a while, but I got an audition coming up in a little while."

"An audition? That's great! Is it a commercial or maybe something a little better?" I was hoping for the best. He was my son, after all.

"Well it's for a play."

"With a touring group?" I tried to sound enthused, while aware it was an unlikely prospect.

"Nah." he answered. "It's a community theater, but they provide a stipend for the cast."

"That's great." I said, knowing it wasn't. I was tempted to give him a taste of his own medicine and tell him it sucks, but I didn't.

"It's pretty close to home too." he added.

"Oh, yeah? So where are you staying now? You got your own place?"

"Not right now. I'm saving up for a decent apartment. I'm staying with a friend right now."

I wanted to tell him to come home, make good with your brother, come see your grandpa, but I knew it would have been in vain. I was certain a plea like that would have been absolutely unproductive. Then, came the moment I thought would come sooner, and had anticipated since he picked up the phone.

"Hey, Dad, I gotta go." he said. "I don't want to be late for the audition."

Well, there it was; the disconnect; the blow off. I was happy to have had *this* much time talking to him at least, but knew he'd want to quit the call as soon as he could.

"Okay." I said. "Don't be a stranger."

"I won't."

"Alright, take it easy."

"Bye."

Having said our goodbyes, we hung up. At least he knew now, I thought. However, I couldn't help but feel sorry I called him at all. It seems I would have been better off not knowing he was waiting on tables in L.A., while hoping for a possible stipend from some unknown theater company. Also, his indifference towards the condition of his own grandfather was heartbreaking. Did I raise him to be so uncaring? The answer to that, was no. I did the best I could with him and Joey. The whole conversation bothered me for a while, but after philosophizing a little, I decided to give Joey a call. His wife answered, and after talking with her for a while, she handed the phone to Joey.

"Hi Joey."

"Hey Dad. How are you?"

"I'm fine thanks. I just got off the phone with your brother." I said.

"Oh yeah?"

When I heard that, I immediately thought of how much he sounded like Derek; same voice, and same uncaring tone. At least Joey had a reason to be callous towards his brother, even if it was still wrong. Anyway, I decided not to bring up Derek's name again. We continued our conversation for about fifteen minutes. We talked about his grandfather in the hospital, for a while. I found Joey to be very sympathetic towards his condition. I could definitely hear a reflection of how he was raised; with dignity, and loyalty to family and friends. This was in direct contrast to what I had heard in Derek. But I knew from years of experience that no two children are alike; even from the same parents and raised in the same way. In the end, he told me he had to get ready for work. I said I had to do the same, but before we hung up, I had to ask him.

"Why do you think the hospital called you instead of me?"

"I don't know." he said. "I just figured they called the first number they could get their hands on, I guess."

Well, there was my answer. It seems my father didn't want any direct communication with me after our last phone call. I guess, I don't blame him. Before letting me go, Joey was sure to request I call his mother to tell her. Reluctantly, I agreed, and we said goodbye.

It had been a while since I talked to Carolyn. I wondered how it would be to dial her number again; weird, I thought. But not as weird as actually talking to her again. That would be awkward as a bulldog in leotards. No matter, I knew it was the right thing to do, so I looked up her number and dialed.

She answered, "Hello?"

The sound of her voice stirred something in me. It was something that had been dormant since we drifted apart. It took me back to the days of being in love with her and wanting to be with her forever. It took me back to when the kids were young and innocent; back to when life was not so complicated. To say I was still in love with her, wouldn't be true. I wasn't. But there's a feeling you get when you visit the past by hearing a song, or a voice. It's a feeling that is undeniable; one that you can't argue with. It was weird but still, the sound of her voice stirred something in me.

"Hi," I said, "It's Ray."

"Ray?"

"Yes. How are you, Carolyn?"

"I'm okay, Ray, how about you?"

I guess every phone call begins with insignificant discourse.

"I'm alright."

"To what do I owe the pleasure?" she asked.

I tried to be delicate. "Well the reason for the call is, I wanted to let you know that my father had a stroke a couple of days ago."

"Oh my God, no! How bad is it?"

"They don't think he'll make it."

"Oh no, I'm so sorry."

Upon hearing that, I remembered it was exactly what Sarah had said when I told *her*. I knew somewhere along our conversation; something would evoke the awkward feeling I dreaded. I had no idea it would be something as simple as her echoing Sarah. Sometimes, life is weird.

"Yeah, I just wanted you to know." I said.

"Where is he?"

"Tisch Hospital on First Avenue; critical care."

"Okay, I think I'll go see him. At least he's getting the best care possible, being there."

"I'm sure he is."

"That's just terrible."

"Yeah." I didn't know what else to say. "Just wanted to let you know." I was sure I had said that already.

"Well thank you, Ray. I hope everything turns out for the best."

That last comment made me feel as though she were no longer in the family; and, of course, she wasn't. I felt bad because of it. We talked for a little while longer, but nothing to speak of. We were estranged, and that's the way we agreed it would be. Funny how even when something is over, you don't consider it permanent. There's always a little longing that things can be undone, and everything would be back to normal. However, life doesn't always cooperate, and you're left making the best of things as they are. Carolyn and I were still friends it seemed, and I was okay with that.

After we hung up, it was almost time to get the day started. I had a couple of classes to conduct, and I promised myself I wouldn't blow up at the students like the night before. I poured another cup of coffee and read the paper until it was time to leave.

# ~A Visit to Tisch~

I got to work on time. In fact, I was a little earlier than usual, so I had a chance to sit at my desk, get my stuff ready, and check my phone messages as the students came in sporadically. I was glad to see a message from Sarah, saying she had a wonderful time the night before. She also asked if we would continue working on her empirical paper. I replied I had the same, and yes, we would work on her paper; over dinner, I added. She returned a smiley face. I loved those smiley faces. I had come to expect them as much as her little purple notes she would slip me without my awareness.

I didn't blow my stack in front of the students this time. I think I was accepting of things a little more. There were some awkward moments when the class was quieter than normal for fear of my wrath or emotional instability, but things seemed to resume normally when the students realized my outburst must have been just a moment in time. Everyone should be allowed moments of reaching the breaking point sometimes. We're all very vulnerable, after all. At any rate, I tried hard not to think about the morning phone call to Derek, and other disturbing thoughts. With that mindset, I was able to conduct class normally and without incident.

Directly after my classes, I went straight to the hospital. I knew my father wouldn't respond or even know I was there, but I had some things to say to him that couldn't wait. I also knew I was going there for me, and not necessarily for him. If he couldn't hear me, it made no difference to him if I was there or not. However, I needed to talk to him before the inevitable happened, if for no other reason than to free some of my guilt.

There's a sterile smell inside every hospital I've ever been in. It's a smell that is clean, but I always associated it with doom and gloom. I sometimes thought how much more pleasant hospitals would be if they smelled like your own kitchen or living room. This one was no exception. From the moment I walked in, I was instantly reminded there were sick or injured people; some of them dying like my father. I knew the staff personnel were doing what they could to help them, but the ultimate fate would be beyond their control. To me hospitals were places where some people waited in a waiting area until they received the news; good or bad.

In case the critical care ward only allowed two immediate family members in at a time to visit a patient, I was sure to tell them I was his son so they would let me in. They told me my sister was in there also. I didn't pursue that, but wondered what they meant, since I don't have a sister. When I entered the room, I saw the one who claimed to be my father's daughter. It was Carolyn. She obviously played it safe also by telling them she was his daughter. Even though I had recently talked with her on the phone, I hadn't seen her in a long time, and I must say she hadn't changed. She was a beautiful woman of fifty-one, with just the right number of highlights in her hair to bring out her eyes. She always took pride in her appearance and I was happy to see she hadn't lost that sense of pride. She stood around five and a half feet tall and was pleasingly plump. She always hated when I said that, but that's married life for you. She obviously looked somber when I came in the room, but that was to be expected.

"Hi sis." I joked, in an attempt to break the somber mood.

"Hi." She said, laughingly, "If that was the only way I could get in, I didn't want to take a chance."

"How is he?" I asked, looking in his direction.

"He doesn't respond. I tried holding his hand and stroking his hair, but no response."

My father, the man who gave me life and raised me, was lying in bed all hooked up with tubes and wires. His mouth was open, and he looked pale and sad. His eyes were closed but I could still see they were sunken in. The left side of his face looked like wax drooping from the top of a lit candle, and every once in a while, one of his eyebrows would twitch. There were two intravenous bags connected to his arm, and I heard and saw hospital equipment monitoring his vital signs; one of them beeping constantly. I also heard one pulling and releasing air every two seconds or so. It was as though it was breathing for him. Having seen enough, I turned my attention to Carolyn. We talked quietly for a while about nothing. We tried to find some common ground on what we used to talk about, but that was in the past and the present made us different. What we had in common was gone. The only thing we had in common at the moment, was grief for a dying man. We were still talking quietly as if to not disturb the man who was barely there. I wondered why. Why were we almost whispering? Was it out of respect, or was it out of fear of disturbing him? I guessed it was just the right thing to do. Finally, the conversation returned to my father.

"Thank you for coming to be with him." I said.

"He's a great man, Ray. I had to see him even if he can't communicate."

"I know. It's like we're talking to him for nothing."

"You never know. They say strange things happen when they're in that state."

"Like a deaf person, suddenly hearing." I added.

"That's right." She went on, "Say what you need to say to him, Ray. Don't hold anything back. I have a feeling he'll hear you even if there's no response from him."

I simply nodded pensively but didn't move towards him. What I had to say was private. She must have read my mind because she immediately began to put her coat on. That was the thing I admired about her. She was always sensible and knew what was appropriate and at the right time.

"Well I was getting ready to go when you came in, Ray. I've been here for a little while now and I have a few errands to run. It was nice seeing you again."

"Likewise." I replied.

We hugged, as grieving people would, and she left. It was nice seeing her again, but I felt a real chasm between us, emotionally. It was as though we had drifted even further. We hardly had anything in common anymore, and I was sure she had met someone since the divorce, which I was fine with.

Being alone with my father, I moved closer to the bed and sat next to him. I took his hand and rubbed it with my thumb up and down, as he used to do with me when I sat on his lap years before. I remembered how it was when my mother died; how my father was at *her* bedside, as I was at his at the moment. I also felt as if, somehow, she was in the room with us. I began to speak.

"Dad…?" I paused for what seemed forever. If he had been conscious, he would undoubtedly have known I was lost for words. Finally, I spoke my mind. "I just want to say that I'm sorry. When we talked on the phone the other day, I was angry and impatient. I realize you did the best you could with what you had when I was young, and I took that for granted." I saw his eyebrow move a little as though he could understand. Maybe Carolyn was right after all. I went on with even more conviction. "No parent deserves a son or daughter who displays such disrespect for them. I know I wasn't always the perfect son, but I want you to know that I'm sorry for the times I wasn't." I thought about something else I would have liked to say if he could hear. "Dad, I know there were times you'd like to take back too. There were times in your life that you're not proud of, I'm sure. I want you to know that I forgive you. I know how imperfect people are. I've studied them all my life. It's these imperfections that make us who we are, though, and that's a good thing. But sometimes we do or say things we shouldn't, and we need to understand that it's just a moment in time. We need to move on and forgive. I don't want you to feel bad about anything you've said or done. Just know, that I forgive you. But regardless of the stupid things we do, as flawed as we are, you're a good man and always have been." I recalled that snowy day when I was younger. "Remember when you were trying to save that poor girl who got hit by a car in that dreadful snow storm years and years ago? I was so proud of you and hoped I would be just like you. You're braver than I ever was."

After having said all that, I felt better about being there with him. I continued honestly with moments that are sometimes overlooked. "We had some great times too, didn't we?" I said, with as much enthusiasm as I could muster. "All the chess games and the stories we'd tell during a storm when we lost our electricity. Remember when we scared mom out of her wits with that enormous fake spider? She broke a window trying to kill it with the broom. Boy, did we get hell after that?"

I found myself smiling just thinking of these things, and it dawned on me; there *were* good times. I wasn't just trying to lighten things up. There were good times, and there were many. I looked at him and saw the quietness in his face. I wondered if he'd heard anything I said. Then I thought I felt his hand squeeze mine. It may have been some reflex brought on by heavy doses of morphine, or a reaction to a sudden itch he couldn't scratch, or it could have been a number of insignificant things. But on the other hand, it might have been something more profound. That thought made me cry.

I stayed a while longer. Eventually, the resident priest came in to administer the sacrament of the anointing of the sick. When it was done, I left. I thought it might be the last time I saw him, but at least I had a chance to talk to him. I left the hospital feeling satisfied I had somehow made amends with my father, but not on a level as superficial as talking to one another. It was on another level I can't describe with words. All I can say is when you can convey feelings without talking, there's no possibility of deception.

When I got home, I reminisced, looking at some old family photos and relaxed knowing it was a good day. I messaged Sarah to confirm our session on the following day, with all the details of when and where. She replied with 'can't wait'. When it was time for bed, I didn't think about how wrong our relationship was. I slept like a baby.

## ~Questions of Ethics~

The following day was a free day for me, as I didn't have any classes to teach. I reached out to some convalescent homes in the area and booked a couple of more gigs to play for their residents. I also got some lessons prepared for the following week.

I met Sarah in the evening for dinner at the La Lanterna di Vittorio. I saw how radiant she looked from a distance away, as I walked toward her. I could see her smile, which emanated from still a fairly long distance. I also admired the way she looked in what she wore, to be honest. It was a simple outfit, but it gave her a look of sophistication and sex appeal. Finally, we greeted each other at the entrance, then went in. She had some folders with her, and I had a briefcase with me, which we brought for nothing, as it turned out. We sat at a table in their gorgeous garden area that we both agreed was very romantic. I couldn't believe how beautiful she seemed that night. I don't know if it was the pink ribbon in her hair, the daintiness in her mannerisms, or the delicateness of her voice. Whatever it was, it was apparent not only to me, but to most of the men in the restaurant. We tried hard to remain discreet. We got the pleasantries out of the way before we ordered and moved onto more important matters. I asked her about her paper. She opened her folders where they were visible to others in the room and said she didn't want to talk about that. She assured me she was progressing fine and that we could discuss it a later time. She was more interested in getting the ramifications of our relationship ironed out; the subject we had put off a couple of nights before. Frankly, so was I.

"I need to ask you a very important rhetorical question." She said.

"Rhetorical?"

"Rhetorical because we both know the answer."

I knew what the question was. "Okay, hit me." I said.

"Is it ethical for a professor to have relations with his student?"

I was honest, "No, it's not."

"So what are we doing here, then?"

I was frank with her, and replied, "I know it's wrong, but I don't care."

She looked surprised to hear that from me; Mr. Prim and proper; Mr. everything-by-the-book; Mr. middle-aged, worldly, sophisticated professor. I, of all people, *should* care. She must have pondered all these thoughts in her mind. Finally, she broke her silence. "The school must have some policy in place against that." She said. "I don't want you to lose your job."

"There's no formal policy concerning teacher-student dating that I'm aware of."

"But it must be implied in other policies concerning professional conduct."

She had a good point. Just because there's no policy, doesn't make it acceptable behavior. Still, I couldn't just disregard the feelings I had for her. Those feelings were real. What I felt was real, and I couldn't ignore that. Just then, I remembered the headline I had read about three weeks before; the headline that read, 'High School Teacher on Administrative Leave' and how I felt reading the news. I remembered thinking how stupid and irresponsible that teacher was, for throwing away his career. But here I was in a similar situation; perhaps jeopardizing *my* career. Yet, I didn't want to think about that. I cared about my job and reputation, but there was something happening in me that was stronger than my sense of rationale. Justification for irrational behavior is a fact of human life, but I never thought I would find myself in a position to justify, or even deny my misconduct.

"Look," I said, "I know it's considered wrong. But who's to say that it *is* wrong? Should we ignore what we feel just because of some obscure, implicit policy?"

"I don't want you to lose your job. I don't want to be the cause of that."

"Is that your only concern; my job?"

"Actually, it is. I don't happen to care what others think."

"You said yourself that we don't know what the future holds; that we shouldn't worry about what might not exist. We may not have to worry about anything."

She had that dubious look again, as though I had just told her the sky was not actually blue, but light salmon with yellow polka dots and violet streaks. I knew what that look was for and she didn't have to say it. It was obvious we both knew that ours, was most likely a relationship that would flourish to some degree. To what degree, we didn't know. At any rate, I tried to explain my true feelings.

"You said you don't care what others think." I said, "Well, neither do I. I'm also not worried about losing my job. This is something we can move forward with without anyone else knowing. I know society says it's wrong, but I'll be damned if I'm going to let a dishonest society that doesn't believe in a moral absolute, tell me what to do and what not to do. I've studied people all my life. I know how fake people can be, how fake a society can be, and I won't let anyone, or anything stand in the way of how I feel."

To that, she asked, "How *do* you feel?"

"I want to continue with what we may or may not have. It's not up to anyone to decide, but those involved; me and you."

"I feel the same way." she said. I could almost see relief in her face.

I tried to lighten up the mood, "Good," I replied. "But don't expect any favoritism in class."

She laughed. "Not even a little?"

"Not even a little."

And with that, we enjoyed our dinner, kept an open mind, and tried not to think about it or bring it up again.

## ~Childhood Fears~

The food finally came, with a bottle of vintage wine. This was an Italian restaurant to beat all others. It was great, and so was the atmosphere. There was a jazz band playing in the club next door, which we could hear from where we were sitting. It was just the right volume for us and provided the right ambience. The lighting was dim enough to see each other well but made the people at other tables seem like shadows. You couldn't ask for a better environment for fine dining and privacy. I promised myself I would go back there again.

She looked reluctant when she asked me how my father was doing. I thought part of her wanted to know how he was, but a greater part of her wanted to know how *I* was feeling about his condition. So, we talked about it; to what degree his condition was deteriorating, but that I was better about it. I told her about how I heard the news and had gone to see him; how I talked to him and he seemed to acknowledge he understood. She was happy to hear all this, and it seemed to have a great impact on her. Then the conversation took a turn that unveiled some truths about us both. We conversed as we ate slowly.

"Tell me about him." she said. "I want to know about him."

"Well, he did the best he could with what he had." I replied.

"No, I want to hear about *him*. What was he like? Did you have a good relationship with him?"

"He provided for us."

She laughed, "That's it?"

"No, not quite."

She raised her eyebrows as if to say, 'I'm waiting'. With that, I decided to not keep anything from her.

"My father was an alcoholic."

"Oh, I'm sorry to hear that."

"Most of the time, he didn't talk much. But when he was drunk, you couldn't shut him up. Some people, when they get drunk, they get depressed and quiet, or giddy and stupid, or whatever. But when my father got drunk, he got mad and boisterous. Nobody liked him."

"How bad?"

"He used to get mad."

"At nothing, I bet."

"At nothing." I went on, "It was as though all the frustrations he felt from recent past, was coming to the surface and exploded into a tirade of abusive language and physical violence."

"That must have been hard on you." She seemed genuinely concerned.

"And hard on my mother." I added. "He would slam doors and scream out obscenities directed mostly at my mother. My brother and I would just hide upstairs and tried not to hear what was going on."

There seemed to be fear in her eyes, as she looked intently at me as I spoke. It was as if she were living the moment of terror I felt when I was a kid. I wanted to reach over and comfort her, but there were other people there to be careful of. I wanted to stop talking, or at least change the subject, but she insisted I continue.

"Why don't we talk about something else?" I said.

"No, I want you to tell me everything. I want to know. Did he ever hit you, or anyone?"

She sounded sincere and thoughtful. She also sounded like she would be a wonderful psychologist someday. I couldn't help but wonder if this particular conversation of ours was a trial run for her future career. I immediately dismissed that thought because I had been in similar situations. Sometimes, you tend to get consumed with someone's personal story if it's tragic enough. You can't help but want to hear more, and secretly try to analyze the wrong, being perpetrated on the innocent.

"I saw him beat my brother once, but he never touched *me*." I replied. "He was very scary. Sometimes he would pass out or just get sick. I couldn't bear to see my father like that. We wanted to help him but were too afraid." She looked as empathetic as I'd seen anyone look. I continued, "So, that was the bad in him, but he also has another side."

"Tell me." she said.

"When he was sober, he was passive and gentle. He didn't say much, but that's not always a negative character trait. It's just who he is. He's a religious man who could quote the bible; book, chapter, and verses."

"There are two sides to all of us, isn't there?" she remarked.

"Sometimes, there are more than two. It depends on where you are and who you're with."

"Agreed."

I ended the discussion of my father on a good note. "I went to see him yesterday and talked to him."

"Oh, good. Was he responsive?"

"I don't know how to answer that. I felt as though he understood what I was saying. It could be my imagination."

Her expression was reassuring, as she said, "I don't think so."

"I like to think he heard me. I'm very happy to have had that chance. I feel like we both had some closure. I also feel that in some way, he was able to apologize to me as well."

She just smiled and responded by looking happy and understanding.

Talking like that, brought me back to those days; back to my childhood. It dawned on me that the perception of a child is not always true to real life. Sometimes things seem worse than they are, and by the same token, a child may not recognize the gravity of other situations. For example, I sometimes thought I wasn't wanted by my parents. In retrospect, I now know there was no reason for me to feel that way. My parents raised and treated me in the same manner as my brother. Similarly, my brother sometimes thought he was adopted. It was a ridiculous notion, since he looked just like me and we both resembled my father. In either situation, we had misconceptions about ourselves and the people in our lives. I wondered how many times these misconceptions break up families, or otherwise create friction that escalate to animosity.

I felt a sense of relief after our talk about my father. There's a satisfaction in knowing that someone understands the pain or joy you've experienced sometime in your life. It felt as though I had just had a very successful session of therapy. I don't know if I felt that way because of my visit to the hospital, or talking about it with Sarah, or a combination of both. I do know I felt relieved, and that's all that mattered. Engaging in any other details or analyses would be a waste of time.

Having said what I wanted to say and what she wanted to hear; I turned the conversation to her. "So, what's *your* story, little lady?"

"My story is boring."

"Try me."

"Well, I was born and raised in Brooklyn."

"I gathered that." I said.

"How would you know?"

"It doesn't take a genius. I know that Brooklyn is a heavily populated Jewish community." I saw the doubt in her face but continued. "I noticed you only eat kosher. What better place to live in, if you're of a strict, orthodox Jewish background?"

"I see." She looked amused. "I'll have to be careful around you. You know too much." she added.

"I don't know too much about *you*."

I knew one thing for sure about her. She liked to play with her hair when she was reluctant or shy about something. She began her finger twirling again, as I had seen her do so many times since we had met. It was something I had come to expect from her, and it was absolutely adorable.

"Okay," she began, "So I was raised by a strict orthodox Jewish man, who insisted on making sure we didn't deviate from our Jewish heritage. He was like that with all of us; me, my mom, and my brother. It was oppressive in many ways. It was like being raised by Abraham himself."

"No ham or bacon, and things like that?"

"No pork at all, but it wasn't just food. We had to adhere to certain practices on Jewish holidays; no electronic devices, or whatever." she said.

By then, I started to understand why she had corrected me so adamantly on that first day of class. She was conditioned to recognize what was right and wrong in terms of her Jewish traditions. She also knew the real truth about the holocaust and her people's history.

"These traditions are sometimes regarded as a hindrance, by today's standards." I said.

"They're a hindrance by today's standards, but we don't use today's standards as reference. By our own standards, these are the right things to do and observe."

That's what I liked about Sarah; you couldn't argue with her. She made you look at your own world from a different perspective, which was sometimes challenging. I wanted to know more. I also thought maybe she was telling me things she had never spoken of with anyone else.

"What about your community; where you lived?" I asked.

"It was a humble home in a stringent neighborhood. Everybody knew one another, but we kept the doors locked anyway."

"Why?"

"Fear."

"Fear of what?" I asked

"I thought you knew everything." she replied, playfully. I just sat there expecting her to go on with her story, but she insisted I try to figure out why they locked the doors. "Go on, smarty-pants. Why do you think we locked the doors?" she asked with a smile.

"Because your neighbors felt safer with you locked up?" I joked.

She laughed one of those belly laughs that only happens once in a while, and you don't experience nearly enough. As she laughed, I looked at her and smiled. For the first time in a long time, I was happy. I hadn't had this kind of silliness in my life since I could remember. I remember thinking how great it all was; my being with someone I could talk to on any level, the atmosphere of the restaurant, the food, the laughs, and everything else. Everything seemed perfect. It suddenly dawned on me how important it was to be silly, to be curious, to be a child.

After her laughter subsided, I said, "Okay, I give up. Why did you lock your doors?"

She became more serious, but not somber. I could tell she was having a great time too, and neither of us allowed ourselves to ruin the mood. She replied, "There are people out there who don't like us because of who we are, or what we stand for, or God knows why. Sometimes, we would wake up in the morning and there would be a sign on our door with anti-Semitic slurs, or sometimes there was graffiti done with paint that said the same things. We'd see swastikas, and outright threats. It was pretty scary sometimes. We just had to be careful and made sure we were safe at night, and even during the day."

"I'm sorry you had to go through that." I said.

"Me too, but like any other situation, it could be worse."

"You're very strong to have an attitude like that."

"I drew my strength from my grandmother." she added.

"I'm sure you did. She must have been a great role model for you, and everyone who knew her story actually."

She replied, "It was scary to hear those stories, though. She made sure we heard what happened as soon as we were old enough to understand. To her, it was important for us to know what happened as soon as possible. I'm sure it was therapeutic for her to tell her story as well."

"Speaking of which, I feel we've just been through some form of therapy ourselves." I said, smiling.

"Yeah, I know what you mean; talking about our childhood fears and all."

"Exactly. When is our next therapy session?" I asked, jokingly.

At that, she laughed again. For some reason, I felt a great sense of accomplishment when I was able to make her laugh. I felt as though she deserved it. I felt she might have had a difficult childhood with all of the hatred inflicted in her neighborhood, and I'm sure, other places where such prejudice was rampant. But mostly, seeing her laugh, made me happy.

When our dinner was done and we were ready to leave, I walked her to her car as I normally did. The night was fairly bright, as there was not a cloud in the sky. The moon's light was reflecting off of the frozen snow, and the stars were radiant with their formation. We tried hard to identify the constellations as we walked slowly. We could see our breath in the air, and the chill of the night made us hold on to each other. We held each other so as to not slip and fall, or maybe it was to keep warm. Either of those two reasons were possible, or neither. Maybe we didn't need a reason. Maybe we just wanted to be close. When we got to her car, we kissed. Then I opened her door and she got in, thanking me.

"My pleasure." I replied.

I waited before closing the door, as she began to speak, "Raymond..." she said softly.

"Yes?" I asked.

"Would you like to come over for a nightcap?"

I knew what that meant. It had nothing to do with drinking wine or admiring her apartment. This was the moment I hadn't anticipated. I guess in the back of my mind, I knew it would come, but it came more suddenly than I expected. She looked at me waiting for an answer with a smile.

"I would love to," I said, hesitantly, "but I have to get up early tomorrow morning."

With that, she nodded, smiled, and said, "I understand. Goodnight, Raymond."

"Goodnight." I replied.

I'm sure she understood what I meant; that I wasn't ready. There's a time and place for everything, and that particular night was not the right time. I reached in and kissed her. We kissed as though we were lovers; as though we didn't want the evening to end; as though we were saying thank you for confiding in me, because that's what lovers do.

When I got home, I found the little note on purple paper. It was tucked into the side pocket of my briefcase. I was trying to remember when she would have had the opportunity to slip this one in, since I hadn't excused myself away from the table all night. It seemed there was no opportunity I could think of. Instead, I resolved to the fact that she shouldn't be underestimated. In any case, this one read, 'Had a great night!'. She didn't put her initials on the bottom, as she was used to doing. She simply drew a heart on this one.

I went to bed that night feeling happy. In all the years I had been in academia, I never once broke any laws or school policies. This was a first for me. Under normal circumstances, I would have reasoned it out logically and followed the proper code of conduct. In this circumstance, I didn't care. I slept soundly until I received a phone call from the hospital at around three thirty in the morning. My father had passed away.

# Week 5

## ~The Wake~

ALL my classes for the week were cancelled for obvious reasons. I took that time to look after the process of taking care of a death in the family; the funeral home, the obituary, the prayer cards, you name it. Funny how everyone has their hand out when someone dies. Everyone wants their cut where there's money to be made. So, the next few days after my father passed away, I was busy making other people richer; a very difficult task when one is grieving. I also found those people I had to deal with, very cold. To them, this was just another transaction; making sure every penny and bank account was accounted for. Oh, to be sure when first greeting them, they acted all empathetic. However, when the formalities were over, it was right down to business; making sure the bottom line was in the right hands faster than a diarrhetic jackrabbit on steroids. They just seemed to have no compassion, or consideration for those whose lives were affected by the loss. So, I made all the necessary arrangements for Thursday. My father's wish was to be cremated, with as little fuss as possible. I arranged for viewing services preceding the actual cremation at the Andrett Funeral Home on Bleecker

Street, but nothing big in terms of a reception following the services. I thought perhaps there might be someone I might go eat with afterwards, if it came to that and if I was up to it. At any rate, Thursday finally came and there was nothing left to do but go to the funeral home and grieve.

Funeral homes are all the same. There's an odor that is disturbing. I don't know if it's the makeup they use to make the deceased look acceptable for showing, but it's an odor you don't smell anywhere else. Whatever it is, it could conceivably give you nightmares about being in a room alone with corpses. Also, the abundance of flowers that are laid out everywhere, are enough to flare up an allergic sneezing fit. There's always someone at the door welcoming you as if you're a willing guest. Upon entering, you sign the guest book no one looks at, then you make your way to the parlor where your loved one is. There, they're displayed like a piece of furniture for everyone to notice and comment on. With flowers all around, your loved one looks like an ornament in some lonely garden. Still, I think wakes and funerals are more dignified than weddings. At least no one plays stupid catch-the-garter games.

People came in and went through the receiving line I was in. I heard all the necessary condoling wishes and expressions. I also heard things like, 'He's in a better place.' and, 'He looks at peace.' I even heard someone say, 'He looks good'. There were a couple of teenage girls giggling in the back; probably talking about who the cutest boy in the room might be. At any rate, I was surprised to see how many people my father knew, and how many were affected by his life. Carolyn was there, of course. I wouldn't have expected otherwise. My brother was not, which was understandable. He was institutionalized at a young age and was in no condition to be there. Joey and his wife were there with the baby, lined up in the receiving line with me. Derek was nowhere to be found. This didn't surprise me in the least. Even if he had wanted to be there, a trip from California to New York is quite a trek. But I was certain he wouldn't have been there even if he lived a block away. The thought of this, made me sad and angry. How could he be so callous? Then again maybe it was for the best, as it would have been awkward at the very least, for him to be under the same roof as Joey and his wife. Finally, the flow of people coming in, started to abate, so I sat down. After a while, Carolyn decided to sit next to me, and we talked for a while. I could see Joey eyeing us every so often.

"How are you feeling?" she asked.

"I'm fine."

"Did you get to talk to him after I left the hospital?"

"Yes, I did. It seemed to me that he could hear me. Even if he didn't, I feel better about things."

"That's good. I know he had his faults, but he was a good man at heart."

"We all have faults. His was no worse than mine or yours." I said.

"Well, he certainly raised a good man in you."

I was happy to hear that. With all our differences, she still respected me at least. Her saying that didn't surprise me, though. She was always a good person herself.

"Thank you." I said, as I thought about everything I was doing wrong at the moment; courting a twenty-five-year-old student of mine when I know full well it's against any school's code of ethics. She must have noted something in my expression. She was always so astute when it came to stuff like that. Whenever I did anything behind her back when we were married, she knew. I'm not sure how, but she knew. When she would confront me on it, my expression gave everything away. Then, she was sure. At any rate, here she was calling me a good man. My expression must have given me away as a fraud.

"What? Don't you believe me?" she asked, playfully.

"Just trying to be humble."

She looked at me. No, she studied me. My eyebrows raised a little as if to say, 'What?'

"You must be hiding something, Ray?" she said with a smile, as if to bust me up about some dark secret I might have.

At that moment, I thought of how Sarah chose to call me Raymond, which I preferred. Hearing Ray just brought back memories of being married again and confronted for doing something wrong. I became incensed. The whole experience of losing my father and getting his arrangements in order, got the better of me. The notion that I *was* doing something as wrong as violating school ethical codes, became a reality I never would have admitted to in a million years.

"No I'm not!" I replied loud enough to be heard by most.

Coming back to my senses and realizing where I was, I immediately composed myself and looked around with a contrite look to make sure everyone who was looking our way, knew everything was alright. Then I saw Joey walking towards us. I prepared myself with possible answers to any inquiry he might have concerning my little outburst.

"Is everything alright, Dad?" he whispered.

I always hated people whispering at me.

"Yes, everything's fine." I replied.

"Everything's fine." Carolyn repeated.

He persisted. "Dad, you want to go outside for a while to get some air?"

That didn't help matters. Why would he think I was the one who needed air?

"Maybe later. Everything's alright, Joey." I replied, calmly.

I said that with an air that suggested he should go back to sit with his family and leave us alone. He took the hint. Carolyn suddenly looked at me remorsefully and began to cry.

"I'm sorry, Ray." she said, sobbing.

"For what?"

"I don't know. Did I say something wrong?"

"No, you didn't."

"This must be a terrible day for you. I didn't mean to make things worse."

"You didn't," I assured her, "Everything's okay."

I put my arm around her as she rested her head on my shoulder, crying. At that moment, I realized she was grieving for my father. Grief comes in different forms and happens at times you least expect. Such was that little incident and I accepted it for what it was. I caressed her hair to soothe her and told her it was okay to cry; it was okay to display weakness in the face of death; it was okay. We held each other as we used to. Just then, someone came in the room wearing dark glasses with a black kerchief over her head. She walked towards my father to pay her respects, then stood near the exit. I knew it was her the moment I saw her. Sarah kept a discreet distance from me but looked in my direction. We made eye contact, then she carefully waved at me and began to twirl her hair with her finger as I expected. I wondered if that was her way of coping with uncomfortable situations. I hoped she knew it was Carolyn whom I was trying to comfort.

So, there I was with my ex-wife crying on my shoulder, my son Joey concerned about my wellbeing, and my young female student waving at me trying to be inconspicuous lest someone figured out we were secretly dating. All this was happening while my father was most likely looking down at me thinking, 'serves you right'. To say my emotions were torn would not be an exaggeration. I wondered if Carolyn still had feelings for me. I wondered if Sarah was feeling a little jealousy upon seeing me with my ex-wife. I also wondered if my relationship with Sarah would be jeopardized. What if she were like Carolyn, with a tendency to discover when I was doing something wrong? It made me question if I was indeed doing something wrong by holding and comforting Carolyn. As these thoughts ran through my head, Sarah turned around and left. Just then, I knew there were many decisions I had made in recent days that were terribly wrong, but I didn't care. If those were wrong decisions on my part, I was willing to live with that. Regardless of how I felt, I couldn't change the past. After all, the past is something you can only contemplate, not recreate. After a while, Carolyn composed herself and apologized for what she called a weakness of hers; crying at nothing. I told her it was alright and was happy she felt better.

The time went by very quickly. Soon, it was time to pay our last respects. Everyone said their goodbyes and proceeded out, until Carolyn and I were the last ones remaining. She slowly approached my father, knelt down next to him in prayer, then exited as well. I then found myself alone with him. I approached him, knowing it would be the last time I saw his face on this earth. Looking down at him, I thought of the old days when everything was so different. I reflected on the good times and bad times; the acts of heroism and courage; the agonizing moments of his failures; the growing aches and pains of his progressing old age. I realized how he had aged so gradually, that I didn't even notice any changes in him. But every once in a while, he would complain about how it sucks to get old and go through the inevitable metamorphose. I also thought about the changes *I* was going through; so gradual, yet certain. In the end, I said a final prayer, said goodbye, and somberly left him to join the others outside.

# ~Family Reunion~

It was flurrying a little, but it wasn't a storm that would have any significant accumulation. It also wasn't too cold outside, being the last week in February. If my father were alive, he would have said it was a fairly mild winter, save for the Nor'easter. To my knowledge, he hadn't complained about his joints hurting or any signs of rheumatism. There was no burial service, as he was going to be cremated. I also made no formal plans for what the church calls a collation. So, everyone made their own individual plans of going their way to acknowledge my father's passing in the manner they thought appropriate. I would make sure to have a mass service offered for him in the coming weeks.

Joey and his family stayed with me the night of the wake, as I wouldn't have them drive back home to Vermont on a snowy night. Even if it hadn't been snowing, I wouldn't hear of it. I also wouldn't hear of their sleeping in some overpriced hotel. I was more than happy to have them anyway, since I hadn't seen them in a while. Talking on the phone is never the same. For better or for worse, Joey was with Carolyn when I invited him to stay with me. I had no choice but to invite Carolyn to at least spend some time with us before going home. She accepted; not to be with me, I'm sure, but to chit chat with her son and his family. She hadn't seen them in a long time, as I hadn't.

When we arrived at my house, I broke out the wine and made a little spread with some wheat crackers, pepperoni, and Monterey Jack cheese. I wondered if pepperoni was kosher, and if Sarah would have eaten such a spread. I figured I had more to learn about her and her traditions than I thought and was eager to. Making pleasantries and catching up with old times, we sipped and munched for a while. I hadn't realized how hungry I was. Funny how when we're involved and preoccupied with a tragedy, we forget to engage in fundamental necessities like eating. We talked about the old days and recounted stories of when we were all younger; accounts that happened before Joey's son was born, before Joey was married, and before he lost some of his hair. The old days came back to us like an old friend we hadn't seen in forever. We welcomed them with open arms and embraced them just as we would our own children; whether they lived a stable life in Vermont or led a dynamic and uncertain life on the West coast. We recounted stories that made us laugh, and stories that made us yearn for those days again.

You would think the opposite, but I had always noticed the not-so-good things of the past make us laugh, just as the good things make us sad. I guess it's because we can laugh at the bad, since we survived them and are able to analyze the stupidity behind them. The good things make us sad because those days are over, and we wish we could relive them as before. Regardless of the reasons, it seems to be a fact of human life. Joey, Carolyn, and I had many such moments of reminiscing that night. It made me wonder if I would look back on that night with sadness that it was over. It turns out I would.

The reality of that night was significant. Occasionally, during our conversations and storytelling, I thought about Sarah. I wondered if she would have fit into our lives had she been there. Here we were talking about such things that had happened before she was born. At that moment, there was no place for her in my life. We had nothing in common. I had more in common with the woman who was no longer in my life; the woman who had cried on my shoulder not more than three hours before; the woman who was the mother of my two boys and the grandmother of my grandson and the one on the way. I questioned the direction in which that night would lead me, and the one in which I wanted to go. As fate would have it, the question would be resolved soon.

At one point, when Joey's son was off playing by himself and we were able to talk freely, Joey appealed to Carolyn and me to reconsider our relationship. I think Carolyn explained it very well. She made sure he understood we were both happy with the way things were. We had our own lives to live, and he and his family would never be excluded from our love and devotion. We were both there if anyone of them needed something, or they simply wanted to talk. But altering our lives to be together again, would not be an option. She made known her feelings towards me, indicating she respected and admired me. But she fell short of admitting she loved me. That's exactly how I felt about her, and this mutual disposition would have us remain close friends. Upon hearing her explanation to Joey, I started feeling better about Sarah and our relationship. I had no one in my life, but Sarah. It dawned on me the memory trips were just distant memories long gone. They were moments no longer significant in my life, unless I wanted to live in the past, which I didn't want to do and felt no regret. I saw Joey's expression as she was speaking. He had the same look he had as a child when we told him he couldn't have sweets so late at night or couldn't borrow the car. He had the same look he had when he was turned down by a girl he wanted to date. His, was an expression of discouragement that made you want to hold him and tell him it's alright. It was a look that made you want to cry. However, I knew time would pass and his demeanor would return to normal soon. I could tell Carolyn felt for him the way I did, but it wasn't enough to change the way we felt about each other.

The evening went on a little while longer, before Carolyn felt it was late enough for her to go home. I thanked her for coming and being there for my father. She thanked me in return for the hospitality. Then we said our goodbyes, and she left. Joey, Francine and I talked for a while longer after their son was fast asleep in a sleeping bag, I'd set up for him. We kept the conversation light, as we all had gone through enough stress for one day. After a time, I set them up in the guest room, and went to bed.

I took the time to message Sarah before I turned the light off. I thanked her for being at the wake and made sure she knew whom I was consoling at the funeral home. I also told her I missed her. She replied and assured me she wasn't worried and trusted me. I was happy to read her message, as she told me she missed me too. We then told each other goodnight, and she added a couple of X's and O's. With that, I turned the light off, said a prayer for my father, and went to sleep.

Before Joey left the next morning, we had breakfast at home. I'd made enough scrambled eggs and coffee for everyone, as well as juice for the little one. Francine asked how she could help, but I insisted she just relax and eat. The conversation soon turned to their new baby who would arrive soon.

"Do you know if it's a boy or girl?" I asked.

Francine answered with a smile, "It's a girl."

"That's wonderful. Have you figured out a name for her yet?"

"We're kind of torn." she said. "We're thinking Ann, Ruth, Mary; something from the bible. But I don't like Ruth, and he's not hot on the other names I came up with. So, we don't know. We're not sure yet."

"How about Sarah?" I asked.

That question came out of nowhere. If I had taken the time to think about what I was saying, I don't think I would have said it. But Francine's response surprised me.

"Oh, I love that!" she exclaimed. "Joey, how 'bout Sarah?"

Joey replied, "Yeah, Sarah's okay."

She repeated, "Oh, I love that name. How come we didn't think of that?"

"I love the name too." I said.

I didn't want to push the name on them. After all, it was *their* child. Last thing they needed was someone meddling in their personal decisions. So, we talked about the baby for a while longer and moved on. While eating, Joey asked me what I was doing with my time these days when I'm not at work. I kept it light. I wasn't about to tell him I was dating one of my students who was young enough to be his sister; that my behavior was against the school code of ethics, and that I didn't care about any of that. I told him I was working on publishing another paper and working with someone on their empirical article. I knew he wouldn't want to hear details about it, as those kinds of papers tend to be complicated and require time for analysis. Also, it wasn't a lie. So, I got away with not divulging some truths about his father he wouldn't respect. For some reason, I didn't feel bad about doing that. It was my life; just as his, was his and Derek's, was Derek's.

# ~Weekend of Reflection~

I spent that weekend relaxing after Joey and the family left. I didn't want to see or talk to family or friends, except Sarah. Also, I was more resolute to go after what my heart wanted, rather than my head. Society would have to survive without the contribution of my principled and just behavior. I was too busy doing what felt right. I hardly did any work other than get ready for the following week's lessons. I didn't read or spend time on future projects. I did a lot of thinking instead. I thought about my childhood and how things had changed for me. I thought about my mother telling me to always remain a good boy, and my father letting me get away with shenanigans my mother would never have allowed if she were witness to them. I thought about my own kids, and how I would have handled some things differently during the years of raising them. However, there were many things I wouldn't have changed. I accepted the notion that people will make mistakes as well as good decisions, which shape us into who we are as adults. I accepted the idea no one should regret who they are. If we can make a difference in someone's life along our journey, all the better.

Sarah and I talked on the phone several times before the start of the new week. We confirmed our dates, while I let her know I still held her accountable for the classwork she owed me. I'm sure she secretly knew I would be more flexible with her than other students. She never once mentioned that possibility, but some things go without saying. I knew in my heart she was in a position to pass with flying colors, and so did she. At any rate, we engaged in sometimes profound, and sometimes silly conversations. It was a refreshing change to be able to converse with someone on more than one level. I felt comfortable talking with her and I could tell she did too. We were able to voice our opinions without fear of judgment. We could also speak openly about our failures, concerns, joys, and ambitions. We reflected on our past and heritage; our relatives, and ancestors; our hopes and dreams. Ours, was a relationship that any sane person would envy. It was growing into something wonderful, regardless of our age, and our circumstance.

I went to church that Saturday to give thanks and to reflect on all I had experienced in the past days. I also reflected on what I sometimes wondered; how an older man winds up with a younger woman, or vice versa. I thought perhaps money might be the determining factor, or maybe security, or the like. Never once did I consider the possibility of having some things in common, or even mutual admiration or attraction, as being the reason. However, as my relationship with Sarah became more serious, I knew it could be much more than superficial desires. It was perhaps a more significant factor, such as love.

# Week 6

## ~Song of the Chickadee~

IT was the last day of February, and a rather chilly day, but sunny. Everyone I ran into, was bundled up to keep warm, including me. Throughout the day, I could hear the song of the black-capped chickadee; the wonderful 2-note whistle that sounds exactly like the first two notes of the song "Cheek To Cheek" from the movie Top Hat. Upon hearing the bird's song, I could almost hear Fred Astaire intoning those same two notes when he sang, *'Heaven'*. Those are the notes the chickadee sings; as if to announce it's in heaven because spring is around the corner. I wondered if Irving Berlin was inspired by the chickadee when he wrote it, or if it was simply an act of God most would dismiss as a coincidence. I tend to think the latter, as most probable. I used to hear that late winter bird call when I was young, not giving it much notice. But as I grew older, I was amazed to hear the same song every day around this time of year. It brought me back to a more carefree time in my life. It made me feel young again.

I couldn't wait for class to begin, that Tuesday. There were a couple of students who were less than desirable, to be sure, which made it more difficult than it should have been. But I knew Sarah and I would meet during our evening class. She and I messaged each other and talked on the phone the entire weekend, but meeting face to face in a place where we didn't have to hide or be careful of not being noticed, was much better. Knowing I would see Sarah in the evening and hearing the song of the chickadee made me feel like I hadn't felt in many years; younger, ambitious, and silly. I ran some errands that day. I also stopped to get Sarah some flowers I would give her when our class was over, and everyone had gone. In my travels, I met some people I knew, some friends, as well as some former students. I'm ashamed to admit I was happy I wasn't seen with Sarah. But discretion is the better part of valor, as they say, and I would have to live a life of discretion until further notice.

I arrived at class a little late. The students were in place and ready when I walked in. There were more empty seats than usual, but I attributed that to what had happened in the previous two weeks and the mid-semester blues. I had promised myself I would apologize for the outburst a couple of weeks prior. I knew it might create an awkward situation, but regardless of that, it was something I had to do. As I walked in, I glanced at Sarah. She smiled at me, as if she had a secret no one else knew. She was exceptionally gorgeous that night, but I couldn't tell you why. Maybe it was the way she made up her hair, or what she wore, or even her happy expression. It could have been any reason whatever, but it didn't matter. Perhaps it was the way I felt, as spring was around the corner. In any case, I thought she looked beautiful. I couldn't help but wonder if she had done something special to look that way for *me*. I also noticed a fragrance as I walked past her. It must have been a combination of wonderful scents such as musk, orange blossom, or white flower. At any rate, spring was not only around the corner, it was also in that very room. As I approached my desk, I saw a package on it carefully wrapped. I slowed my pace as I got closer, and immediately looked at the entire class. Most had the same smile I noticed on Sarah when I walked in. After a while of looking at them and wondering what the mystery was, I looked back at the package and noticed the tag on it. I was sure it was from all the students offering their condolences, as Sarah would not be so indiscreet as to give me something like this in front of everyone. I looked at the tag, which read, *from all of us*. I then turned back to the class.

"Should I open it now?" I asked with humility.

"Yes," was the consenting response.

As I unwrapped it, I could sense the tension in the room from the others. They must have wondered if I would like whatever it was. I opened the little box and pulled out a coffee mug. The words on it read, *Dr. Dina, most beloved professor at NYU*. I stared at it for a while, trying not to get too emotional. I was reminded of the movie 'To Sir with Love' and imagined myself cast in the leading role. Finally, I held it close to me and looked at the class.

"Thank you so much." I said, as they mumbled various expressions of acknowledgement. I continued solemnly, "I really appreciate the gift. It's wonderful." I took a deep breath. "I also want to apologize for my behavior a couple of weeks ago. I should never have yelled at you like a madman." I heard some grumbling from the class but held my hand up to signal them to let me speak. They did. "There's no excuse for losing my temper the way I did. Maybe I was under stress, but it's still not a reason. I vow to never do that again to anyone. I hope you can forgive me."

Most of them responded in some way, making sure I knew they didn't hold it against me and at the very least, my apology was accepted. Then Sarah spoke.

"Dr. Dina, we forgive you, but no forgiveness is necessary. Most of us here would have done much worse if we had been in your situation. We don't want you to worry about it anymore." Then, she paused and said, "We love you."

Sarah and I looked in each other's eyes for a long time. I thought about those last three words she spoke. I hoped she meant to say much more than to express the class sentiment. I hoped it was a feeling that was more profound.

I continued the class and the students were engaged as ever. I tried not to look at Sarah too often lest I aroused any kind of suspicion from the others. I began to feel as if she had an advantage over me, as she could look at me all night without giving the wrong impression. It sometimes made me feel a little uncomfortable. This was a feeling I rarely got when lecturing, but it felt real that night. In any event, I was satisfied with the way things were. The chickadees were singing, and Sarah looked beautiful.

# ~Nightcap and Ripples~

After the class was over, the room emptied out and Sarah stayed. Her walk was slow and deliberate, as she strolled in my direction. We looked carefully about, before we kissed. I then asked her if she had anything to do with the mug I had gotten as a gift. She, of course, denied it but I knew better. I thanked her anyway. I asked her to come with me to my car before we left. Her eyes grew wide with suspense, as she gave a little smile that was telling of her amusement with the mystery. She agreed, and we walked out together. When we got to the car, I presented her with the flowers I had bought earlier that day. She was elated.

"Oh, they're beautiful," she said, "but you shouldn't have."

"I thought you deserved something beautiful to compliment how beautiful *you* are."

"Well this is not the first time I've accused you of being wrong."

We laughed. "No, you're right about that." I replied. "But I still maintain I'm right about you."

"Thank you."

"My pleasure."

She gave me a hopeful look, as she asked, "Nightcap?"

I had heard those words from her before but felt totally different when I first heard them from the way I felt that night. A couple of weeks before, I guess I wasn't ready to fully come to terms with our relationship. That night, I was. I wondered if I might have been too preoccupied with my father's condition a few days before. That night, having had closure, I felt it was behind me and that notion somehow gave me permission to move forward with my heart's desire.

"I'd love to," was my simple reply.

She gave that smile again and said, "Great."

I followed her home. Her apartment wasn't far from the school, and were it not for New York traffic, we would have arrived in a matter of thirty to forty minutes. Finally, we arrived a little after ten o'clock at night and the air was getting quite chilly. I held her close as we walked to the door. By the time we entered, I had goosebumps. I wasn't sure if they were a result of the cold, or the anticipation of being alone with Sarah in her apartment. In any case, my senses were alive.

Her apartment was rather small, but well adorned with a woman's touch. I could tell she had a flare for color coordinating and choice of proper garnishing. The place was a bit chilly, as I had expected for that time of year. We went directly to the living room, which was dressed in humble furniture, a television, and a small stereo. There, she invited me to sit on the sofa, as she walked to the kitchen to pour what I suspected to be red wine and put her flowers in some water. She then returned with the wine glasses and sat close to me.

"A toast." I said, as I raised my glass with hers. "To meaningful relationships."

"Here's to a wonderful man whom I admire and cherish." she replied.

We sipped our wine, then she remarked it was chilly in the room. I agreed but told her it was fine. At that, she got up and went into the bedroom to get a blanket.

"Are you that cold?" I asked.

She didn't respond. She merely sat back down next to me and covered us both up to our necks with the blanket. It made me feel like a little kid playing some made-up game. We were close enough for me to feel her sweater against me. I could smell her perfect aroma emanating, as she played with her hair. The irrational part of me could have sworn her soul was visible through her eyes. The rational part of me tried hard to resist any temptation to doing something too soon. I tried to speak but couldn't think of what to say. Still, anything said would have sounded ridiculous in contrast to our perfect situation; too perfect to be real. I don't know why, but there was a sudden feeling of elation inside of me. I felt my youth return as though I had discovered some secret to eternal life. It may have been the warmth I felt under the blanket next to her, or perhaps it was the privacy the blanket offered, even though we were completely alone. It may have been her eyes that revealed her soul. It may even have come from a feeling of being wanted and needed by someone who couldn't possibly need someone like me. Nevertheless, I couldn't refrain from taking hold of her firmly and kissing her with all the sincere passion I never knew I possessed.

After we kissed, I thought I saw want in her eyes. It was as though she were asking for something she needed. As I gazed at her, I considered if the want in her eyes were only a reflection of the want in mine. Was she feeling the same as I was or was it simply a look of consent, allowing our feelings to be recognized? It didn't matter. *We* were what mattered; where we were; as we were. She took my hand and led me to her bedroom. She glanced at me frequently as we walked, and I felt a disquiet nervousness as my heart was pounding. All the while, she looked calm and resolute. Once in her room, she held my hand and pulled me closer to her. At that moment, I lost all rational thought. I picked her up in my arms, slowly carried her as we kissed, and carefully lowered her onto the bed. She insisted we turn off the lights. I didn't question it, as I could understand whatever the reason was. I, in fact, felt a little more comfortable with the lights off as well. I wasn't sure why I felt this way. It may have been, perhaps, the uneasiness of being with someone who was thirty years my junior, or the fact that I simply shouldn't have been there for a hundred other reasons. On the other hand, it may have been the simple reason she gave; it was more romantic, which I agreed with. In the darkness, her fragrance seemed more prominent. The feel of her skin against mine was something I hadn't felt in forever. I felt her body rise and fall as I kissed her neck and slowly moved to her breasts. I felt every soft curve she was endowed with, as her hands roamed to caress my chest and work their way to my hips. All my senses were aroused as a blind man being able to see again, or a deaf man being able to hear again. I suddenly became a man able to live again. I heard her sigh as she did when she first held me that night in the classroom to console me.

All the while we were making love, she reached for a tissue to wipe my face, as it was covered with perspiration despite the chill in the air. I felt our hearts beating in unison as though we were lovers in a classic and timeless literary piece. All the poetry and love songs of the world put together, couldn't have expressed how I was feeling. Some emotions are beyond words, but what I felt that night transcended not only words but expression itself. A simple man might have said I was in love. Given the way I felt towards Sarah that night, I was not about to argue with a simple man.

In the heat of the moment, I forgot who I was. I no longer had two sons who would never speak again. The negative memories of my childhood had ceased to haunt me. The loneliness of my life was suddenly dissipating, and happiness seemed to increase as the ripples in a pond during a summer rain. Finally, those ripples overtook me and in the heat of the moment, I became one with Sarah Goldman.

As the intensity passed, we lay there holding each other tightly. Our breathing was brisk and seemed to be attuned, as it slowly returned to normal. I didn't want to let go. We had experienced something wonderful together and I didn't want it to end. Finally, I laid down next to her, while she turned the light on. The light was dim and warm, as I turned to face her and kissed her. Suddenly, I was reminded of the dream I had a couple of weeks before, and how Sarah speculated I was after something I couldn't have. I thought about my job and my faith. What we did was wrong in so many ways, but I didn't care, nor did she seem to care either. What about *her* faith, I wondered? I knew what her father would say about the very prospect of doing something so totally against her upbringing. Was I guilty of tarnishing an innocent soul? I must have seemed obviously preoccupied because as I was pondering all this, my concentration was broken with her question.

"What are you thinking of? Is anything wrong?"

"No, nothing's wrong." I replied.

"You seem concerned."

"I'm not."

"Raymond, this was wonderful. I don't want to think about anything else tonight. Okay?"

I could tell she was serious. I knew what she meant, and I agreed with her totally. For the rest of the night, I vowed not to think so much, and let life happen.

"Okay," I whispered softly.

We talked for a while, then fell asleep in each other's arms.

# ~Accident or Intent~

It was very early when we woke up and found ourselves still very close together. We had no idea of how cold the room was until she got up to take a shower. Only then, did we notice how warm we kept each other from the winter morning. As she carefully sat up and put on her robe, she insisted I stay in bed and wait for her to return. After her shower, she made coffee and came back with our drinks. We sat up in bed and talked, as we sipped our coffee.

"How'd you sleep?" she asked.

"Like a baby. How about you?"

"Same."

We sat there looking at each other as though we had ventured into unexplored territory, wondering what other new experiences would happen upon us.

"Last night was wonderful." I said. "It was something I don't regret for one moment."

"Not even a little?" she joked, showing a tiny space between her thumb and index finger.

"Should I?"

"No."

"Then, let's not."

She whispered, "Okay," then we kissed.

As I was sipping my coffee, the conversation took a serious turn. She looked at me and asked, "You felt the scars last night, didn't you?"

It took me by surprise, yet I should have known nothing gets passed Sarah. She must have known the subject would come up eventually, so she initiated the conversation.

"On your legs?" I asked.

She simply nodded. To pretend I didn't feel something on her legs, would have been an obvious lie. Sarah deserved better.

I answered, "Yes, I did."

"I'm sorry. Is that a turn off for you?"

"Absolutely not." I waited to make sure there was no doubt in her eyes. Then I asked the question I knew the answer to. "Is that why you wanted the lights off last night?"

"Yes. My legs look awful."

I gently brushed the hair back from her eyes, and replied, "Don't ever feel self-conscious with me. What happened, if you don't mind my asking?"

"I was hit by a car when I was little."

"Oh my God, that's awful."

"I was in the hospital for a few days recovering from multiple fractures. Most of the damage was done to my legs, but they were able to fix them to the point where I could walk normally again. I spent almost an entire school year walking on crutches."

"How did it happen?" I asked.

"We're not sure. The driver sped away."

"They never caught 'em?"

"No. Some witnesses said that it was a man at the wheel. He was swerving on the road before he hit me. Some believe he might have been drunk."

All I could do upon hearing that, was shake my head in disbelief. How awful it is when someone has total disregard for another human life, I thought. This wasn't some accident caused by a blinding snowstorm, it was caused by someone allowing themselves to reach a debilitating state and getting behind the wheel. I never understood the mentality of some people's decision to endanger someone else's life simply because their weakness is more important. But then again, how could someone in a drunken state, rationalize and reason with any kind of intelligence? It just isn't fair for someone to fall victim to such disregard. The act of driving under the influence of any substance is barbaric. However, it became more so, after learning of Sarah's incident; of her being a victim to such a crime.

"My father thought it may have been a hate crime, and not so much a drunk driver." she added.

"You think that's a possibility?"

She spoke without hesitation. "Yes, I do. There were many times I can remember when our house was the target of hate crimes because we're Jewish. The house was the target, but *we* were the ultimate target. Some people wanted us hurt or even dead."

I didn't know what to say. If drunken driving could be explained away with some far-fetched justification, this could not. Part of me wanted to believe it was not a hate crime. It hurt inside to even think someone could hurt Sarah deliberately because of her heritage, her faith, or some other reason that had nothing to do with her.

"I'm sorry. I wish you didn't have to live through that." I said.

"It's over. You would tell me if it bothered you, right?"

"It doesn't bother me in the least, and yes I would tell you."

"Thank you."

She smiled and seemed relieved upon hearing me say that. I could tell it bothered her a great deal, and I could only imagine the kind of life it would be to constantly make sure no one saw your legs because of scars. They must have been a constant reminder to her of how irresponsible, or even evil some people can be. I decided to change the subject so as to not dwell on the scars on her legs. I was also very curious as to why she wasn't in a relationship with someone else; perhaps someone her own age.

"Sarah?"

"Yes?"

"Sometimes I wonder why you're not in a relationship, and why you're involved with me."

"What do you mean, involved with you? Why wouldn't I be?" she asked.

"You know why. I'm fifty-four years old and you're a young, beautiful woman with the world at your feet. Anyone your age would be happy to be in a serious relationship with you."

"Age doesn't matter to me. I told you that. Does it matter to you?"

I persisted, "It doesn't matter to me, but I'm sure it does to a lot of people."

"No one cares about them."

"I know you're right, but I guess I'm not sure what you're seeing in me." I said. "It's obvious why I'm attracted to you. You're young and full of life. When I'm with you, I feel the same way. There's a real reason for such an attraction. But, I'm not so sure of what I have to offer to make you want *me*."

"Does everything need a reason? Do you need a reason for liking a particular shade of color, or breed of dog?" She answered her own question, "No, you don't. People take these things for granted and don't question it."

"You know what I see in you. What is it you see in me?" I asked.

"I see a great man who makes me laugh and has a great head on his shoulders, unlike guys my age who are not mature enough to know what makes a woman happy." Then, she pointed her finger at me in jest. "Now I don't want to hear any more of that, mister."

She gave that look again, as a mother would when offering her final warning to a misbehaving child. In any event, she made her point. No one is in a position to judge and at times, shouldn't question what feels right. As I thought that, I couldn't help but ponder on the significant difference between what feels right and what is wrong. I was suddenly brought back to earth as I felt her hand give my knee a little squeeze.

"You hear me, mister?" she asked, half-jokingly.

"Yes ma'am," I replied.

That made her smile. Upon seeing her smile, I knew the answer to my previous question. Why was she attracted to me? Because I made her happy, and that's exactly what each person on earth is entitled to. I wasn't about to deny her happiness because of some societal foolhardy conclusion. We talked a while longer, and finally it was time to get ready for the day. I had a couple of classes to teach and she had her other class she was writing her empirical article paper for.

"We haven't worked on your paper in a little while." I told her.

"I'm doing alright with it. All I needed was someone to bounce ideas off of and get me motivated."

"I'll want to read it before you submit it."

"You'll be the first." she said.

"By the way, how are you doing with tutoring Natania?"

She looked reluctant to tell me. "I gave it up a few weeks ago."

"You gave up the job at SCO Services?"

"No, but I'm not tutoring Natania anymore."

"Why not?" I asked.

"I couldn't continue, knowing it was wrong."

I looked at her amazed. She knew exactly what I was thinking. What *we* were doing was even more wrong.

She replied, "I know what you're thinking. Talk about irony, huh?"

The irony was too real. She had given up tutoring Natania on a matter of principle; thinking it was unethical. Yet, she was in bed with her professor. I kissed her on the forehead and told her she did the right thing. That didn't seem to help. At that, we both looked a little guilty and decided not to talk about it anymore. I couldn't help but think whether she would, in time, give *me* up. She was, after all, someone I had come to know to have a discerning sense of what was prudent. It seemed to me, as well, there was another factor at play. How can two people continue in a relationship where there was a thirty-year difference in their ages? In just a few years, she would be in her prime and I would be eligible for senior discounts at restaurants. I decided not to think about that anymore and enjoy the happiness I had at the moment. After a while, we got dressed, ate a little, then I left to start the day.

I taught my classes as usual that day but for the first time in a long time, my students must have noticed how extraordinarily happy I was. A person's moods are usually conveyed to others with a simple look or expression. No words need be spoken. I'm sure some of them wondered what was up. I'm willing to bet some might have wondered if Dr. Dina got laid the night before. To that, I have no comment other than to say that in a crude way, they were right. However, it was so much more.

In my travels that day, I came across Sarah's latest little love note sitting in my coat pocket. The little purple note read; *you were wonderful.* It was signed only with a heart and smiley face. It made my day.

## ~Evening of Surprises~

That Thursday was a day off for Sarah and me, as we didn't have any classes scheduled. I spent the afternoon entertaining at a local nursing home and she did some shopping for dinner we would have that night at my place. At around five o'clock, I called her to make sure we were still on for dinner. She told me she was ready, and I should brace myself for a surprise. I thought it was a coincidence, as I had a surprise for her as well. I gave her directions to my place and waited for her.

I answered the door with a big smile as I saw her in the doorway. She looked beautiful as always, but there was something special about her just then. Her hair was made up and flowing more than usual. Her face was radiant as she smiled from ear to ear, and her skin seemed to appear silky smooth, almost provocatively daring you to touch it and feel her softness. Her sweater showed her bare slender neck, revealing clusters of curls from her hair flowing on each side. Her perfect body from the neck down gave evidence of her ability to wear any attire and not put it to shame. As I greeted her, I saw she was weighed down with some grocery bags in her hands. I took them from her, and we proceeded into the kitchen. There I kissed her, and then she pulled out a bottle of champagne from one of the bags.

"Was that the surprise?" I asked.

"Well, one of them." she answered with a grin.

I started thinking about how relationships are so dependent on having fun and anticipating little surprises here and there. I wondered how many relationships didn't last because of the absence of these simple human necessities. It's a simple formula, I thought. All one needs to do is to provide a little excitement in someone's life, no matter how small the excitement is. These important facts of life, I learned from Sarah. She was the answer to my happiness and provided the answers to the most important questions of life.

"I have a surprise for *you.*" I said.

"Really? What?"

She had the exact reaction I had when she surprised *me.* It was the look of a little child finding out they can stay up until ten o'clock; the look of a puppy anticipating a treat; the look of a proud parent learning of their child's accomplishments in school.

"I made reservations at the Red Coach Inn in Niagara Falls for us." I announced.

Her eyes grew wide open. "What?" She asked in total amazement.

"A suite for two." I replied.

"When?"

"Spring break is coming up in a couple of weeks, and I thought it would be nice to go away with you and forget about school and work."

She ran to me and hugged me tightly. "Thank you. Oh, I can't wait!" Then she kissed me as if I had saved her life.

"I didn't know how you'd react to that. I didn't know if you thought it was appropriate."

"It's a wonderful surprise, Raymond, and I can't wait."

We stood holding each other for a while, then she proceeded to make dinner. At that point, I considered myself the most fortunate man in the world. I had it all; youth, excitement, and happiness. I lit some candles, poured the champagne, and toasted before we ate. Our dinner was a simple chicken and broccoli stir fry she made with crushed garlic and fresh grated ginger. As we ate, I couldn't help but notice how beautiful Sarah looked. She even ate with a certain appeal. I looked and admired the way she could exhilarate me by the simplest of movements. Once in a while, she would look at me and smile, as though she knew how her natural mannerisms were affecting me. I didn't know what she saw in me, but we had already gone through that discussion. Whatever it was, I didn't want it to change. I was happy and didn't want anything to interfere with that happiness. It dawned on me then, she suddenly had become my world.

In all the excitement, I completely forgot about her reply when asked if the champagne was the surprise. She had told me it was one of them. I would find out soon enough what the other surprise was, but at that moment, I could think of nothing other than how wonderful an evening it was. During dinner, we had light conversation. We talked a little about my gig at the nursing home earlier that day. We also talked quite a bit about how she was doing with her empirical paper. She asked some detailed questions about it and I put her on the right track. I wondered if she was asking questions because she needed help, or to make conversation. In any case, it seemed she was almost done and ready to submit it to her other professor. It also seemed she would make quite a good psychologist someday.

Finally, dinner was over. I cleared the table and we sat in the living room. She noticed my guitar in the corner and asked if I could play for her. It had been a while since I'd serenaded someone with that guitar. Playing for some residents in a nursing home was far from serenading a young beauty whose admiration for me seemed exceeded only by her love for her grandmother. I must admit I was a little shy, but she insisted. I reluctantly picked it up and played. As she said she wanted to hear something meaningful, I thought I would be a hit if I played the most romantic and thought-provoking songs I knew; "Annie's Song" by John Denver, and "Mr. Tambourine Man" by Dylan. As I played and sang to her, I would have been blind not to notice her reaction. Her expression was one of enthusiasm and surprise, but also wonderment. She had a glow about her, and her eyes seemed to smile. To say she was impressed would be an understatement, as hers was the greatest response of my musical endeavors. She almost seemed to have witnessed some revelation or something. When the songs were over, I looked at her with a smile as I put the guitar down. I then, got the biggest kiss of my life.

"You were wonderful!" she exclaimed.

"Thanks."

"No, I mean you are really good; better than some of these so-called celebrities."

I thanked her again but assured her it was nothing. She made a big deal of the fact that no one had ever sung for her, and that it made for a very special evening. After she'd gotten over the unexpected surprise of my singing to her, she became more interested in the whole concept of entertaining people.

"You only play nursing homes?" She asked.

"Yeah convalescent homes of all kinds."

"What's it like?"

"It's really something to experience."

"Must be depressing a little."

"When I first started, it was a bit hard to take." I replied. "These people hardly see anyone. Even those with family, don't get many visitors. It's like they're put there and forgotten. This is what makes playing for them so worthwhile."

"I'm sure. It must be a real treat for them, especially hearing someone with an outrageous voice like yours."

I laughed when she said that. Of all the compliments I had ever received, I'd never heard I had an outrageous voice.

"Outrageous?" I asked, laughing.

"Yes. I had no idea you were so good."

"I don't take compliments very well." I said.

"Just telling you the truth."

"Thanks."

"Tell me about the residents."

She was being the ultimate psychologist, being full of curiosity and intrigue. I reflected for a moment, then began to describe my experiences.

"When I first started, I was surprised at how open they are about their situation."

"What do you mean?"

"I would overhear some of their conversations. I heard one ask another one time if they had decided whether they were going to be cremated or buried when they died."

"Oh no, that's awful!" she asserted.

"Well to them, that's their life. That's their future."

"I just feel so bad for people in those places."

"But the joy is visible in their faces when I'm playing for them." I added. "At least they have *that.* I'm sure it's not just me. I'm sure they're ecstatic when anyone comes to entertain them."

"They must be." she said.

There was a certain look she had when she was interested in what I was talking about. It was a look that was unmistakable. She seemed genuinely interested. Some people stare right through you when they haven't the slightest interest in what you're saying. Some don't even care if their glazed look is at all obvious. Not Sarah; her attentiveness was absolute.

I continued, "Some don't get along, and in a way, it's kind of funny. You can tell when they don't like each other. They pick on each other and actually get pretty mad. Just like anywhere else, some get along and some don't. They live together, after all."

"I'm sure."

"But it's pretty tame. They're in no condition to start a physical confrontation or anything. It's usually just mouthing off and swearing a few words."

She nodded. After a moment she asked, "How do they react when you play? They must sing along to songs they know."

"Some look like they're sleeping, but all of a sudden, you see their feet tapping or their lips moving to the lyrics."

"That must be something to see."

"It is. Some look out of it, but they're not. Some obviously, are more alert than others. Those are the residents who applaud, but I never got a standing ovation." I said, jokingly.

She laughed at that.

"That would be something to see, too." she said.

"Well, you don't need a standing ovation to know how much they love it."

"How was it today when you played? Anything special happen?"

"Actually, yeah. There was a resident who came up to me after I was done. Do you know what she wanted?"

"What?"

"She had a basket full of greeting cards. They weren't cards that were sent to her, they were just cards with nothing in them that weren't sent yet. She wanted me to have one."

"Oh, that's sweet."

"She had picked one out especially for me because there was a picture of a cat on it. She said it was her favorite because of the cat, and she wanted me to have it."

Sarah gave a little half laugh and half 'aww', as if to say how cute and sweet that was. At the same time, her eyes were sad because she knew the woman was probably in that place because of dementia or something.

I continued, "One time, this one woman approached me to say she loved me."

Sarah smiled and shaking her head, said, "That's adorable."

"I thought so too until I realized she was mistaking me for her long-lost love."

"Really?"

"She was telling me that she still loves me, and she had heard I got married. She said the other woman was very lucky." Sarah nodded as if to agree with her. I went on,

"She was telling me that I hadn't changed a bit, and that I could visit her anytime, as she would still be there for me. Then she took my hand and pulled me closer to her. I thought she would simply give me a hug, but she kissed me on the lips. That's when I knew she was seriously mistaking me for someone in her past; a lost love."

Sarah's eyes began to water. I wasn't sure if she pitied the woman for her dementia, or whether there was some secret love Sarah had lost in *her* past. Whatever the reason, the haze in her eyes made her look that much more beautiful to me. We talked a little more about the residents, then moved on to other subjects that seemed to take on new importance. We talked about things we forgot about, things we wanted to forget about, and things we took for granted. Our discussions were much more than small talk or insignificant dialogue, they were meaningful. These conversations were more consultations than anything. I attributed that to our line of work, but how odd it was to have met someone I could confide in. It was as though we needed each other at that particular moment in time, and we took advantage of every opportunity.

The evening wore on and it was time to turn in. She asked if she could stay, and I insisted she did. If I had any sense at all, any normal male DNA, I would not and did not let her go that night. I would have been a fool to pass up an evening spent with such a beauty and intellect. As we walked into the bedroom, she excused herself to the bathroom. I waited there, sitting on the bed wondering what she had in store. When she came out, I suddenly realized what that other surprise was for me. There was no question. She was wearing a very short and flirty, white lace robe partly open at the top. It was held in place with a white ribbon tied around her waist.

"Wow!" I exclaimed.

She laughed and proceeded to stroll towards the bed, where I was sitting. She sat next to me, stroking my hair.

"Surprise." she said, in a kind of melodic whisper.

I was speechless and felt like a little kid in a chocolate-tasting factory, not knowing what to taste first. I finally felt I should say something; anything. "Does this have anything to do with the midterm I'll be giving you on Tuesday?" I joked and felt ridiculous for having said something as stupid.

She smiled but didn't say a word. She simply stood up in front of me and pulled on the bow of the ribbon around her waist. Her robe opened to reveal a matching G-string, and nothing else, as the ribbon fell to the floor. I knew Sarah was beautiful, but I had never imagined the true beauty she was blessed with. The rest of her was just as perfect as what I had come to know. I suddenly felt guilt at the fact I didn't deserve her. I wanted her to know that and felt compelled to tell her so. I didn't know what to say, but I began to speak anyway.

"Sarah..."

She interrupted me with a gentle finger to my mouth. All I could do was just sit on the bed in amazement. When she moved her finger away, I tried to speak again, but she bent down to kiss me before I could utter the next syllable. I felt the softness of her lips and could smell her perfume that filled my senses. Next, she realigned herself and stood in front of me for a moment, smiling. Noticing my gaze and burning desire to touch her perfectly shaped bosom, she approached me, stood straddled over my legs, and pressed the firmness of her breasts to my face. With all the animal instincts in my body, I buried my face deeper and caressed her softness with my cheeks, and soon began kissing every inch of her breasts. As I took in the texture and scent of her cleavage and listened intently to the pounding of her heart, I reached behind her legs with both hands and slowly inched my way upward to the cheeks of her well-rounded bottom. Caressing her curves, I heard her breathing deeper and heavier. Her hands reached behind my head and pulled me deeper into her bosom, while gently gripping my hair. Overwhelmed with passion, I took hold of her and hastily dropped her down to the bed. She giggled at that, as I began to kiss her on the neck and take in her alluring scent. Soon, I could hear her sigh again, which made me want her more.

We made love that night with the light on, and no inhibitions. There were no worries about my seeing the scars on her legs. We didn't worry about our professional situation, or the question of breaking rules. I felt as though I was suddenly set free after years of captivity, and she was my liberator and deliverer. We looked into each other's eyes and never wondered about right or wrong. Finally, we kissed and held each other tightly as we reached the height of our passion. It was a night I would never forget.

# ~Joanne~

I woke up in the middle of a light sleep, that night. I'm not sure what caused me to wake up, but sometimes these things happen. I looked over at Sarah and watched her sleep for a while, making sure to not disturb her rest. To disturb a restful sleep as she was in, would have been a sin against God and man. She looked as peaceful as a kitten lying close to its mother and in total comfort. After a while, I turned my gaze to the ceiling I could barely see in the darkness of the room. I thought of how often I looked up at that ceiling in the middle of previous sleepless nights caused by whatever reason. However, I never imagined gazing up with one of my students beside me; one whom I had made love to a couple of hours before. My mind wandered. I thought of years past and the girl crushes I had, that invariably happen in those elementary school years. There was a girl who lived a few houses down on our street. Her name was Joanne and she was probably the first crush I can remember that bloomed into love. Although, I'm not sure I could call it love, as there was really no interaction that would lend to such distinction. But the distance she kept from me was painful; painful as any love gone wrong could be. She was good friends with my best friend, Gary, as they both went to the same school. I went to a different school, which made it difficult for a shy kid like me to approach such a sweet girl as she was. I would ask Gary every once in a while, to mention my name to her, but he would have no part of that. Oddly enough, I understood his reluctance to get involved in those days. He told me he wouldn't want her to start hating him for making her feel uncomfortable. However, as an older man with much life experience, it was hard for me to understand his reasoning. What harm would it bring, I thought? I would have been happy to help *him* out with *his* love endeavors. In any case, I was on my own when it came to getting close to Joanne, which didn't leave me much hope. I used to walk to and from school, as my school wasn't that far from home. One particular day found me wandering from my normal way home and making believe I was lost in the wilderness. So, I arrived home from school a little later than usual. When I arrived, I saw Gary and Joanne get off their bus in front of my house. There was my chance, I thought. I could finally break the ice and maybe talk to her. Maybe she would notice some charm in me that would attract her. I called Gary's name and waved to him, as I was running towards them. When I got about twenty feet away, Joanne turned and started walking towards her house in a quickened pace. I stopped dead in my tracks and watched her walk away. I saw how beautiful she was even as she walked away from me. I thought about how much I could care for her if she gave me the chance. At that moment, however, I realized I had experienced a hopeless situation. I could no longer imagine us together and maybe living happily ever after. I thought perhaps Gary had talked to her about me after all, and she had made up her mind about us. Whether or not he did, I never knew. In any case, the pain was real. I felt like crying. Of course, one never cries in front of his best friend in the sixth grade. I watched her walk away from me and disappear behind the front door of her house.

After she was gone, I went home as well. One never cries in front of his best friend.

After reminiscing about the days gone by, I returned my gaze to Sarah. Her position hadn't changed. It dawned on me then that I was as happy as I could ever be despite my first crush walking away from me decades before, which seemed so devastating at the time. It also occurred to me if Sarah were to leave, I would feel the same deep-seated pain as I had felt when I saw Joanne walk away. As I looked at her, Sarah suddenly stirred a little and I heard her sigh a little sigh. I smiled at how contented she seemed. I was happy to know I was making a difference in her life. I kissed her on the cheek lightly so as to not wake her. I then closed my eyes, and after a little while, fell asleep next to the woman I loved.

# Week 7

## ~Chiming of the Clock~

AS my relationship with Sarah grew, we spent more and more time at home; either her place or mine. We would have dinner at home and not spend so much time eating at restaurants. We would of course, spend more and more nights together. Wherever we were, we were ever vigilant so as to not be recognized by anyone we knew. We were living a discreet life, but happy doing so.

We woke up late on the day of the seventh class we had together. It was the week I gave the midterm. I assured her she would do well on the exam. I also reminded her to submit her empirical paper to the other professor. It was, after all, the reason we got together. It would be a shame to have spent all this effort on the paper and fail to submit it on time. She assured me she was all set and ready to submit it. Again, she made coffee and we stayed in bed for a while. We had our normal morning talk about how we slept, and so on. Then, the conversation turned into another one of our more serious conversations we frequently had. I asked her to talk about some of her past love encounters, which she didn't seem to mind talking about. I thought we had come to the point where we were both pretty comfortable with each other and didn't have to worry about being judged. Candor was not a problem with us, as we knew from our profession that talking openly can be a healing experience.

"I had a strange relationship about three years ago." she said.

"Tell me about it."

"Only if you promise to not use it against me, if we have a spat."

"What could we possibly argue about?" I asked.

"I always assume something will eventually get me mad, when dealing with men."

We both laughed, but somehow, I knew she was only half joking.

"I promise to not use it against you or ever throw it back in your face." I saw a doubtful look in her eyes.

"Promise?" She asked, smiling.

"I promise I won't do it in public, only when we're alone" I added jokingly.

She went to slap my arm playfully but spilled some of her coffee instead. We laughed, as she tried her best to clean up her mess. I found myself having more fun than ever, since becoming personally involved with Sarah. For that, I was grateful to my instincts for allowing our relationship to grow. Finally, after more kidding around, she started talking about her mysterious encounter.

"About three years ago, I started roaming on the internet. Not a dating sight or anything like that, but just looking around when I was bored."

"Why were you bored?" I asked.

"I was alone; no one to be with."

"How can someone like you, with all your beauty and intelligence, ever be alone?"

"You give me more credit than I deserve." She continued, "Anyway, I wound up in this chat room. I wasn't chatting with anyone, but just watching what other people were writing. Then all of a sudden, someone messaged me for a private chat."

"It was this guy?"

"Yeah, his nickname was MysteryMan."

"What?"

She repeated, "MysteryMan." I reacted surprised for a moment. She looked at me curiously. "What's the matter?" she asked.

"Oh, nothing. Go ahead, continue."

"Is something wrong?" she insisted, still giving me a curious look.

"No, of course not. What was *your* nickname?" I asked.

"Lilly."

I paused again. "Pretty name." I said.

"Yes, it is. So, he asked me for a private chat, and I thought it wouldn't do any harm to play along and talk to someone I didn't know."

"Do you still think there's no harm in it?"

"I think there's real potential harm. I wouldn't fall for that again." She said.

"Live and learn, right?"

"Yeah."

"So, what happened?"

"Well, at first it was pretty innocent. I would ask questions and he would try to evade the answer, which made me more curious about this MysteryMan. It was also a lot of fun."

"They have ways of luring you in." I said.

"Well I thought I would go so far, then backpedal when it got too weird. It didn't turn out that way though."

"What do you mean?"

"I eventually got involved emotionally."

All I could picture upon hearing that, was if MysteryMan had known her, he wouldn't have taken advantage of this naive and pure woman.

"Did you ever meet him face to face?" I asked.

"No, I knew enough to stay away from that, but it was strange. After a time, I really felt love for him."

"It's very common to fall in love with someone you don't meet. As long as they make you feel good, your imagination takes over from there."

"That's true. Talking to someone on the internet allows them to take on any persona they like; male, female, or even lie about anything else for that matter. They can make you feel whatever they want you to feel without commitment."

"How did those feelings start?" I asked.

"At first, it was just nice to talk to someone who seemed to understand me. Then it got to a point where, whenever I saw his nickname on the website, it made me happy. Eventually, I started associating other things with the conversations we were having."

"Like what?"

"It's stupid but there was a song I used to hear as a little girl that sounded very much like the chime of our kitchen clock. I loved that song. Sometimes we would chat, and the clock would chime, as it normally would. Soon, whenever the clock would chime during the day, I would think of him."

"It's not stupid, it's very real." I added.

"It got so bad that I started depending on him. We even exchanged anonymous emails we had created. Whenever something was wrong or it was a bad day, I would look for him. Whenever something good happened that I wanted to share with someone, I would look for him then too. I really felt like I was in love with him."

"I think you were."

"You think so?"

"I know so. I'm glad you didn't get hurt though. What else happened?"

"He was also a musician. One day he surprised me and emailed me a song he had written for me. He mentioned me by name in the song."

"Lilly?" I asked.

"Yes, Lilly."

"How did you feel about the song? Some would find it a little creepy."

"I cried when I heard it. It was beautiful." she admitted.

"Can I ask you a more personal question, Sarah? You don't have to answer if you don't want to."

"Of course."

"Do you miss him?"

After a moment of hesitation, she answered, "Yes, I do. I do, even though I know he played with my emotions."

"So, you resent him a little."

"Of course. How would you feel if someone played with *your* emotions?"

I didn't answer. "Did he reveal anything about himself?" I asked.

"No, not really. After a time, he revealed some things about himself, but never too much to give anything away."

"And you?"

"I kept everything about myself a secret. I was afraid something bad could happen, so I kept very private."

"That's good."

"He would remember my birthday and email me little ecards"

"How long did this go on?"

"A couple of years. That's why I had no reason to believe he wasn't serious about me. I was sure he loved me too."

"What finally happened?"

"He finally decided to stop the relationship. I think he knew it was headed nowhere, and it could only end with someone getting hurt; most probably me."

"So, he told you?"

"No, he gradually stopped going on the website to meet me. After a while, I got the message and emailed him saying I understood. Eventually, he wrote back to say goodbye."

"If you were sure it was legitimate, why didn't you meet him?"

"I was afraid." she replied. "I cried when he wrote that final email. I knew it was the end of our relationship, such as it was."

"And now?"

"And now, when I hear the clock chime, I think of how I used to feel about him; someone I've never met."

"Some people get divorced because of such emotional love with someone they've never met. Unfortunately, it happens."

"I know. It's very easy to imagine the love of your life and have someone feed that imagination."

It was from this conversation I understood how vulnerable Sarah was. I couldn't help but think if *I* were feeding into her vulnerability at that very moment with *our* relationship. I didn't want to entertain any notion of that thought, though. It hurt too much. All I could picture; was how I would feel if Sarah suddenly decided our relationship was headed nowhere and could only end in someone getting hurt. In our case, however, the one who would get hurt would be me; hurt badly. I leaned over and kissed her. I wanted her to know I understood, and her relationship with this MysteryMan was not ridiculous at all. It was normal for her to experience feelings she wanted to experience through an imaginary friend or lover. I also wondered if she was hurt because of his decision to put a stop to it, or because she hated herself for carrying on a love relationship that didn't really exist. I guess no one wins in this situation, even if both parties are sincere. She thanked me for listening. She said she had never told anyone for fear they would judge her. I told her I would never do such a thing. God knows I had made my share of bad decisions in my life. We held each other for a while. There was total silence. She had confided in me and told me something no one else knew. She'd realized her mistake and I realized how she felt being in a relationship with an unknown, she knew she would never meet. I also realized *I* now was the one she needed, much like she needed him. What I'm sure she didn't realize was how much I needed *her*. There was something else she didn't realize; something I had learned from her confiding in me.

Never in my wildest dreams, would I have suspected destiny to play out as it had; much like the chances of someone winning millions from a lottery whose odds of winning are 1 in 150,000,000, and yet someone always wins. As fate is unpredictable and as elusive as a butterfly caught in the summer breeze, it can also take hold of you and make your heart beat twice as fast as falling in love. Not only had I learned about Sarah's vulnerability, but also about our relationship; present and past. Sarah was Lilly. The same Lilly I had known, three years prior; the same Lilly I fell in love with online. What *she* didn't know was what I couldn't tell her for fear of resentment; for fear of destroying what we had. As fate would unexpectedly have it, I couldn't tell her *I* was the MysteryMan she fell in love with.

## ~From Ambivalence to Awakening~

After our morning talk, it was again time to get ready for the day. As she was getting ready, moving from this room to that room, all I could do for the longest time was stare; not looking at anything in particular, but just stare into nothingness thinking about what was revealed to me. How could this happen, I thought? How could I keep this from her? Would it be so horrible to let her know? Yes, it would be if it jeopardized our relationship. I knew it was best to try to forget it and consider it a moment in time that no longer existed. It was time to move on and think about the present. So, I did my best to forget, or at least ignore.

I thought about school, the class she was taking with me, and about the up and coming exam. I hoped she studied for the midterm. I knew I would be lenient with her, but I wished I didn't have to put her through the burden of studying.

When Sarah had finished with her getting ready and making sure she was presentable again, as she put it, she was off to her morning classes and I was left to wonder about many things that had happened in recent weeks. I thought mainly about my relationship with Sarah, but I also thought about my family; namely Joey, Derek, and yes, even Carolyn. I still considered her family even after the divorce. I guess it was due to years of familiarity that comes with years of wedded bliss, as well as the years that weren't bliss. Old habits die hard, as they say. It pained me to think of Carolyn as an old habit, but honesty is sometimes painful. I thought about picking up the guitar and writing a song for Sarah. I dismissed that thought right away, as composing music has to be inspired. Otherwise, the music is most likely not worth listening to. Not that Sarah didn't inspire me; she did. I simply didn't feel like writing, or doing anything that required much thought, quite frankly. I also didn't want to seem like a copycat. Ironically, what MysterMan did was something that was special to her, and I wasn't about to hijack that sentiment.

My thoughts started drifting, then, to thinking about the whole MysterMan relationship. What would Carolyn say about that, I wondered? She would likely say Sarah was 'one of those'. I knew what Carolyn meant when she said things like 'one of those'. My ex was not one to have an open mind about others and the naive decisions people sometimes make. She would discard her story as either made up, or simply stupid. There was a time when I could bring her around to consider the feelings of others, but that ended with our relationship years before the divorce. At any rate, I still thought of her as a good friend and had fond memories of the experiences we went through together.

I thought about calling Joey to see how his family was, but I thought it would lead to small talk, which requires too much effort. It's a sad state of affairs when you don't want to talk to family on the phone because it sounds too much like a lot of work. Nevertheless, sometimes you feel that way as much as you don't want to. Feelings are hard to deny, though, and I thought it would be better to call him at some other time.

I entertained the notion of calling Derek for about half a second. That call would have been a mistake. I would wind up leaving a voicemail that would have quickly been deleted, I have no doubt. I was sad after thinking that, but then realized what I had thought a moment before; honesty is sometimes painful.

I finally settled my thoughts on Sarah. As I thought of her, I looked around and saw my house empty. It was really quite a big house for one individual to live in. I suddenly felt as though home wasn't really home anymore. It felt empty without Sarah. Over the past few days, she had turned my house into a home. The meals that were prepared were great, the conversations we had were thought-provoking, and our intimate moments were rejuvenating. These thoughts made me want to avoid thinking about how our relationship could suddenly fail for whatever reason. I wasn't sure how I could survive such a life-changing occurrence. It dawned on me, then, I may have been more vulnerable than Sarah. So, I couldn't possibly tell her about the man she met online; the one she resented.

After a while, it was time for me to get some work done. I poured myself a glass of white wine and sat in the living room in complete silence; no music, no T.V., no distractions whatsoever. The sound of silence was so incredible, that I made no attempt at rushing to get my lessons done. I found myself closing my eyes and taking in the tranquility. I saw darkness, but knew the sun was shining through the window. I could feel the warmth on my face, but still feel the chill in the room and the goose bumps on my arms and legs. The taste of the wine was sweet and sour. It felt cool as I swallowed, but the alcohol warmed my stomach. As I drank, the smell of the wine replaced that of the coffee Sarah had made earlier. I could hear the silence of the room, interrupted occasionally with the sweet sounds of nature outside. The sound of birds and the occasional wind were soft through the closed windows that kept me safe from the elements of winter. I felt at peace and totally relaxed. I was alone, but not lonely. In all my days, I had never taken the time to indulge my senses to their full potential, as this moment. I credit Sarah for waking the senses in me that were dormant up to that point in time. This is the happiness everyone seeks, I thought. Soon, that peace would be replaced by the hustle of the day. But for now, I was in heaven as the song of the chickadee would affirm.

Eventually, as life would have it, I had to come back to earth and get ready for the day. I also became aware, for the first time in a couple of weeks, I should have been working on my next empirical paper. I'd been distracted and knew it. I didn't mind, though, as I had been happier than I'd ever been.

In my travels through the house before leaving, I discovered another note from her. This one, I found in my bathroom cabinet. It was on purple paper of course. The note had nothing written on it, but a lipstick kiss she had made with her own lips with hearts all around. This note, I kissed, and her fragrance surrounded my senses.

# ~Anxiety and Jealousy~

I arrived at the university before class began with much time to spare. It was about five twenty in the afternoon and class didn't start before six. Considering I was one to be late quite often, my colleagues would have wondered what was wrong, had they seen me in class before my time. I guess that's the kind of effect Sarah had on me. I found myself not knowing what to do with myself when she wasn't around. That particular time, I had decided to leave for work sooner than usual just to have something to do. At any rate, at least I had time to prepare to give the midterm exam every one of my students were in no hurry for. As six o'clock drew nearer, the students started to straggle in one by one. As each came in, I saw the same lackadaisical look on their faces as the previous drifter. It didn't upset me in the least. I was used to seeing that kind of enthusiasm at mid semester, when students are assessed to make sure they've learned something from all of their wonderful work. When Sarah came in, however, hers was a pleasant face to behold. She seemed happy to be in class, but I detected a hint of apprehension about how successful she would be with the midterm. She, of all people, should have known enough not to worry. I was the one grading the exam, and she was the one who had awakened my senses to make me feel alive again. Such a gift cannot be ignored and must be repaid; ethical violations notwithstanding. I tried to ease her anxieties with a look of confidence, as if to say, 'don't worry about a thing, I'll take care of it'. But that didn't seem to communicate too well. I didn't want her to worry but I couldn't very well make it known to the rest of the class I would grade her paper with the love she deserved. So, I decided to play the game and carry on as if she would receive no favoritism from me. I told the class they could leave as soon as they were done with the exam. I wouldn't normally do this to my other classes, but I was anticipating Sarah to take her sweet time and be the last one done so we could be alone. As time progressed, the students finished one by one and left. I kept a close eye on Sarah. She sometimes looked puzzled at some of the questions on the exam, and at other times, seemed to flow through it like it was second nature to her.

There were still a few students left in the classroom, when suddenly, Sarah got up and brought her paper to my desk. At first, I thought she had a question about the test, or more likely found some typo I overlooked. However, she simply dropped the paper on my desk, gave me a smile, and walked to the door. Stunned, I watched her as she was leaving. It was then I noticed my young neo Nazi student watching her leave as well. He seemed to follow her every stride towards the door. I recognized the look he had as his gaze followed her. It was a look I had seen many times; a look of want, or need, or lust.

"Mr. Russell!" I exclaimed, "Keep your attention on your work!"

Sarah stopped in her tracks and looked to see what was going on, as well as everyone else in the room.

"I am," was his response, "I just wanted to see who was leaving, that's all."

"I want my students to concentrate on their work, not allow themselves to be distracted."

"Okay." he said.

There was a hint of insubordination about his tone. I took his answer to be a little arrogant. I shouted back, "Do we have a problem?"

He quickly responded, "No."

After this short confrontation, Sean Russell put his head down and continued with his exam, while looking up at me every so often with disdain. I simply looked back at him with a similar response. I also looked around the room for anyone else who might have that look about Sarah. Everyone had returned to their exam work so as to not exacerbate a fragile and volatile situation, to be sure. I looked at Sarah, and she looked at me. She looked indifferent from my viewpoint, as she turned and left. I saw her close the door behind her and felt the same pain I had felt decades before when my childhood crush had done the same. I was suddenly taken with an anxiety of my own. I felt anger that someone might look at Sarah the way I did. I felt panic at the prospect of losing her. I wanted to get up from my desk and run after her but knew I couldn't. I felt even more anxious because of that reality. Then as I looked up towards the door, I saw Sarah through the window looking at me from the hallway. She was smiling. She waved at me and blew me a kiss. I looked around the room and made sure no one could see her. As everyone was busy with their midterms, I looked back at Sarah. She was laughing and shaking her head at how jealous I was. I smiled at her, as she blew me another kiss and left. I turned back to look at the class. Everyone was working and seemed totally oblivious to my exchange with her. I felt foolish, but also justified to be angry.

Finally, the last of the last had left and I was sitting at my desk in an empty room that, just moments before, was filled with students anticipating the worst and hoping for the best. I sat looking at the pile of fresh new papers on my desk, representing the midterm grade I would give to those who desperately needed to pass this course. I looked particularly closely at Sean Russell's paper. It looked like crap; mistakes left and right with too much of his own opinion inserted where it shouldn't have been, as well as not using the proper terminology in its right context, and full of typos. The essay portion was not well written either, nor was it conducive to a professional empirical paper. It was missing the critical elements required, and even the penmanship was horrendous. As I looked for more faults with Mr. Russell's paper, Sarah walked in.

"Hi." she said.

I looked up. She was radiant with a smile from ear to ear. After a moment of shock, I replied, "Hi."

"Are you quite over your jealous rage?" she asked.

"I don't like anyone looking at you…"

"The way you do?" she looked proud of herself to have been able to finish my sentence.

"That's right." I said with a little anger in my voice. More anger than I would have liked.

"Don't you know you have nothing to worry about?"

"Don't I?"

"No, you don't."

I looked down. I must have looked like I was pitying myself because she came closer and with both hands, raised my head so my eyes could meet hers.

"I don't want to lose you." I said, probably looking like a frightened puppy. I was shaking my head, but it seemed my whole body was shaking as well.

"You're not going to lose me."

With that, she gave me a kiss; a passionate kiss that could not have been mistaken for anything other than true love between lovers. I held her tight as we kissed. Then, she took her hands and began to stroke my face the way she did when we made love. All the while, I thought about how I hadn't told her I loved her yet, in all the times we were together. But I knew just then, I *did* love her. I let her stroke my face as I gazed into her eyes. I was so moved by being with Sarah that I completely forgot we were standing near the door. My eyes moved to the window of the door, and there I could see some students walking; moving to and fro. I immediately broke my hold of Sarah and motioned to the window. She quickly separated herself from me and tried to look inconspicuous and innocent.

"You think someone saw us?" she asked.

"I don't know."

"I don't want to get you in trouble"

"I know." I replied. After a moment, I continued, "Come on, let's take this outside. You go first."

She agreed and left. I then got my papers in order, grabbed my coat and put the lights out as I exited the room. I was locking up when I heard a voice a few feet behind me.

"Good night, Dr. Dina."

I knew that voice. I had heard it almost every week in class. We had had a discussion about his bigotry towards anyone who was of a different origin. I turned slowly to meet eyes with the person I was sure had said good night. It was Sean Russell. I wondered if he had seen me kissing Sarah.

Trying not to appear too anxious, I tried to stay cool and replied. "Good night, Sean."

"I'm sorry about what happened in there." he said.

"It's quite alright. All is forgotten."

"Is it?"

"Yes, it is."

"I was just looking at Sarah when she was leaving, that's all. Is there a reason I shouldn't have been looking at her?"

"No reason at all. I just wanted you to concentrate on your work."

He continued as though I hadn't said a word. "I mean, if you don't want me to look at her again, I won't. I wouldn't want that to affect my midterm grade."

I looked at him knowing full well he knew something was going on between Sarah and me. His, was a hateful expression. His lips were curled ever so subtly as to make it obvious he was trying to hold in a smile; a smile of perhaps knowing something he shouldn't know. I realized there was the distinct possibility he had seen us kissing just a moment before. Why else would he have been standing in the hallway seemingly waiting for me? This was unsettling. I began to wonder about my future with NYU, with Sarah, and with my reputation that had endured up to this point, a track record of being untarnished and without blemish.

I replied, "You can look at whomever you wish, young man. The only thing that will affect your grade is the effort, or lack of, you've put into your work. Is that clear?"

He smiled and said, "It's perfectly clear. Everything is perfectly clear. Good night, Dr. Dina."

With that, he left. I stood there at the door for a while, waiting and thinking. Waiting for what? I don't know; perhaps to have enough distance between me and Sean. But what I was thinking, was sure. I didn't trust Sean Russell. I had seen him interact with his friends and overheard some conversations. From what I'd heard, he was the type to start trouble and must have been a bully in his younger days. I had also heard him use racial slurs to describe certain groups and talk about them with violent tendencies.

Eventually, I hurried outside to Sarah. She was waiting in her car and flagged me down immediately when I came through the exit door. I wondered how much I should tell her as I approached her car. As soon as I got there, she greeted me with a kiss. I kept a close eye on my surroundings, as I didn't want anyone to see us; much less Sean.

She must have noticed there was something wrong with the way I looked, as she asked me, "Are you okay?"

"Yes, I'm fine."

I decided then and there I shouldn't mention my run in with Sean. I didn't want her to be worried as I was.

"You want to go somewhere?" she asked.

"No, I have some papers to correct, along with a million other things."

"A million other things?" She was beginning to sound as she did when I was trying to keep my father's condition from her. She had a tendency to draw something from you that you wanted to keep secret. There was no getting away with anything when she wanted to find out what was wrong. When I didn't answer, she repeated her question with that look only a mother or lover could give. "A million other things?"

"What I mean is there are so many things to get ready for, before we leave." I said.

"Oh, okay. I'm glad to hear you say that. I was afraid you might have changed your mind."

"Never."

"So, when will I see you?"

"I'll call."

"Are you sure there's nothing wrong?" she insisted.

"I'm sure."

I looked around before we kissed good night, then she was off.

I knew Sarah enough to also know she didn't believe me for one second. I'm not sure what she imagined at the time; probably not something as grave as what had transpired just moments before. I myself couldn't imagine how severe things were or would get. I wasn't even sure if anything dire would ever come of all this. Could it be all in my mind, I thought? I dismissed that arguable question right away. Something had gone wrong and it wasn't my imagination. How far it would go would depend on Sean and possibly his friends if he had the audacity to spread rumors, that is. Even if he hadn't seen me kiss her after class, just my jealousy alone when he was staring at her was enough to convince any young impressionable individual that I, at the very least, had some interest in one of my female students. Even in our advanced class of "Mind and Society" as well as in the hallways of the university, two plus two equals four.

## ~Mother of All Nightmares~

I arrived home a little past ten o'clock that night. All the way home I kept thinking of my career and the decisions I had made in recent weeks. What also kept coming back in my thoughts were Sarah's words when she asked, 'A million other things?' There weren't a million other things to do when I got home. There was only one thing I could do. As soon as I stepped through my front door, I dropped everything I was holding and ran to the bathroom. I made it just in time. There, I spent the next few minutes vomiting. When I thought I was done, I went into my bedroom and sat on my bed for a while to process everything that had happened. It's amazing what people put themselves through without seeing it coming. I thought I was so clever to believe I could keep living a discreet life with a secret; a secret that could end my career and disgrace me in front of my colleagues, friends, and worst of all, my family. People looked up to me. They expected me to provide a good example of what it's like to attain success and happiness, while still making time for myself. I felt guilt, remorse, and shame. At the same time, I was in love with Sarah even if I hadn't told her so. I wanted to keep that love alive because it's what kept *me* alive. After an hour or so of these thoughts going through my mind, I found my way to the bathroom once more, as I thought I would throw up again. I didn't, but the nausea never went away that night. I decided to gather up all the strength I had and take a shower. I let the water run down on me for the longest time and never really washed up. Just the sound and feel of the hot water on my face felt wonderful. It was as though I was rinsing the past few hours away. After my shower, I went directly to bed and tried hard to get some sleep. Even as my mind was racing, sleep would eventually come. But it would not come before a few repeated trips to the bathroom, which wound up being false alarms.

In the short period of time I was asleep, it was the kind of sleep everyone dreads; the kind where you're aware of your surroundings all night long. You're even aware of the time, if that makes any sense. At the same time, you're sleeping deeply enough to dream some nonsense meshed with the reality of the day. It was a horrible night, but my nightmare made it even worse. If I recall correctly, it was the worst nightmare of my life. Walls seemed to turn to some kind of muddy substance that was being flung all over the place by no one in particular. The muddy walls then dissolved to reveal mountains of sulfur, as I heard whispers I couldn't make out. There were many voices saying nothing in particular; just whispers. I found myself floating past the brimstone and back in that abandoned house from a previous dream, where the whispers were silent. The house was the same as I had dreamt it before, and I experienced all the same sensations. The furniture was the same, as well as all the rooms. I wound up being in the same room where I saw the dark hole in the wall. It was still there, but not empty as before. When I looked in, there was a face I couldn't recognize. Eventually, the face came into focus and I could see it was Sarah. When I called to her, her features gradually and slowly changed to those of someone else; that someone was Carolyn. She began to scold me for doing what she called the unmentionables with a dirty whore. Carolyn suddenly became whole, standing in front of me, and was wearing the white lace robe worn by Sarah just a few hours before.

"Is this what you want, Dr. Dina?" I heard her say, in a sultry voice I had never associated with Carolyn.

She began to disrobe, as I looked away and found we were not alone in the room. I saw Sean Russell smiling, as he was looking at Carolyn taking off her robe. Carolyn suddenly became Sarah again and walked towards Sean while looking at me. Her grin was evil.

"Will I get a good grade for this?" she asked me.

In a rage, I answered no as I pulled her back to me. Sean became incensed and started after me. I began to run but couldn't move. As he approached me, I tried to fight him off but couldn't. The more force I used to hit him with, the less I could swing my arms. I was afraid for my life. Sarah and Carolyn then became two separate individuals and they were laughing at me, saying I would get what I deserved. Suddenly, the walls began to dissolve again into that muddy smear as before. I then found myself in the classroom with my students present, as well as my two sons and father. Everyone, including Sarah, was pale and motionless as wax figures. Sarah looked dead as a corpse with eyes open. Suddenly, my father came to life, looked at me with sunken eyes, and began repeating over and over again, 'I'm ashamed, I'm ashamed, I'm ashamed'. It was then, I woke up in a cold sweat and found the beddings had dropped to the floor. I looked around me and saw darkness. I turned the light on, sat up in bed, and felt that wave of nausea smothering me again. After a while, I decided to get up to sit in the living room. As I sat in the dark with my eyes closed, I heard the clock on the wall chiming two o'clock. I immediately thought of Sarah's MysteryMan encounter because of the chiming of the clock, which made me feel worse. I also thought about how long of a night it would be for me. I wasn't sure if I was back to reality, or if I was still experiencing a nightmare, or perhaps a little of both meshed together in some forsaken place. I took some deep breaths, tried to relax, and stayed in that sitting position, in and out of sleep, until I heard the clock chime seven.

## ~Posters in the Dark~

To say the rest of the week was filled with anxiety, would be an understatement. I muddled through it, however. I tried to avoid talking to Sarah about the jealousy episode just prior and tried my best to concentrate on the trip we had planned. I was able to get through most of the midterm papers, and as I had expected, didn't think much of the results from most of the class. Sarah's, however, was perfect. I mean that with the most objective truth possible, given our relationship. Were there times when I thought she could have explained in greater detail? Yes, there were, but it's easy to overlook mistakes when you love someone. It becomes rather easy to explain the deficiencies away as a student's interpretation and justify what would otherwise be considered a lack of detail. In any case, I gave her an A+. I tried my hardest to be lenient with Sean Russell's paper, but again looking at it objectively, I feel confident he got what he deserved.

I did take some time on Thursday to stop by the school to get a feel for how things were; if Sean had indeed taken it upon himself to tell anyone about me and Sarah. I wasn't sure if he saw us at all, but if he did, the question of whether he would spill the beans, was incessantly on my mind. I stuck my head in the office door of the department chair. There was no one there, nor did I expect to see anyone. We're all busy, I understand that. I sometimes wonder why, then, I looked in that office, knowing full well finding anyone would be unlikely. Perhaps I was feeling desperate to find out if I still had a job, or worse yet, would wind up on the front page of the local paper. Part of me was glad there was no one there, and as it turned out, I didn't meet anyone of any significance who had the authority to decide my fate with the school. I stopped by my classroom. I'm not sure why. It was empty as it should have been. I peeked in the door window from the hallway and could imagine what Sean might have seen. If he was there when Sarah and I kissed, he definitely saw it all; with all of its incriminating, unethical, and embarrassing reality

As I peered in, I could feel the blood course through my veins. My head felt a rush of elevated pressure. There were no lights on. The blackness of the room gave an impression of lifelessness; of what it might be like to be alive in a coffin buried in the ground. I tried hard to see the walls and the various posters I had hung up; posters depicting the chemically induced effects, positive thoughts have on the brain; posters full of optimism. But I couldn't see them or even imagine what they would look like to me in this emotional state. Would they have seemed like insignificant and unproven rhetoric you hear when someone is trying to make the best of a bad situation; trying to make you feel better about something awful that happened? Would they have appeared to be a reflection of how you look when you're at your best, knowing full well it's not how you really look in the morning when you've spent the entire night being nauseous from guilt? Rather than seeing the posters with their fake idealism, I found myself happy to be staring at blackness; dismal as it may have been. That was a truer representation of what I felt. However, I couldn't just walk away not knowing my fate. I couldn't walk away with uncertainty hanging, and my neck hanging alongside of it. I couldn't walk away without doing something; something right; something wrong; it didn't matter. It was then, I decided my best course of action.

My hand shook as I unlocked the door. I walked in my classroom and turned on the lights. The posters on the walls were as I expected; optimistic, yet as fake as a physician appearing to be all-knowing, while being clueless and trying his damnedest to figure out what the hell could possibly be wrong with his patient. As I walked to my desk, I could feel my heart racing, as the next few minutes could very well decide my fate. At least it would be decided by my own actions and on my own terms, not someone else's. I was okay with that. When I finally reached my desk, I turned my computer on. It took way too long for it to boot up because of my own impatience, but I was finally able to access the school's personnel file. As I searched, I saw names I recognized as my current students. These names seemed to be spying on me and telling me they were silent witnesses to my actions. I didn't care. Neither was I willing to let my conscience decide my fate. I paused when I saw Sarah's name and looked at it for a while. I felt as she might have felt when she saw the name of her online love, a couple of years before. I felt the same happiness and the same ache in my heart. I longed for her to be with me, but there were more immediate things I had to do at that moment. So, I continued to scroll. I finally came to the name I was looking for, with all the pertinent information about him; address, phone, email, and everything else about my friend Sean Russell. I stared at his name for a while also and thought about all that had happened in recent days. As I pondered all this, I became more resolute to go ahead with the only option available to me before it was too late. I picked up my phone and checked for messages. There were insignificant messages and junk mail that caught my attention, but soon realized I was only stalling. Finally, I dialed Sean's number and heard the phone ring on the other end.

"Hello?" His voice sounded weak, as though he had been woken up from a deep sleep.

"Hello," I said, "this is Dr. Dina."

"Dr. Dina? Oh, what can I do for you?"

"I like to give my students an update on their midterms before Spring break, that's all. Calling is better and more personal than email."

"Oh, okay. So, how'd I do?"

"Not too well, I'm afraid."

"What was wrong?"

"We can go over those details when we get back from break."

"So, you called just to say I sucked at it?"

"Well, there are just too many oversights in your paper to go into detail right now. I found a few questions that seemed to be misunderstood. The written portion was also lacking."

He began to sound worried, if not desperate. "Listen," he said, "I need to pass this course. I'm on the last leg of my graduate program and I can't start failing now."

"I understand that, but what can I do?"

"Did I fail it?" he asked.

"I'm afraid so."

My body was shaking when I told him that. I don't know if I was shaking from fear, anger, or if the room was simply too cold. I hoped he hadn't heard it in my voice. At any rate, there was total silence on the other end of the phone. He was thinking; maybe plotting, I was sure. I became anxious in anticipation of his reply. After a long pause, he began.

"Listen," Another long pause. "Let's be honest about a few things and try to work something out."

"What do you mean?"

"I saw something a couple of days ago in your classroom."

"I'm not sure what you mean." I replied.

"I saw you making out with Sarah Goldman." Well there it was. He *had* seen us kiss, but I also figured he hadn't told anyone yet. I had a feeling I knew what was coming next. I kept silent and waited for his next move. "You know it's a violation of school policy, don't you?" I stayed silent and waited for him to finish. He continued, "I'd hate for you to lose your job and be disgraced publicly. So, I think maybe you could find it in your heart to look at my paper again and see if what you thought was wrong at first glance, was actually correct all along."

"I see." I said.

"So, what do you think? Should you take a second look?"

I kept silent for a while, processing the whole situation and getting angry at what was unequivocal blackmail. Here I was with my student threatening to blow the whistle if I didn't pass him. I gave it some thought. I could easily have turned the tables, telling him I would pass him if he didn't say anything. But there was no guarantee with that kind of agreement. Besides, he got me mad as hell with his arrogant threat. I decided to go with my original plan, which would make his silence more absolute. It was my turn.

"Sean, listen."

"Yes?"

"In the written portion of the exam, I didn't find a citing page."

There was a pause.

"What do you mean? I gave you one. Anyway, what does that have to do with what we're talking about?"

"Well *you* say you gave me one, and I say you didn't. I explicitly told everyone to cite your sources, and you didn't."

"So? What are you saying?" He sounded confused.

"Plagiarism is grounds for dismissal." There was more silence. I could hear him breathing. It was heavy breathing. I finally broke the silence and continued talking. "It would be a shame if you were to be expelled from school so close to finishing your degree, don't you think?"

He finally answered with desperation in his voice. "I'll still tell everyone, and you'll lose your job."

"Go ahead." I said, "There'll be a long investigation process. I'll just take early retirement before the process begins. You, on the other hand, are not in the same position I'm in. You'll have to find another school and perhaps be subject to answering why you were expelled from NYU. This would be a permanent record in your file." I waited for a while to hear his response, which never came. I continued. "So, tell me again what you saw on exam day."

After a while, he said, "I don't know what you're talking about."

I elaborated slowly and deliberately. "The day of the exam after everyone was gone; what did you see when you looked in the classroom?"

He replied carefully, "I just glanced in as I was walking by and saw you at your desk correcting papers."

"Are you sure?" I asked.

"Positive."

"Good." I said, followed by a moment of silence.

"Can I have my exam back?" he asked.

"No. I'll go over it with you, but I like to hang on to them for future reference, if you know what I mean."

"Okay, I get it." After a moment, he asked, "Did I pass?"

I thought for a moment. "I don't know yet." I replied and hung up.

With that, I had sunk to a new low in my life. It was because of Sarah I had done all of this unethical, immoral, and now illegal business. However, I couldn't blame her. She was the cause, but not the perpetrator. She was the coveted jewel, but not the thief. She was innocent in all of this, and I was not. Somehow, I knew I would someday have to pay for my sins. But for now, I did what I had to do and hoped it would go no further or get any worse.

After I was able to contain myself a little, I shut everything off, stepped out, and locked the classroom door. I took one last look inside the room through the door window and again saw blackness. However, this blackness was especially dark. I couldn't see those optimistic posters, but knew they were there. They were a constant reminder of things that exist and are true, but you refuse to see. They reminded me too much of my dangerous situation with Sarah, I refused to acknowledge and put an end to. But I couldn't help it. I wanted, rather, to live in the dark and not be accosted with the truth. After a while of looking at darkness in the room, I turned to leave. On my way out, I noticed a poster on the bulletin board announcing another convention for professors for the last week of March. I gave it a resentful look, as I walked quickly past and made my way out the door.

I texted Sarah and told her I was on my way to pick her up and grab a bite to eat; not that I was hungry, with my stomach all in a knot. She immediately responded with a smiley face followed by a little heart, which made me feel better about things. I smiled and drove off. I promised myself I'd try not to think about the events of the last couple of days and try to focus on my going away with Sarah; a well-deserved vacation away from work and home. Although the bad thoughts crept in once in a while, I kept myself pretty busy making a list of things to pack. I made sure to not bring up what had happened, as that certainly would have ruined the vacation. What she didn't know couldn't possibly hurt her.

The following day, I called Joey to tell him I'd be away on business for about a week; that I would be leaving tomorrow. I didn't want him to start wondering where I was, should he have been in need of reaching me and I couldn't answer the phone. All was well with him and the family, so it was one less thing to worry about. I also hadn't heard any further from Mr. Russell, which was fine with me. Tomorrow couldn't come soon enough, I thought, as my vacation with Sarah would officially begin.

Sarah and I left Saturday a little after noon. I told her to bring her birth certificate or passport in case we wanted to cross the border into Canada. She loved the idea. She also made sure to let me know she didn't want to fly there, so I drove all the way. It was a seven-hour drive, but better than taking a Greyhound for ten. We stopped along the way for about twenty minutes to grab something quick to eat, so when we got to the hotel, we weren't hungry in the least. Both being exhausted from the ride, we unpacked quickly and decided to retire for the night. She took a shower, during which, and unbeknownst to her, I slipped something under the bed. When she came out, we made love before sleeping like babies until morning.

# Week 8

## ~The Morning Sun~

SHE woke me up from a sound sleep, that morning.

"What's the matter? You okay?" she asked.

I tried my best to come to life. I slowly opened my eyes and realized I was with Sarah. When I was feeling somewhat coherent, I replied, "Yes, I'm okay."

"You were jumping and shaking in your sleep" she said.

"Sorry, I had a bad dream."

"It must have been pretty horrible for you to jump like that. What was it?"

"To tell you the truth, I don't remember."

I tried to sound convincing, but she knew better. She gave me that look again. One thing about Sarah, is you could never hide anything from her. If there was something wrong with me, she knew it. She also knew when to stop inquiring though, so as to not upset me anymore than I was; but not this time. For a while, she just held me tight, which made me feel as safe as I've ever felt. We were lying there holding each other. The light of the morning sun shone through the cracks of the window blinds. The room was dark, as the blinds were down, and I could hear the sound of the heater humming its steady tone. Sarah's hair smelled like a Spring shower, even as she tried her best to fix it in an attempt to hide the messy hair of a good night's sleep. She was worried for nothing, I thought. She was beautiful no matter how disheveled she looked.

"Can you tell me what the dream was?" she asked. "And don't give me the same bull of not remembering. That, doesn't work with me." I waited for a moment, hesitating. She persisted, "Please."

It was a dream about a most negative outcome from my deception to her, my virtual assault on Sean, and everything associated with my general behavior and life-changing decisions. I couldn't possibly tell her about my dream without disclosing the events of the last few days. I also couldn't lie to her and make something up. She didn't deserve that kind of deception from me, even to save her from having the same worries I had. So, I changed the subject altogether, by whispering something in her ear; something I should have told her weeks before.

"I love you, Sarah."

She was completely taken by surprise, as she gazed in my eyes for what seemed like forever. I savored every moment of her smile. Her glow became as bright as the sun shining through the window blinds, and her batting eyelashes fluttered like a butterfly bathing in the morning dew.

She whispered back, "I love you, Raymond."

We kissed. I was truly and deeply in love with her. This was not the same feeling you get when you're infatuated or impressed with someone or how they look. This was real, complete with all of the emotions that come along with being in love; the fear of losing her, the jealousy, the ecstasy, the happiness, and many other emotions that are beyond human ability to explain. After we kissed, I reached under the bed and retrieved a present I had bought for her.

"Happy Spring break." I said with a smile, as she took it.

"A book?" she asked.

"Yep."

She read the cover, "Spellbound!"

"I saw you have some of her books but wasn't sure if you have this one."

"I don't. I was meaning to pick it up, but I never did."

"Well, there you go. You have it now."

She looked at the front cover for a while, ran her hand over it as if to polish it, then turned it over to read the synopsis of the story. There, carefully taped to the back cover, was a little box containing a diamond necklace. She opened the box as her mouth opened and remained that way for the longest time. Nothing was said, until I simply started laughing at her astonishment. Finally, she broke her silence.

"Oh my God, Raymond!" she exclaimed.

"It's not much, but it's from me to you."

"Not much?" She was practically in tears, "I love it, Raymond."

After a moment of looking at it some more, she carefully removed it from its box and asked me to place it around her neck. She then gave me a passionate kiss, after which she gazed at the necklace again. The diamond was glimmering from the faint sun rays through the blinds of our window.

"Oh, I love it so much." she repeated. "Thank you."

"You deserve something as beautiful." After a moment of looking into each other's eyes, I joked, "I hope you like the book too."

"I do." She hesitated, then asked delicately, "Will you read to me?"

"What?"

"I'm serious. I want you to read to me."

"Why?"

"I want to hear a beautiful love story coming from you. I want to hear your voice behind the words." After seeing my look of amazement, she persisted, "Please?"

"Only if you're serious."

"I couldn't be more serious."

Upon seeing how sincere she was, I surrendered. "Okay, I'll read to you."

As she handed me the book, I saw the childlike wonder in her eyes. I wondered if parental love was missing in her childhood, or if she was just that much in love with me. Either way, I was happy to oblige and make her happy. Seeing her happy was liberating for me; all my troubles swept away like the sand caught up in the ocean tide; like the darkness of night replaced by the golden light of the morning sun. I turned a dim light on and began to read to Sarah. She listened intently and held me tight, as her necklace reflected the light and the morning rays.

# ~My Brother~

We were getting ready to go out for breakfast that morning, like we would the rest of the week. As we were about to leave the hotel room, she told me to wait a minute. I waited at the door and looked at her inquisitively as she went back to the dresser, fished in her pocket book, pulled out a pen and the little purple notepad, and began to write. I knew at that moment she was writing me a little note I was accustomed to receiving from her. I wondered for a while why she would be writing in front of me. I was usually used to finding these notes in some hidden places on my person or in my school bag, but not this time. It soon dawned on me the notes were no longer a surprise, but a well expected little present from her. I waited. When she was done writing, she came over to me, placed it in my coat pocket, and said let's go.

"Wait a minute," I said, "can I read it?"

"Not yet," she replied.

"Why not?"

"I like that suspense look in your face. It's so sexy."

"When can I see it?"

"When we're in bed tonight."

Surrendering to her wishes, I gave her a dirty look as I put the note back in my coat pocket, gave her a kiss, and we left the room.

We made our way to the Canadian side of Niagara Falls, where I wanted to treat Sarah to a kosher breakfast at a restaurant called Top Nosh not far from the border. To say she was impressed, would be an understatement. I had a feeling she had never left the country, or perhaps never even left the state. I was right. This seemingly worldly young lady had very little traveling experience. This made our trip even more interesting, as she was amazed at the least of places we visited. We sat down, placed our breakfast orders, and held hands as we talked. We had the usual 'How'd you sleep? I'm famished, it's a beautiful day' and that sort of conversation. Then it got personal again, as it always had in the past few weeks since I'd known her.

"Tell me about your childhood." she said.

"There isn't much to tell."

"That's what everyone says, but everyone has a story that's interesting even if they don't think so. I'm sure you do, especially."

"Oh really?"

"Yes."

I waited and thought for a while. "Okay." I replied.

"Don't think about what you think I want to hear. Just tell me." she said.

"Like what?"

"You told me about your brother a while back. You said your father beat him and he was institutionalized."

"Not a pleasant story."

"Still, I want to know." She looked at me with wanting eyes as if this kind of knowledge would somehow make her a better person. Perhaps in some way, it did. She persisted, "Please?"

I couldn't resist her childlike curiosity. I reluctantly recounted the story. "My brother came home from school one day crying in fear. My mother asked what the matter was. He told her he had seen some pigs on the school bus that were following him. My mother thought he was talking metaphorically; that he had run into some bullies who wouldn't leave him alone or something of that nature. But she soon learned he was being quite literal."

"He was delusional?" she asked.

"Yes, he was. He was seeing things. That marked the first sign of his condition."

"What was the diagnosis?"

"Well in those days, the doctors did the best they could with the knowledge they had."

"Didn't they use chlor...?" She tried hard to remember the drug.

"Chlorpromazine." I said.

"That's it." she replied, making an I-should-have-known face.

"Well, the drug was discovered around that time, but I doubt it was widely used right away."

"So, what did they do?"

"I don't really know; having been as young as I was. I'm sure they probably just sedated the worst cases and institutionalized them."

"Is that what they did to your brother?"

"Yeah. I remember that day. I was too young to be in school, so I was home when he came home. He was hysterical and my mother tried her best to calm him, to no avail. Finally, she called the local doctor. In those days, doctors made house calls. She described his hysteria, so the doctor came ready with a syringe to calm him down. When the doctor walked in, my brother completely freaked out. I watched my brother crying and screaming, as they were trying to hold him down. Then I saw the doctor give him a shot in the arm. I don't know what it was, but my brother immediately became limp and passed out. The doctor said it was a sedative. He advised my mother to have him placed where he could get twenty-four-hour care."

"I'm sorry. It must have been awful for your whole family."

"It was, but he had ups and downs. Some days were better than others."

"You must have been afraid at that age?"

"Yes, I was. I was afraid of him because I didn't know if he was dangerous. At times he talked violently; saying he wanted to kill so and so. Most of the time, though, he was passive; just laughing to himself and things like that. But I was also mainly afraid that it would happen to me. It was a real fear of mine; knowing that if it happened to my brother, it could happen to me. Sometimes, I would hear things and looked around intently to make sure there indeed was something to hear. As it turns out, I was being paranoid for nothing."

"Well, who could blame you? You were just a young boy seeing what his brother was going through."

"It took me a while to get over it."

"I can only imagine how your parents felt, too."

"My father hated the fact he wasn't normal."

"Was that the reason he used to beat him?"

"I can't prove it, but I'm sure that's what it was. My mother, on the other hand, was more emotional about it."

"*I* would be."

"My brother wasn't sick all the time, though. There were times when they would institutionalize him for months at a time, where he would get better. Then, he'd come home and didn't appear to have any symptoms but was heavily medicated. He'd be like that for a few months, but then relapse and have to be taken away again. He knew when he would relapse too. He'd be living a fairly normal life at home, then all of a sudden he'd start acting strange."

"Like what?"

"Like he'd look for the milk in the oven or the cupboard, then finally realize it was in the fridge. He'd also look for a glass in the wrong places. He became lost, gradually. That's when my mother would start talking to my father about placing him again. When things got bad enough, they made the decision and it was up to my mother to tell my brother."

"Did he suspect he was going away again?"

"Yes, that's what made things so bad. She would start telling him he had to go away again, and he would tell her he knew. He knew he was lost and started getting worse."

"But when they're like that, aren't they oblivious to the fact they have a problem?" she asked.

"He wasn't that far advanced with his symptoms. He knew there was something wrong with him, and that it was getting worse. The idea was to place him before it got too bad or let him become a danger to himself or others. So, she would make the necessary arrangements and schedule a date to bring him. I remember having such mixed emotions about his being placed."

"Of course." she replied.

"I felt bad for him, but on the other hand, I was afraid with him around the house."

"It must have been awful bringing him."

"It *was* awful. I had to go one time."

"What happened?"

"As I said, I wasn't in school yet and my mother couldn't find anyone to watch me, so I had to go that particular time. On the way to the facility, he was completely aware of what was happening and began to cry. He didn't put up a fight. He knew it was for his own good, but he cried like a baby. At one point my mother told him to stop because it made *her* cry and that made driving the car difficult. When I heard her say that, I cried too."

I noticed her eyes start to water as I was speaking. It was reminiscent of the day she spoke of her tutoring sessions with Natania. Fortunately, our food was ready and being served, so naturally the conversation ended there. After the server left, I decided to veer off a little and try to bring her lovely smile back.

"If I didn't know any better, I'd say that waiter has a thing for you." I said.

"Oh, really?" That smile began to show.

"Yes, really. Looks like you have a bigger portion than I do. Just for that, I'm going to read that purple note you gave me this morning."

"No, you don't."

She began to laugh, as she warned me of the terrible calamity that would befall me should I have the brashness to even glance in its direction. Mission, accomplished, I thought. She was back to her smiling self. We ate and laughed, as we usually did. No more was mentioned of my brother and the hell we went through because of his condition. But I knew her well, and knew it was a story that would stay with her a lifetime.

When we were done eating, she excused herself to go to the lady's room. I was looking over the check and signing it, when I heard a notification on her phone. I hadn't realized she had left it on the table when she left. The notification got my attention, and I instinctively looked up to see it sitting there with the screen lit up. I'm not one to spy but in this instance, I couldn't help but see what was in front of me. Her phone was facing the other way, making the text upside down from my viewpoint. But I thought I recognized the last name of the sender. The screen light extinguished before I could read the full name, but I had seen enough. Now, I'm not big on social media, and believe it's mostly a waste of time. On the other hand, I can understand why it might be appealing and even fun to someone who was thirty years younger than I was. I began to think if she was able to communicate with some faceless individual in a chatroom for a couple of years, she'd be more than able to carry on an online friendship of sorts with someone else she actually knew. I struggled with that notion against the possibility I was being too protective, or more to the point, completely jealous. As I saw her walking back towards our table, I tried hard to keep my feelings in check and keep a smile. I think I was successful, since she didn't seem to notice anything was wrong. I didn't want another scene I had displayed in class after her midterm exam but couldn't help feeling awful inside. I was sure I had caught a glimpse of the sender's last name, or at least a few of the letters. Even seeing it upside down, I was sure I had seen the name Russell.

## ~The Uncle~

We enjoyed the sights on the Canadian side and visited a few shops for some souvenirs before we made our way back to the New York side. We then found a beautiful view of the falls and sat for a while.

"Sarah?"

"Yes, Hun?"

It was the first time she had called me Hun. I was never big on little pet names, but that made me feel good. It was as though her calling me that, confirmed our relationship as serious; like the first time you squeeze a girl's hand and she squeezes back. I just sat there, looked in her eyes and smiled for a time.

"You going to tell me what's on your mind, or should I get my crystal ball?" she quipped.

"I'd like to have an honest conversation about our relationship." I said.

"Why do you want to be so serious?"

"It's hard for me to understand why you're with me and not some younger man."

"Oh, come on." she gave that not-again look.

"Please." I said.

"I love you, Raymond."

"I know there's a reason for real love, but still I'd like to know why. Why me, and not someone else?"

"What prompted this? Why are you so insecure with me?"

"You fell in love online a couple of years ago. Could it happen again?"

"No."

"How do you know?"

"Because I'm happy with *you.*"

"Aren't there guys who flirt with you every once in a while? What about the guys in your classes; in *our* class? They're more your age." I felt guilty about trying to extract information about her feelings towards Sean.

"I wouldn't be comfortable with them."

"Maybe you would."

"I can tell you with complete confidence I wouldn't be."

"Why not?"

"I dated very few guys before you. My most serious love was that ridiculous MysteryMan."

Upon hearing that, I suddenly felt a stabbing pain in the upper part of my stomach; nothing serious, I was sure. But it hurt like hell. Fortunately, I was able to keep my composure so as to not reveal any discomfort to Sarah.

"Why very few?" I asked.

"It's not important."

"It is to me."

"I don't feel comfortable around men; never have."

"Why? Did something happen?" She hesitated. I gave her a persistent look. The same look she was so used to giving me when she wanted the truth from me at all cost. I repeated my question, as the pain in my stomach finally abated. "Did something happen to you?"

"Yes." she said, finally.

"What?" She didn't answer. She just stared straight ahead at the falls, whose raging sound must have been reflective of what she was feeling inside. "What happened?" I insisted.

After a moment, she looked at me and parted her lips to speak. Nothing came out. I held her hand in comfort, as I knew she had been hiding something; a childhood incident, perhaps. Soon she began to speak; softly at first, in her reluctance. But soon disclosed her story in full confidence in me.

She finally softly disclosed, "I was raped as a child." Upon hearing this, I couldn't speak or respond. I could only convey my empathy through eye contact. From her look, I saw she knew how badly I felt for her. "My uncle." she added, with a tremble in her voice.

"I'm so sorry." I replied.

"I was no more than nine years old." We both stared at each other with a glance worth more than a thousand words. Nothing needed to be said, our expressions said it all. No words could possibly convey the emotions we felt at that moment. After a while of silence, she continued, "My parents had gone out for the evening. I think it was their anniversary. I don't remember, but my uncle was babysitting me. I hadn't noticed anything strange, but then again, what would a nine-year-old notice anyway?"

"This wasn't your fault." I assured her.

She continued without acknowledging what I'd said. "I remember it was getting late. It was dark outside. He told me to take a bath before bed, so I started filling the tub. As I was getting undressed, he came into the bathroom. At that point, I had everything off except my panties and was embarrassed that he would see me this way. He assured me he just wanted to make sure the water wasn't too hot. He came in and waved his hand in the water, and said it was just right. He then, splashed some water in my face, playfully laughing. I laughed too, out of courtesy. I didn't think it was funny and felt very uncomfortable. Then he left the room. When the tub had enough water, I shut it off and sat in."

I found myself wanting her to stop talking about it. I knew something like this is too difficult to relive. "You don't have to tell me anymore if you don't want to." I assured her.

"It's okay." She continued, "Soon, he came back in and I tried my best to hide myself. He stood above me and asked what it was that smelled so good. I told him it was my mom's bath oil. He then asked if it was soft. I told him yes. Then, he bent down and touched my arm. He started rubbing my arm up and down, saying how soft it was. I told him I had to finish, but he didn't respond. He just kept rubbing my arm, and I started feeling like I was going to cry. He must have seen that in my face because soon after, he smiled, started out the door, and shut it behind him." I waited to see if she would go on with her story. I didn't want to push her. Frankly, I would have been happy to not hear the rest. But she continued. "When I was done, I didn't have a change of clothes with me, so I came out with a towel around me. He looked at me scurry by, as I hurried to my bedroom, got in pajamas, and quickly got into bed pulling the covers over my face. It was then, I heard the creaking sound of his footsteps."

"You don't have to say anymore, Sarah."

"He told me it's a game adults play, then he got on top of me. I couldn't move. I screamed but there was no one to hear me. It was awful. It hurt." Her eyes were misty.

"Sarah."

As I said her name, she came back to the present as if woken from a bad dream. I held her tight, as she whispered in my ear. "You're the only man I can get close to. I don't know why, but I'm afraid to get close to anyone else. You're the only one."

"Why is it okay with me?" I asked.

She simply replied, "I don't know."

I whispered, "You can feel safe with me. I'll never hurt you."

She let out a heavy sigh upon hearing my words, and holding me as tight as possible, began to cry on my shoulder. After a time, she was able to compose herself, which surprised me at how strong she was. We eventually were able to enjoy the rest of the day sightseeing, and gift-shopping. Her story left me to wonder why she didn't tell anyone of her attacker, then I realized it was easier said than done. Many cases of rape go undisclosed for fear of some kind of backlash even from friends and family. I, in turn, felt there was no need to bring up what I had seen on her phone that morning. One emotional experience was enough for one day, I thought. I still felt uncomfortable about the prospect of Sean Russell messaging her by phone. Could it have been an attempt to tell her of what happened between him and me, and not so much trying to get close to her? I didn't know. But I decided I'd have to let it go, as well as many other thoughts, and make our trip as pleasant as possible.

As we lay in bed that evening, I asked if it was the proper time to look at the note, she had written earlier that day. She didn't say a word, but rather got up and retrieved it from my coat pocket. She danced toward me and handed it to me with a smile. I waited until she got back in bed before I unfolded it and read it. It read, '*Please, sing to me*'. I looked at her with a smile, folded the little note and put it aside. Then, I sang to her until we were both tired enough to go to sleep.

# ~A Much Smaller Scar~

I was tired but couldn't sleep for very long. My mind kept wandering. The street light shone through the cracks of the window blinds. I looked at the part of my hand that was illuminated by that light and saw the tiny scar I had gotten there when I was seven years old. I remember thinking how it pales compared to the scars on Sarah's legs from the car accident. The fact that physical scars last a lifetime, as do emotional scars, became manifest in what I saw in the quiet of the night. It made me think about how we never really forget when we get hurt physically or emotionally. All the more reason to not expose any truths about Sarah's online affair. I reflected on what she told me; how she'd reacted and was affected by the whole episode. I thought about what *I* went through during our little online game.

It was around the time Carolyn and I grew apart. Suddenly, we had very little in common, and didn't see eye to eye on many issues. She had started making up her hair differently and dressing to impress. Impress who, I thought? Most likely someone else but me. At any rate, I started feeling a little more independent myself. I was also familiar with chat rooms, from hearing my students talk to one another. One would invite so and so to this or that website and meet up. Not that I had any interest in those kinds of activities, but I knew of them from conversations I'd overheard at school. One day, after Carolyn got mad about something or other and stormed out, I decided to explore one very popular website I had heard of and see what my students were up to. It was a place where you could specify your location and chat with local people. I was sure to not use my real name but came up with MysterMan instead. To my surprise, I didn't notice any of my students' names on there. It then dawned on me they probably wouldn't be using their real names either for fear of spying eyes, or just to remain anonymous. I looked at what was going on for a while and got the hang of how to navigate the website. I soon was drawn to one named Lilly. With the help of online instructions, I asked Lilly for a private chat. I was stunned as she accepted my request, and soon found myself communicating with this unknown individual. It was a game. I was able to fool this person into thinking I was some intriguing and mysterious man with unlimited ability to razzle dazzle the one on the other end. It was fun to me and was surprised to learn Lilly was feeling it too. We played the flirt game for a little while, then decided we should meet in this same room again. It wasn't my idea, but hers. I certainly wasn't a big fan of deceiving people, but it seemed okay to do, as everyone was doing it as well. If I had known of Sarah's vulnerability, I would never have continued that pseudo relationship, which I knew could never exist in reality. However, I did continue and felt a certain satisfaction with myself; not only with fooling someone into thinking there was an actual relationship, but also with the knowledge that I was somehow getting even with Carolyn's indifferent feelings toward me, which seemed to grow with each passing day. I remember writing the song I recorded and emailed it to her. I took every bit of information I had about her and wrote about it with a lovely melody. I guess in some way, I fell for Lilly as much as she did MysterMan. How else would someone be inspired to write a song about someone? On the same day I sent it to her, she replied with astonishment. She told me she loved it and cried when she'd heard it. I didn't believe that then, but I do now. All the while, I had no clue as to how Sarah was affected, nor did I care. It was a game. I thought it was as much a game on the other end as well. I remember thinking I shouldn't divulge too much information about myself, or at least not true information. After all, I had a reputation to uphold and a family I knew I shouldn't disgrace. So, it went on for quite a long time until I decided enough was enough. As she recounted to me, I gradually went on the website less frequently until I received an email from her saying she understood.

I lay there in bed with the love of my life sleeping next to me, knowing I had deceived, and tormented her. I looked back at my little scar that was exposed by the street light. Then I looked further down towards one of Sarah's legs, which was exposed over the bed covers. *Her* scars were not illuminated by the street light. They were in the dark but were much more visible than mine. Her physical scars were greater than mine. The cause of those scars was more painful than mine. So were her emotional scars. I thought again how we never really forget when we get hurt physically or emotionally. I had hurt Sarah but couldn't apologize for it. I didn't want to lose her. It was that simple.

# ~Imagination of a Lonely Woman~

The last thing I remembered when I woke up in the morning, was looking at Sarah's scars. I was now looking at Sarah sleeping peacefully next to me. Her eyes twitched when I kissed her nose. I kissed again, and they opened.

"Good morning." I said.

"Good morning." she replied, with a hand covering her yawn.

"What would you like to do today?" I asked.

"Whatever you want. As long as we're together, it doesn't matter what we do."

I gazed into her eyes. After a moment, I brushed my hand on her cheek, which showed the wrinkles of a good night's sleep.

"What song were you reminded of when you heard the clock chime during your online encounter?" I asked.

"*That* was out of the blue."

"Just curious."

"Curious, or jealous?"

If she only knew, I thought. Who was there to be jealous about; myself? Although, I guess in some way, jealousy wasn't so irrational. After all, isn't there cause for jealousy when a woman wants you to sport a goatee because of some celebrity she likes who wears one? She still winds up with you, only modified to look like some other guy.

"A little of both, I guess." I joked.

"It was a song I used to hear my mom sing to herself; something called Tall Trees in Georgia."

"What's it about?"

She had a look of reminiscing, as she answered. "A lonely woman."

I gave a sympathetic smile. "Was that you, at the time?" I asked.

"Not at the time of the encounter, but I would reflect on how lonely I was before then. Then, I had someone I could talk to and confide in. Still, the clock chime brought me back to the days when I *was* lonely."

At that, I left it alone and changed the subject. But I never forgot her words, nor the title of the song. I thought I owed her the courtesy of at least listening to the song. I was curious about it, and how close to the melody of the chiming of a clock it was. I was also very curious about something else.

"You didn't know what he looked like?" I asked, knowing the answer.

"No."

"You must have pictured him in your mind, based on his responses and the little you knew of him."

"I could imagine him; how he looked, and even his facial expressions."

"Can you describe him to me?"

"Why?"

"Curious."

"No, I think we ought to leave that alone."

"Just humor me."

After a moment of studying me and assessing whether any danger or awkwardness would come of it, she replied, "Okay."

Her description of the infamous MysterMan was not me, which was exactly what I expected. She described him as someone having very little in common with me.

From his height to color of eyes, everything was as far from describing me as one could imagine. This didn't surprise me in the least. It stands to reason she would imagine this individual as the man of her dreams; and not me. Everyone, especially in childhood, has had a mental picture of what the perfect significant other would be like; from looks to personality. No one, conceivably with very few exceptions, have had the good fortune of finding that person in their lives. She must have noticed a look of disappointment in my face, because she stopped dead in her tracks and kissed me.

"*You're* the man of my dreams." she said, softly.

"But I don't have blue eyes." I replied jokingly, referring to her description of her dream soulmate.

She laughed and gave another kiss for good measure. It dawned on me just then that Sarah didn't look as I pictured Lilly either. I guess I was just as guilty as she was, when it came to imagining the perfect woman. What I wondered though, is why she never mentioned her roots, or her association with the holocaust and her grandmother when she was with her online MysterMan. I guess she was more selective and prudent than I thought she would be with a faceless individual, which I commended her for. This only confirmed how important I was to her, having confided in me face to face as she had. As we got closer, however, I started remembering familiarities between her and Lilly; little things like her interest in how people behaved, and her interest in pursuing her education in psychology. I just hoped it wasn't the case with her about me. I stayed awake until late on many nights during our stay, trying to think of some things I might have said to give her a clue. But to be sure, I was very careful about disclosing anything personal about myself during our little online affair. At any rate, that was the last we talked about MysteryMan for the rest of the vacation. I had a feeling prying too much into the matter would arouse suspicions and questions I didn't want to discuss or answer.

To that end and in the previous couple of days, I became more comfortable and confident with Sarah. There were times in the previous weeks when I'd felt undeserving of her affection, but that had changed. It changed with the honesty behind her past; the pain she had gone through; the lack of trust she had with other men. It finally occurred to me I was, indeed, someone whom she wanted to be with. I decided to savor every moment of that thought.

The rest of our time together at the Falls was wonderful. We had a great time and I tried hard to keep it that way. I didn't want to think about anything other than the fact that we were happy with each other. At times we felt like a couple in love on a honeymoon. We did the normal sightseeing, gift shopping, and adventure-seeking things people do at these places. We watched the sun rise, and the sun set every day. We counted stars and felt the cold air on our skin, while snuggling to keep warm. On the last night we stayed at the hotel, we didn't sleep at all. We just lay there talking all night. It was wonderful. In the back of my mind, however, I knew those moments would end. They would end soon. During the course of our conversations, the mention of going back home to the old grind, would sometimes rear its ugly head. But I was always successful in deflecting to another thought; a more pleasant thought. I had to. I needed to. What potentially awaited me back home, would come soon enough.

# Week 9

## ~The Tallest Tree~

IT was Sunday. Spring was in the air. It was that time of year when you feel hope coming back to life after a cold and dark winter season. The chickadee songs were all around, reminding you you're as young as you want to be. The trees were budding, promising you a spectacular view of green leaves that would eventually become even more beautiful, as the summer turned into fall. The sun was warm on your face, and for the first time in weeks, you felt more energetic. The temperature was warming, and a light jacket would suffice; not a thick and heavy coat. Spring was in the air.

We made our way back home, taking our time to stop occasionally to eat or simply look at what nature put on display. We made sure to enjoy every bit of what we had. We talked and laughed, but never cried. The crying, as necessary and important as it was, was behind us. We were as happy as a couple could be, and never once looked back with remorse.

On our way, we stopped at an old farm somewhere near Cortland that sold fresh fruits and vegetables. It turns out the merchant who owned the farm also gave buggy rides. It was something we hadn't done yet, so we decided to take the owner up on it. He got the horses ready, and away we went. The ride took us to remote parts of the landscape one can only see from a distance. The hills were vast, and the air was fresh. The reason we held each other so tightly was not because of the turbulence of the ride, but because it felt right. Then, we saw a cluster of astonishing pine trees on top of a hill about a quarter of a mile from a stream in the middle of nowhere. We asked the driver to stop for a moment, so we could take a quick walk. He had no problem with that. He stopped the ride at the stream to let the horses drink, as Sarah and I walked to the trees; taking photos of the beautiful landscape as we went. We took in the aroma of pine as we drew closer. The trees were flawless, as if no one had ever dared walk on such sacred ground to touch any of them for fear of damaging them. It was then I heard Sarah sing for the first time. She sang softly, *tall trees in Georgia...they grow so high...they shade me so…* Upon hearing her, I stopped walking. She turned back to look at me, smiling. After a moment, I went to her and kissed her passionately. No words were spoken, because there were no words needed. No words could relate what we felt. We then continued to walk to the trees. We picked out the tallest tree of them all and approached it.

"Can this be our tree?" she asked, with glowing eyes.

I gazed at her for a while, taking in her innocence, then picked up a sharp rock from the ground and began carving our initials on it. "Now, it's ours forever." I said.

She simply responded with a smile.

We stayed there a little while, but I could have stayed for an eternity. I'd never felt so alive before that moment with her. If there is such a thing as a soulmate, she was the one; the only one. Eventually, it was time to return to the buggy and continue our ride, but not before taking a photo of Sarah standing next to our tree. She stood there next to the tallest tree with rays of sunlight shining through its branches. But mostly, she was in the shade; shade that protected her from the harshness of reality and made her look more beautiful than ever. Nothing ever came close to comparing with that moment I had with Sarah next to that pine tree.

We finally returned and continued the ride, with the driver educating us on the history of the place, as we went. He might as well have been talking about any nonsense indiscernible to the human ear, because we were too much in awe of our surroundings to care. It was a life experience I would never forget or come close to experiencing again. But before I knew it, we were back in the car and on the road to home.

The old grind eventually returns, as much as you don't want it to. Sometimes it returns subtly, and other times with a vengeance. But sometimes it returns with a gradual intensity that you never see coming. Such was what happened in the coming days. Don't blink, they say, or you'll miss what's coming. I should have blinked. Perhaps, I should have kept them closed.

# ~The Whole Truth~

It wasn't something she wanted to talk about. I knew that, but the subject couldn't lie dormant. If Sean Russell was intimidating her somehow, I had to put an end to it before it got out of hand. I was sure I saw his name on her phone a few days before. I hoped I was wrong. I wasn't. On the way home, I had to tell her what happened; my conversation with Sean; how he wanted to blow the whistle on our relationship. I would also have to tell her everything; including my threat to have him expelled from school with a made-up story about plagiarism. I didn't know what she would think of me then. Would that be the last straw that would push her away? I couldn't bear the thought. But I couldn't bear the thought of his threatening her either.

"Did you get a strange message from someone in our class the other day?" I finally asked, while keeping my eyes on the road. I didn't really want eye contact.

"What do you mean?"

"On your phone. Did you receive a weird message when we were eating breakfast at the Top Nosh restaurant?" I wasn't looking at her, but I knew what kind of look she was giving *me.*

"Yes, I did. But how did you know?" she replied.

"You left your phone on the table when you went to the lady's room. I heard it ding and looked up. I didn't mean to look. It's just something you do instinctively."

"I know. But why do you ask?"

"I thought I recognized the name of the sender."

"Let's drop it." she said.

"Who messaged you?"

"It's not important."

"Please, it *is* important. Please tell me."

"It's just that guy in class, Sean."

"What did he want?" I asked.

"My, are we jealous again?" she joked.

I wasn't in the joking mood. "Sarah, please." I finally looked at her. She must have noticed the serious look in my face, because *her* look became serious too.

"He just wants to talk to me about something."

"About what?"

"He didn't say. I assumed it was school work."

"How did he get your number?" I was really curious about *that*.

"We all shared numbers when you gave us that group project to do. Remember? What is the matter with you?"

I hadn't remembered, but she was right. I had encouraged the groups to share numbers so they could communicate outside of school and get things done. I remember thinking it was a good idea at the time; not anymore.

"Listen," I said, "I don't think it's a good idea to get mixed up with him. He's trouble."

"I'm not getting mixed up with anybody. What do mean trouble?"

This was a side of me I never wanted Sarah to see; a side I was ashamed of. We were fine; happy. We had a great vacation. We confided in each other and shared our best and worst secrets we would never tell anyone else. But there we were trying to remain calm in a stressful situation, and in which I would have to divulge something ugly. It was then, I finally told her everything; the phone call I had with Sean; the threats made on both sides. I apologized to her for being dishonest, and a coward. I warned her about things she was naive to. I was completely honest; maybe too honest. Normally, I wouldn't be so telling for fear of losing the relationship with someone, but Sarah was different. I felt I could be totally honest about everything with her. There was a part of me that feared losing her, but deep down inside, I knew I wouldn't. Our love was too strong. As I was revealing all this to her, I heard the sound of another notification coming from her phone. She picked it up and looked at it. She remained silent.

"Is it him?" I asked.

After a moment, she answered, "Yes."

"What does it say?"

"He wants to meet me. There's something I have to know. That's all it says."

"Don't reply." I urged.

"I won't. What are we going to do?"

"I'll take care of it when I get home. Don't worry." I might as well have been talking to myself, because she was staring out into space not listening to what I was saying. I repeated, "Don't worry."

She looked at me and gave a worried smile. "I'll try not to."

The rest of the way home was pretty quiet. We were careful not to analyze too much. Lord knows, that can lead to unwarranted anxious moments. We still talked about it, though. She was sure to let me know she wasn't upset about what I had said to him. But she was obviously worried; not for herself, but for me. She even asked if we should take a break from each other to let it pass. At that, I replied a resounding no! I would not have some juvenile bully dictate what I should and shouldn't do; whom I should and shouldn't see. I assured her I would take care of it, and I meant every word.

It's moments like these that make me think of when I was just a child; back to the days when there were no worries, and not a care in the world. When you're that young, you don't think of life-changing moments. You simply go on living your life thinking about play and the needs of the present. You don't even have to worry about what you're going to do the following day. All there is, is the pleasure of enjoying a beautiful spring day as you watch a caterpillar crawling on the ground; wondering how in the world it could soon become free to fly. But not knowing how, was okay, because there was not a care in the world.

## ~Joey's New Job~

I knew exactly what I was going to do when we arrived. I just didn't know when I was going to do it. Until then, I warned her not to reply to any of his messages, as harmless as they might sound. She agreed. I knew she had the good sense of staying away from trouble, but it never hurts to make sure. As I was thinking that, the next thought that popped into my head made me sad. She had been taken in once, I thought. It was a moment in her life that would make a permanent impression on her. What was sad about that, was I was the one she had been taken in by. I was sorry for the whole MysteryMan thing, but it was too late and not something I could apologize for.

I dropped her off at her apartment when we arrived home. She had a few things to do and look after, and so did I. So, we went our separate ways for the time being, but not without my reminding her to be wary of any messages she received; especially from Sean. She told me not to worry about that and went on her way. As I watched her enter the house, I felt almost hopeless. I felt as I used to feel when my kids were sick with the flu or something, and there was nothing I could do about it. Nothing I could ever do would make them feel better. All I could do was be there, which was of little help as far as I was concerned. Such was the feeling I had at that moment with Sarah. There was little I could do to make things right. All I could do was deal with Sean directly, without knowing the kind of backlash it would create. Regardless of that, I knew what I had to do and was determined to get it done.

When I got home, I looked around to familiar surroundings. There's nothing like coming back home after some time away; the comfort of knowing where everything is, of taking a shower in your own bathroom, of resting your head on your own pillow; the smell of familiar things like candles that were lit before leaving for vacation; the sound the floor makes as you're walking on it. All of these things were signs of finally being home. As much as the vacation was enjoyable and would be desired again at some other time, there was still no place like home, as the saying goes.

After I hung up my jacket and put my things in order, I noticed I had messages on my answering service. Most were of no significance; sales calls and scammers claiming to be from the IRS telling me I would lose my house if I didn't return their phone call within seventy-two hours. My favorite was always someone claiming I had viruses on my computer and being so gracious as to offer to help, while I sit in front of the monitor and tell them whatever sensitive information they want to know. Just hitting the delete button on those calls is not satisfying enough. Too bad there aren't more vengeful repercussions to the scammers when deleting their messages; like maybe getting diarrhetic cramps for a few hours. I did get another phone message I was happy to hear, however. Joey had messaged me to tell me he had some good news to share. So, I poured myself some white wine and dialed his number. After a couple of rings, he answered.

"Hello?"

"Hey Joey, it's dad."

"Oh hey, dad. How was your trip?"

"It was wonderful. Nothing like getting away to clear your head a little from the routine of everyday life."

"That's great."

"Well, what's the good news?" I asked.

"Well, I got a promotion offer at work."

"Really? That's great!"

It's good to hear good news in the midst of worrying about other stresses of life that one can always do without.

"Yeah, they want me to oversee the marketing departments of a chain of corporate offices." he replied.

"Are you serious? More money, I hope."

"You bet. This is exactly what Francine and I have been hoping for."

Hearing the name Francine brought back memories of the incident with Derek. It made me sad to think Derek was no longer part of the family, seemingly. Still, it was time to think about more pleasant things at that moment. I was talking to Joey and that was a good thing.

"I hope you're thinking about accepting the offer." I said.

"I'm definitely accepting it. It's going to be official sometime next week."

"That's wonderful, Joey. I couldn't be prouder of you."

"There's only one catch." he said.

There it was. I knew nothing could ever be perfect, or at the very least, somewhat acceptable. There's always something that happens to make good news, not so good. So, I asked, with great trepidation, "What is it?"

"I have to relocate."

My heart sank. Nothing prepared me for that. I suddenly felt very alone. After a while, I finally broke the silence. "Where?" I asked. I braced myself for the worst. I knew I'd have a hard time accepting the fact that Joey would have to move somewhere where I would hardly ever see him again.

"Seattle."

I tried to stay calm. "Wow, that's pretty far." I said, trying my best to sound matter-of-factly. But I think my tone revealed the shock I was feeling deep inside my bones.

"Dad, I'll come visit."

"Of course, you will. Don't worry about me. You take care of your new job and your family. I'll be fine."

"I wish it was somewhere closer, but you know how it is with these places. They need you somewhere, you take it or leave it."

"Well, you take it. You deserve it." I replied. Then I thought I'd better change the subject before I cried. "So, how's the family?" I asked. There goes that small talk again. We talked for a while longer about things that didn't matter. Then, we finally said goodbye.

"I love you." he said.

"I love you too." I replied, before hanging up.

That hurt. The family I thought I had, was gone. It was bad enough losing Derek, but it was also something expected. Ever since he was a young man, I knew he would someday leave and not regret it. He sometimes made it clear the family stood in his way. But suddenly, it was Joey's turn to leave and take my grandson with him, not to mention my new granddaughter, yet to be born. There were no ill feelings, thank God. But still, he was leaving, and it seemed the final chapter in my family's life. I didn't feel much like getting anything done after the phone call. If memory serves me right, I don't think I even unpacked anything. All I remember doing was staring at the wall for the longest time. After a time of staring, I simply sat down with my head in my hands, as someone would with a bad headache. I also remember thinking everyone was gone; my mother, father, Derek, and now, Joey and his family. Joey was leaving. Not that he lived very close, he didn't, but at least it was a drive away. His moving to Seattle was too far. For that matter, even if it was closer, I still wouldn't see him much. His job sometimes required traveling abroad. I was sure he would travel even more with this promotion. I was right.

Eventually, I went to bed and closed my eyes. I wasn't tired but it seemed the best place to be to not do anything or talk to anyone. I did finally fall asleep, though, and my last thought before I did was, although I had lost everyone, I still had Sarah; at least for the time being.

## ~Warning Sign~

Next morning, I woke up with a tightness in my chest. I tried my best to talk myself into believing it was heartburn or anxiety, but the more I tried, the more I feared the worst. I had trouble breathing, which was not a good sign, but not a deciding factor for diagnosing a heart attack. Anxiety will bring on labored breathing, I thought. I decided to go to the ER anyway. Whatever it was, it wasn't good. I felt good enough to drive myself as opposed to calling the rescue, knowing full well it wasn't the greatest idea I ever had. But I felt if it was nothing at all but indigestion or something, I'd be wasting a lot of money paying for transportation to the hospital. At the time, it made sense to me. So I grabbed my jacket, got in the car, and went.

When I got out of the car and carefully walked to the entrance of the hospital, I felt myself feeling better than a few minutes before. The symptoms of whatever it was, were starting to abate and my breathing was no longer labored. I went in anyway. The waiting room was directly opposite the entrance and there was no one at the check-in window except the lady behind it. My reluctance must have been apparent, as I walked to the window to talk to the woman sitting there. I explained what my symptoms were and told her I was feeling much better. She immediately called for a wheelchair to take me in, as though she hadn't heard the latter part of our conversation. I was feeling better, I told her, but that fell on deaf ears. Before leaving the waiting room in my new ride, I looked around to see the poor individuals waiting to be seen. There was an overweight middle-aged man wheezing and coughing. He was with someone who appeared to be his wife, since she was always nagging him about the fact that he should have seen a doctor sooner, so they didn't have to deal with the ER. He didn't respond to those claims, but rather just gave her dirty looks in between coughs. A little further down the same wall of chairs, was an obviously pregnant woman who seemed to be alright. Perhaps she was with someone else who was taken in already. She kept looking at me, probably trying to figure out what my ailment was. Maybe I looked a little pale; who knows? On the other wall, was an elderly man with what seemed might have been his daughter. He had a cane and looked to be in pain, as the daughter was on her phone. She may have been texting someone, or perhaps playing an online game. I'd like to think whatever it was she was doing, was not in total disregard to her father's plight. To engage in the worst-case analysis of situations is sometimes unfair. I'm sure she was messaging a family member to tell them everything would be okay with him. I can only hope, because God knows people can be cruel.

Someone finally came to get me with the wheelchair, as the woman at the window had requested. He was a slender gentleman I would have trusted with my daughters, if I had any. He came to me smiling and asking how I could be made comfortable; asking if I was in any pain, and questions of that nature. I told him I was alright, and I didn't really need to be wheeled in. But he insisted with a warm and encouraging smile, as he said it didn't hurt to be on the safe side. I was not in any position to argue, so I sat as he took me in through a set of doors, on which was a sign that read *Thank you for not smoking.* I was immediately transported to one of the emergency rooms.

A doctor came in with two nurses, who tended to me right away. They hooked me up to an IV and an EKG that reminded me of the equipment my father was connected to before he died. They proceeded to take my blood pressure and check other vital signs. As the equipment was monitoring and returning results, I saw the nurses whose demeanor was becoming less urgent, begin to relax. I took that as a good sign. I heard them talk among themselves and nodding. Then the doctor made an announcement that I was happy to hear.

"You have a strong heart, it seems." he said, "How do you feel?"

"I feel okay now. Just a little nervous, that's all."

"Perfectly normal after any episode of uncertainty." he replied.

He then proceeded to ask me about my symptoms, and various other questions to determine the possible gravity of my condition. I assured him the symptoms had dissipated; that I wanted to come in just in case it was something serious. He commended me for that and then asked a question I didn't want to admit the answer to.

"Is there anything going on in your life that you think could bring on any anxiety or contribute to digestive problems?" he asked.

What went on in my head was, *oh yeah, doc. I'm sleeping with a girl young enough to be my daughter. Oh, and she's one of my students. I'm also about to do something illegal with some kid who's threatening to blow the whistle on us. Oh, and another thing, my family is gone and I'm alone, scared, and guilt ridden and sometimes I just want to cry or die, whichever comes first.*

Instead, I answered, "No, I don't think so."

"Well, we'll observe you for a little while and see if everything remains the way it should. In the meantime, we'll keep the IV in case we need it. Just lie back and try to relax." he said.

One of the nurses said, "If you need anything, I'll be right around the corner. Okay?"

"Okay, thank you." I replied.

At that, one of the nurses disconnected me from the EKG and they proceeded out of the room. Lying in the room alone, I thought and came to terms with the probable notion that I was making myself sick. I had allowed myself to be in a predicament I couldn't handle, and my body was starting to shut down because of it. Funny how your body tells you when you've had enough; that you're overdoing it. Warning signs can come in different forms. I thought briefly about taking a leave of absence from work and kept that course of action as a possibility but didn't want to rush into any rash decisions, especially when I was in no condition to do so. I would address that at a later time, when I was sure my health was okay. But for now, the first order of business was to relax and take it easy like the doctor advised.

When all was said and done, the doctor released me but not without my promise to follow up with my primary care physician. He had concerns because of my elevated blood pressure. I promised I would, but never did. I attributed the high blood pressure to be a normal occurrence when one goes to the emergency room with chest pain. I resolved to myself I would just take it easy for the rest of the day and be good as new the following day, when I would meet Mr. Russell for our next class. In retrospect, I now consider my decision to not follow up, to be a poor one. But such is life.

The rest of the day was spent doing nothing and got a little boring, to be honest. I talked to Sarah on the phone, but didn't tell her what happened with me, for fear of her reaction and worrying for nothing. After all, I was alright. She told me Sean tried to reach her a couple of times more, and she made sure to let me know she hadn't responded to him. We talked about our perfect vacation and how happy we were to have found each other, despite everything. After our talk on the phone, I decided to search and listen to the song she had sung on our little expedition to the pine trees on the way home. I found it, and immediately listened to it intently. It was a beautiful song. I could tell why it had made such a significant impact on her, and how she associated it with the chiming of a clock. Much like the chickadee sang *Cheek to Cheek* every early spring, the chiming clock would reverberate the first few notes of this song's melody. It was sad, but beautiful with everything it represented; Sarah being lonely, our having found the tallest pine tree, and the shade it provided for such a fragile soul.

# ~Trevor Adams~

When I said I knew exactly what I wanted to do concerning my friend, Sean, I meant every word. I wanted to confront him and make sure we could come to an agreement, depending on how reasonable of a person he was. If not, I would have to have him expelled. But somethings just don't go according to plan. Tuesday was finally here, and I was ready to conciliate with my nemesis. Having relaxed the day before, I felt well enough to carry on with my regular routine. Class would go on as usual. I was prepared. I would try to remain objective in my opinion of all my students, which would prove to be the most difficult task of my adult life. However, I couldn't let any bias thought, cloud my judgement of right and wrong. But I remained steadfast to what I knew had to be done.

Sean Russell was very much like a kid by the name of Trevor Adams I used to know and hate when I was in high school. He was a good-looking guy with dirty blond hair, blue eyes and a strong square looking chin. The hair on his chest was fully visible through the button-down shirts he wore, which he didn't fasten all the way to the top. This kind of conspicuous virility was unusual for a boy his age and all the girls admired it. All the boys, on the other hand, envied it. I just hated it. Not because I was envious, but because it perpetuated his arrogance and made him all the more hateful. He was a tall, muscular type who loved all sports. Being the star quarterback of the high school football team, he also had his pick of any girl in the school he wanted to date, none of whom would dare turn him down for obvious vain reasons. This was another reason for my hatred toward him. A guy like me had little chance of getting a date without the added competition. But as much as I hated him for all the attributes mentioned, I really hated him because he was a bully; a bully who could get away with it because of who he was. No one dared take on old wonderful Trevor. Not even the faculty because they knew how important the football games were against other school teams. We have to have school spirit, after all. He liked girls, but he would bully any boy who was smaller than he was, which most of the male student population including me were. He loved to pick on me. My stature compared to his, was night and day. Gym class was his favorite time for bullying guys like me. What greater opportunity to pick on a guy, than to be in front of other sports-minded guys and being emphatically critical about size and athletic ability? If gym class wasn't bad enough, the shower after the class was magical to a guy like him; snapping wet towels on our asses as we tried to hide our private extremities, lest they become the laughing stock of the entire school by way of gossip. I hated Trevor Adams and so did many others. He knew it and was proud of it, which made him even more hateful still.

Years later, as fate would have it, I met up with Trevor at a restaurant. My friends and I were in the mood for tacos, so we walked into a local Mexican restaurant. Who, but Trevor would walk in with some friends a little while after we were seated and eating, unbeknownst to me? They ended up sitting fairly close to where we were, as it turns out, but I hadn't noticed them walking in at all. I was with my friends without a care in the world, when Trevor walked up to me at our table. He looked at me a while and made sure I could see him clearly when I looked up. Then he spoke.

"Hey, Ray." he said. "Do you recognize me?"

I looked at him carefully and eventually made the connection. His, was a face I could never forget. After a moment of coming to grips with who he was and where he was, I responded, "Yeah, you're Trevor from school."

"How you doin'?" he asked.

"Alright." I said, hesitantly, expecting him to dump a glass of water on my head or debase me in some other degrading manner.

"List'n, I'm real glad I ran into you after all this time. Since high school, I been really feelin' bad 'bout what I did to you in school. I been feelin' like I wish I had the chance to apologize and say I'm sorry for what I caused."

I saw the sincerity in his face. He didn't have to come over and say that. I hadn't looked up at him when he walked in, so he had no reason to feel he should come over and at least say hi. No, this was sincere. I believed him when he said it had been bothering him for a while. Lord knows I've felt the same about certain things I'd said or done when I was younger. Here was an earnest, heartfelt emotion from someone who couldn't have a warm feeling in his bones a few years back.

I replied with some level of apprehension, "Oh, don't worry about it. It's okay." I still didn't trust him and didn't know what to expect next.

"I know what I did and how I felt about you and some of the others. I just want you to know that I feel bad 'bout it and I'm sorry."

I tried to make light of it and said with a welcoming smile, "Apology accepted, but not necessary."

At that, he held out his hand to shake mine. Years back, I would have spit in his face. But at that moment, however, I simply shook his hand and knew I was granted a wish I thought would never come true; for him to make good with the things he had done, which caused so much pain.

# ~Lines Crossed~

I had asked Sarah to do me the favor of skipping class that Tuesday night, to which she agreed. Sean Russell was not in class either when I got there, which I had mixed emotions about. I was glad I didn't have to put on a facade and make believe he was just another fine student of mine. By the same token, I wished he had been there so we could straighten a few things out, like leaving Sarah alone. I began my lecture about the significance of group behavior, social perception, conformity, aggression, and most importantly, prejudice. It was towards the end of class and in the middle of a group discussion that Sean came in late without saying a word and proceeded to just take his seat in a disruptive manner. I believe it was done deliberately, which I didn't appreciate. He took his seat and just stared at me, almost daring me to say or do the wrong thing. I would ignore him as best I could, but not before I gave him the attention, he so desired from the class.

"You missed my lecture on prejudice Mr. Russell. You of all people should have been here for that." I said, in an attempt to embarrass him for his rude disruption and emphasize his obvious bias towards certain groups of people.

He said nothing. All he did was stare. The rest of the lecture was just as awkward, until the end of our session. Finally, I dismissed everyone and stood near my desk as I watched them leave. As all the other students proceeded out with an expression that seemed to indicate they knew something was wrong, Sean stayed in his seat. I hoped they weren't privy to any details of what was going on, but even if they were, it wasn't something I could control. Finally, everyone was gone, as I stood there with Sean looking at me.

"If you're trying to intimidate me with that look of yours, it's not working." I said.

"I'm not sure what you mean." was his response.

I ignored his game of innocence. Instead I talked about his midterm paper. "You did a very poor job with your midterm, Sean, and that's not counting the plagiarism. So, I'd be playing it cool if I were you."

"I already told you I didn't see a thing that day. I was just passing by the classroom and looked in and saw you sitting at your desk"

"I'm talking about those dirty looks you're giving me. I also know you're trying to get in touch with Sarah. Why?"

"That's between Sarah and me."

"She doesn't want to talk to you, so leave her alone."

"I have school work I need to talk to her about."

"I want you to leave Sarah alone. Don't message her, don't call her, and don't go near her."

"Don't worry. Why would I want to go near that Jew bitch anyway?"

He saw my face change when he said that, which made him smile. He now knew how to get under my skin.

"You had better watch what you say about her." I commanded, angrily.

"You like that kike bitch, don't you?" he slurred, nonchalantly.

I became enraged. The mere thought of someone referring to her as something as vile as that name made my blood boil. I approached him slowly.

"You call her that again and you'll wish you never did." I said, slowly and furiously.

He just laughed and said, "She's a kike and I can't wait to get my hands on her. I'll show her what a real man..."

I didn't give him a chance to finish. I grabbed him by the collar and stood him up so our faces were so close, I could smell his putrid rotting breath. It made me hate him even more. All the while I had him where I wanted him, all I could think about was my childhood bully, Trevor, and how much I wanted to hit him. While holding him by the collar, all he did was show an evil smile that sent chills right through me. It was as though I was confronted with pure evil. It was then, he had the nerve to finish the sentence I had prevented him from finishing.

"I'll show her what a *real* man feels like." he said, as he stared at me in defiance.

My vision went dark with rage. I heard the impact and the cracking noise it made, but I wasn't sure what part of his face I hit. When my vision came back into focus, I saw him half on the floor and half leaning on the wall near the exit door. His mouth was open in an attempt to breathe, while blood was pouring out of both nostrils. His left eye was beginning to turn a yellowish tint, which soon would turn into an impressive shiner. He used his sleeve to try to contain his bleeding, and before long, his entire shirt was scarlet red. While he sat there for the longest time trying to handle the pain and control the bleeding, I thought about walking over and giving him a kick in the teeth but was able to contain myself while depriving myself of the pleasure. Just then, a random student I didn't know looked in through the door window. All he saw was me standing there and I was happy with that. There was nothing suspicious about my standing there in my classroom. Then he opened the door to inquire if I was alright. I guess Sean's impact with the floor and wall was loud enough to be heard outside the room. I, myself, had not heard anything, save the impact my fist made on his face as it happened, but I was also blind with rage. Upon opening the door, he immediately saw what happened. He looked at Sean, then looked back at me, and repeated this motion until the reality set in. I heard him ask, "Sean, are you alright?"

It dawned on me, then, he was a friend of Sean's if he knew his name; witnesses, I thought.

Sean answered, "Yeah, everything's cool. I'm fine."

To mitigate the situation, I added, "Yes, he's fine; just an accident."

By then, Sean had gotten back up on his feet with the blood that was dripping from his nose, which would presently begin to abate. The student who had suddenly witnessed the result of a violent situation, looked at us both again in disbelief.

Sean looked at me and began to scream, "You're done, Dina! I'll have your job and your pension when I'm done with you! And wait 'til I see your bitch!"

With that, he left with his friend as the friend continued tending to him and inquiring about what happened. I heard their voices fade as they walked down the hall. I thought I might have heard one of them say they needed to tell someone.

I stood there for a while just looking at the blood on the floor where Sean had landed. I stood, stared, and wished it hadn't happened. Many questions went through my mind just then. I wondered what would happen to me and my career. What did he mean to do to Sarah? Did he mean to hurt her in some way or just tell her a bunch of lies that would jeopardize our relationship? These questions, I didn't know the answers to, but it was time to face reality and all of its consequences. We had both crossed the line in a big way. I hated him for the anti-Semitic slur he called Sarah. I hated myself for having lost control and probably destroying my career. It was surreal and hoped it was a dream. It wasn't. After a while of thinking about gloom and doom, I went to the lavatory to get some wet paper towels. It was then I realized my hand was hurting badly. I wondered if the cracking noise I'd heard when I hit him, was his nose or my hand or both. With paper towel in my good hand, I returned to the classroom to clean the blood spill. In the process, I thought about how I used to tend to Joey when he had a bloody nose as a child. As I scrubbed, I cried and missed my family more than ever. I also feared for Sarah.

# ~Happy Place~

Everyone has a happy place. When I was younger, maybe eleven or twelve years old, I would sit by the brook near our house and let the sun shine on me. It warmed me in the early spring when there was still a chill in the air. I would watch the water flow and take in its song of peace as it made its way to whatever destination awaited it. Occasionally, there appeared a frog or some other creature enjoying the water and the sun as I was. I wasn't the type to run after it to capture it or maybe harm it, as some of my schoolmates loved to do. It would go on its merry way without a care in the world, much like me. It's sometimes hard to remember those carefree days with all the running around you must do as an adult just to keep your wits about you and fit into society's mold. But when you get a chance, slowing down and thinking about a time when you had no care in the world, brings you to a new level of happiness. You eventually, however, must come to terms with the fact that those memories are in the past and you're even further away from them as the distance from the East coast to the West coast. Just then, you experience a sadness as real and absolute as the joy those memories bring. The longing and yearning are as real as the feelings of comfort and security. The world is cold and unfriendly. Its ways are riddled with a history of war, hatred, and disasters brought upon by those who occupy it. But with all of its negative state of being and uncertain narrative of much needed peace and love, one thing is as sure as the sun rising in the East; everyone has a happy place.

If there was such a place for me at the moment of my encounter with Sean, I could not find it nor could I remember its existence. If it even existed outside my imagination, if it even existed within the reality of life, if it even existed only for my wellbeing and rejuvenation, it had fled quickly; as quickly as my fleeting youth.

# ~For All Eternity~

It was a tumultuous rest of the week that proved to be the worst of days. It turns out I had two hairline fractures in my hand. I don't know if Sean had a broken nose and would never find out. As the doctor wrapped most of my hand in some sort of cast, I felt the same tightness in my chest as a couple of days before. This time, though, I would ignore it and chalk it up to another episode of anxiety or indigestion. Fortunately, the symptoms subsided on their own again.

I never got a visit from the police, so I felt confident Sean did not press charges. Lord knows he had an eye witness and enough evidence on his face to do so. Then I thought, why would he bother? It would result in my spending maybe one night in jail and receiving some community service sentence or something. That was a slap on the wrist compared to the harm he could actually inflict by seeking to ruin my career and reputation, which I expected would happen for sure. But I had other things that needed my full attention at the moment before the shoe dropped. As I knew and expected, news travelled quickly on social media. Sarah had heard about what happened through her online friends, and she wanted to know if it was true. When I got home from getting my hand bandaged up at the clinic, Sarah was waiting for me outside my door. I saw her face wet from her tears, as I approached her. Before I reached her, she ran to me and hugged me tightly. After a moment, she looked at me with very sad eyes.

"Is it true?" she asked.

I couldn't answer right away. I waited for what must have seemed an eternity for her. I saw the sadness and worry in her face, with creases above her eyebrows and her head shaking slightly in an attempt to become ready for total denial. As she waited for my answer, she began to twirl her hair, as she had a custom of doing.

"It's true." I finally confessed.

"Why didn't you tell me?"

"I didn't want to worry you."

"I would rather have found out from you instead. Don't you know that?"

"I'm sorry. I should have told you."

"Oh my God, Raymond, what are we going to do?"

"This is on me, Sarah. It doesn't concern you. You don't have to worry one bit."

She responded with tears streaming down her cheeks, "What do you mean I don't have to worry? I love you. I don't want anything to happen to you. Don't you think that's going to affect me?"

I just held her tightly and said, "I know." After a moment, I took her hand. "Come on, let's go inside."

We walked in and I closed the door behind us. It took us a while to get a grip on everything that had happened, as I explained everything to her; from when Sean walked into the classroom to the time he left with his friend. I didn't tell her what he said about her, though. I didn't want her to fear anyone or anything, as I was sure what he said were just words to intimidate me. I explained that he would probably make trouble for me with the administrators, but didn't know how it would all play out, or how much trouble he would actually cause. I also explained how I have good friends at the administration level and could conceivably walk away with a reprimand or written warning. But no matter what trouble he would cause, I made sure she knew I was willing to face it, knowing I still had her by my side.

"You'll always have me." she responded.

"I know, and I'll always be there for you too, sweetheart. I won't let anything bad happen to you, ever."

"What if he calls the police?"

"I would have found out about that by now. He won't. Don't worry."

She gave a little sigh as I was used to hearing from her over the previous several weeks. We sat and held each other for a long time, not saying a word. We remained silent for about twenty minutes for sure. We were quite content to remain close and provide support for each other for such uncertain times. After our quiet time, I pulled out my phone and scrolled through the pictures until I happened upon the photo, I took of her next to our tall pine tree we had found on our way back home from vacation. We found ourselves smiling a hesitant smile, as we tried hard to think pleasant thoughts and put the previous hours behind us. We fantasized over the tall tree and perfect love; how I would come to her rescue, were she ever trapped in a dungeon by some evil Victorian villain. I would snatch her from his grip, as I made him pay for his monstrous deeds, then run away with her to where there would be warm sunlight miles away from any danger; where there would be real love, and not make-believe love; where there would be no one but the two of us sharing a life of fantasy. We would make a home in the midst of the tall pines and the stream, where she would wipe the perspiration from my brow and kiss me, and I would love her for all eternity. We laughed a little, perhaps at the silliness, or maybe it was a nervous laugh. It was difficult to be sure. Soon, to her amazement, I began to softly sing the song I had heard her singing; the song that reminded her so much of a few years before when she had fallen for an online love; the song that represented a happier time; the song that brought us both back to the time when love seemed to be just a game, but soon flourished into something that was so much more. When I began to sing, she cried.

She gladly accepted my offer for her to stay with me that night. She knew well I didn't want to spend the night alone with my thoughts. I knew she didn't either. As it turned out, we didn't sleep all night. We talked. We looked deeply into each other's eyes and read each other's minds, but mostly, we talked. It was an evening we both needed and wished it could have lasted for all eternity.

## ~It's A Long Way to Seattle~

We weren't hungry enough to eat in the morning, so I made some coffee and tea. We didn't know what the day would bring. Would everything go undetected and just go away, or would it bring disaster? I guess sometimes the suspense of not knowing is worse than the actual consequences, as bad as they could be. I didn't want us to dwell on impending developments, so we tried to enjoy our time as much as possible while we were together. She finally showed me some pictures of her as a child with her parents and grandmother. In all the pictures I saw, I never saw her grandmother smile. I asked Sarah about it.

"Bubbe never usually smiled." she said.

"Bubbe?" I asked.

"That's the Jewish name for Grandmother."

"Oh, I didn't know."

"Yeah, I can't really remember her ever smiling too much. I'm thinking it was because of what she went through, and all."

"As much hell as she went through, she's very lucky to have made it out alive."

"I wouldn't call it luck, actually. She told us there were many times she wished she was one of the ones chosen to die because she had seen enough atrocities committed."

"Terrible."

"Yes." she replied, softly.

I brushed the hair from her cheek to expose more of her beauty and kissed her. Just then, my phone began to vibrate and play the tune I had programmed for incoming calls. We looked at each other. I could see the fear and uncertainty in her eyes and wondered if she saw the same thing in mine. I looked down to see who was calling. It was Joey. I could feel the expression in my face change drastically, to that of a look of surprise and then despair. Sarah noticed and became very concerned.

"Who is it?" she asked with a quiver in her voice.

"It's Joey, my son who lives in Vermont."

"Oh good." she replied with a sigh of relief. "I thought maybe it was someone, like an administrator from the school."

I knew why Joey was calling, but I didn't tell her. It was time for him to pack up his family and leave. I wasn't in the mood to hear that, so I simply didn't answer the phone. The incoming tune played for about ten seconds, when it finally stopped.

"Why didn't you answer?"

I gave her the first excuse I could think of. "This is *our* time right now. I don't want anything to disturb what we've got going right now, that's all."

"What if it's an emergency, or something?"

"It's not." I replied.

She gave me that dubious look she had occasionally, when she knew she wasn't getting the truth out of me. "How do you know it's not? Were you expecting his call?"

I took too long to answer that. Was I expecting his call? If I said no, how would I know it wasn't an emergency? If I said yes, why would my expression change to one of surprise? She had me and we both knew it.

"Call him." she insisted.

"Sarah, I know what it's about. He just got a job promotion and he's taking his family out to live in Seattle."

She just hugged me at that moment. She knew he was the last of the family I had. She knew I would be left here with no one.

She whispered in my ear, "You still have me." I looked at her and smiled. "Call him and go visit before he leaves." she said.

"He doesn't want to be bothered with me."

She insisted, "Yes he does, or he wouldn't have called. Do it." After a moment's thought, I nodded in agreement. She continued, "I'm gonna get going now. You take care of what you have to take care of." With that, she got her things together, gave me a kiss, and left.

As soon as she was gone, I called right away. The phone on the other end rang for what seemed forever. Finally, Joey answered.

"Hello?"

"Hey Joey, it's dad."

"How are you?"

"Just fine, Joey. How about you?"

"Okay."

"So, what's up?" I asked.

"Well…"

There was a long pause and I knew he had bad news for me. "Go on, Joey, just tell me."

He hesitated and finally said, "I just found out I have to move tomorrow." There was reluctance in his voice.

"Tomorrow?" I asked.

"Yeah, they've been developing a new product line and it's ready to sell. They want me to be on the next flight to Berlin with the vice president of the company. I was supposed to move, in about four days but now there's a rush on things because of the CEO's schedule and they can't afford to wait."

"What about Francine? Don't they know your wife is pregnant?"

"Well she's not due for another three weeks. But at the first sign of any change, I'll take the first flight back. They know that already and they're okay with it."

"Well, they better be. What about all your furniture and everything else?" I asked.

"The movers have been shipping it out over the past few days, so I really have nothing left here anyway."

It broke my heart to hear him say he had nothing left here. I know he meant his possessions, but suddenly, I felt like I wasn't in his life anymore. He had nothing left to stay for. His life was in Seattle.

I tried my best not to sound choked up, "Well, you do what you have to."

"I was hoping we could get together one last time before the move, but I got blindsided. I'm sorry, dad. But I wanted to say bye before leaving."

I knew before I called, I'd be hearing him say he was leaving, but I thought we'd have a chance to get together one last time. I guess that's the way things go sometimes. At least he wasn't leaving without saying goodbye, much like his brother had. I wanted to cry, but I didn't want to discourage him or make him feel guilty.

"Well I'm glad for you, Joey, and I'm very happy about your job. It's a wonderful opportunity and I couldn't ask for better for my son."

"Thanks, Dad. Hey, but how are things with you?"

I wasn't in the mood for small talk. My son was leaving. Anyway, he didn't know any of what had been happening, so I didn't offer any information about it.

"Oh, just fine. You know me; just working and keeping busy with boring stuff."

As I was saying that, I heard him move away from the phone to warn his son about not getting too close to something or other, and also heard other commotion in the background. He was busy with the move. I'd been there myself; the whole family just nervous about being in a new place as well as the confusion and anxiety of moving. As much as I hated to think about it, it was time to say goodbye so he could take care of things on his end.

"Hey listen, Joey, I hope you have a great trip, and everything is smooth sailing. I'll call you."

He hesitated, then said, "I love you, Dad." His voice sounded different; as though he was holding back tears. I hurt at the thought.

"I love you too, Joey." He must have heard the same struggle to get the words out, as I had heard from him. I suddenly worked up enough control to finish the phone call without crying. "You take care of your family, now." I said with great enthusiasm.

"I will."

"Okay, don't be a stranger."

"I won't."

"Okay, bye."

"Bye."

I hung up the phone, and just like that, my son Joey was suddenly out of my life.

The little boy in me, emerged out of the depths of nowhere and surfaced front and center. I recalled the time my mother took my brother and me strawberry picking somewhere, miles from our house. My bowl was not very full, when I decided to stray a little to find the bigger berries. I strayed too far, as I found myself completely lost and alone. The fear I felt was too enormous for a little kid to experience. I began to cry out with tears flowing down my face, as I thought I would be lost forever; never to see my family again. Fortunately, my mother had heard the cries and found me.

These were my feelings after ending my call with Joey. I looked around, as if lost, and was filled with panic. I could feel my pulse pounding in my head. After a moment, I lay myself down in bed and cried out loud; loud enough to worry the neighbors, had the windows not been shut tight for the winter season, but not loud enough to be heard by the mother of the little lost boy picking strawberries.

I eventually messaged Sarah to tell her I wasn't feeling well, and I would see her in the morning. She responded in her usual understanding way, and after our mutual affirmation of love for one another, I went to sleep an exhausted man.

## ~Flower of My Life~

That Friday morning was the day I received the call from the Director of Graduate Studies at NYU. It was short and sweet. I was to meet him in his office first thing on Monday morning. I inquired about the subject matter of the meeting, and he simply replied it was an internal matter that required our immediate attention. I knew exactly what it was all about but didn't pursue the conversation. I acknowledged him and confirmed I would be in his office promptly at 7:00am on Monday.

I hung up the phone and thought for a moment; not about the phone call, but about how Joey and his family must be on their way by now. My career was no longer a priority in my life. The next few days would take me in a direction I couldn't control, so I decided to worry as little about it as possible. There was only one priority left in my life, and that was my relationship with Sarah. I messaged her and we made plans for the day. She asked if my hand was feeling better, and if I had called Joey to go see him before he left. To that, I replied a simple yes. I then took a shower, shaved, and got ready to pick her up at her place.

I was determined to make this a perfect day for Sarah; *the* perfect day. It was of the utmost importance that the day be perfect, as I had a feeling the next few days would be turbulent. On my way to pick her up, I stopped by the flower shop to pick up something special. I didn't want the normal dozen roses for a blue lady, I wanted something much more; something that would speak of eternal love and personify how I felt about her. I asked specifically for a bouquet of a mixture of the most romantic flowers I could think of; a combination of Stargazer Lily for our St. Valentine's Day we spent together weeks past, Pastel Carnation for her more subdued and introverted charm, Deep Red Camelia for our special perfect day, Blue Iris to represent the Goddess that she is, and a single Red Rose in the middle for the love and affection I have for her. The entire bouquet was adorned with myrtle, and fern. It was beautiful. I also stopped to get a box of Godiva Kosher Truffles, and a bottle of champagne. I wanted everything perfect.

The diamond necklace I had surprised her with during our vacation, made her lovely neck sparkle in the sunlight, when she came through the door to greet me with a kiss. Her eyes were radiant as usual, but became more so, to see the flowers I had brought. She admitted she had never seen such a beautiful arrangement, then took the time to put them in some water. As she was pouring water into a vase, I looked on her end table and was happy to see a bookmark halfway down the book I gave her. She'd been reading it and I felt good about having chosen a gift she enjoyed. When she was finally satisfied with the placement of her flowers, she seized a sample of the truffles, and we were on our way. She asked where we were going, to which I replied we were going to our perfect day. At that, she smiled.

As I mentioned before, it was a very mild winter, save for a few snow showers and the big Nor'easter. That day was no exception. It felt like spring; more like the end of the month of May instead of the end of March. So, we pretty much left our coats behind, in favor of sweaters. It was the time of year when puddles replaced snow mounds and the air had a clean smell, which gave life to the singing birds and the scurrying chipmunks.

We had breakfast at the Sunflower Cafe, after which we took a walk on the Riegelmann Boardwalk. The view was spectacular and couldn't ask for a better day. We made small talk, and I didn't mind doing that with Sarah. Small talk was not a waste of time with her. It was interesting and usually led to laughter or a smile.

"How's your hand?" She asked.

"Oh, it's fine. As long as I'm careful with it, it doesn't hurt at all."

"Have you heard any more about this whole ordeal?"

"No, and I'd rather not talk about such things today. Today is for us, not anyone else. Let's not talk about work and school, but just enjoy the day together. Okay?"

"Okay." she agreed.

We could hear the waves hit the shore, as we walked. The rumbling of the ocean against the rocks and sand added to the ambience, and we lost ourselves in the moment. We stopped for a while to hold each other and look in each other's eyes. She looked as though she were a model walking down the runway of a fashion show, with her hair flowing in the breeze of the morning.

Just then, she kissed me, looked back at me, and said, "I need to tell you something."

She looked serious. "Of course," I said with concern. "About what?"

"MysteryMan."

My wonder must have shown in my face. "Why would you want to talk about *him*?" I asked.

She replied carefully, "Because I know it was you."

I remained stunned for what seemed an eternity without moving or speaking. I just looked at her, not knowing what to do. I looked in her eyes to see if there was a hint of hatred towards me. There was none. I looked to see if she was playing an innocent game or joke, knowing full well I couldn't possibly be that guy. I saw nothing to indicate she was playing with me.

"What are you talking about?" I asked, trying to maintain a credulous tone.

"I appreciate you trying to spare me, but I'm not mad. In fact, when I started suspecting it, I thought it was very sweet, not to mention incredible." I was speechless again, and just stared at her shaking my head. She continued, "The first time I suspected it, was when you played those songs for me; when you sang to me at your place. I could hear in your voice the same voice I heard in the song my MysteryMan wrote for me. And now, it means so much more than it did then." I remembered. I sang those two songs and then I got the kiss of my life from her. I was still speechless. "That's why I brought up the whole MysteryMan thing a week later. I wanted to see your expression. And believe me, you were very surprised when you heard me say MysteryMan." She went on, "So, that was a giveaway, and so was when you talked about your brother who was unstable, as you called it then." she added. "And of course, the way you talk and the words you use."

Yes, I *did* talk about my brother and some of the things that were happening at home when he was young. I had forgotten that. She was also right about the way I talk.

"But what really gave it away was you talking in your sleep." I stared at her, as she continued, "You were talking about how happy you were that I loved the song you wrote for me as MysteryMan."

"You're not kidding, right?" I replied, hoping things wouldn't turn out too badly.

"No, I'm not. You mentioned the song by its title." She looked at me for a moment, then said the title of the song I had written for Lilly, my online friend of a few years before, "Flower of My Life."

My heart sank.

She continued, "In the song, you sang of Lilly, the flower of my life, the lavish color of my life."

She didn't look resentful at all, but I wasn't sure if this would be the end of everything we had. I choked up as I began to apologize. "I'm so sorry." I said, with the most remorse I'd ever felt.

"Don't be sorry. I'm as much at fault. Besides, I loved you then and I love you more now. We made a game of it, and now we have the real thing; the love that matters."

"But you told me you were so hurt." I said.

"I was, but that's in the past now."

"You told me you resented the person who played that game with you. You resented me."

"I said that, again, to see your face. I don't regret a moment of the time we spent together online, just like I feel blessed for the moments we have now."

"Still, I'm sorry." I said.

"That's the last time I want to hear you say you're sorry. Are we clear?" She had that motherly voice again; the tone of voice you don't dare argue with.

"We're clear." I replied. "Why did you wait so long to tell me you knew?"

"I wanted to see how long you'd keep it from me. I don't think you were ever going to tell me." she said. She was right.

After our walk on the boardwalk, one that was to be the most revealing in all the time I'd known her, we took a ride to the Coney Island Lighthouse, where we stayed until it was evening.

As we listened to the crashing waves, watched the sunset, and saw the light of the lighthouse getting brighter as the twilight sky changed from orange to dark blue and darker still, we talked and laughed about how ridiculous we were to be playing emotional games. We were both guilty of the same thing, and I was relieved in so many ways. I didn't have to hide that secret from her anymore, and we could talk freely about how we felt. As strange as it seems, we were also able to relive old times together. When we were online friends, there were many times we would get on a personal level of how we felt at those particular moments. To relive those times, was as reminiscent as looking at old pictures. In the darkness of the night, illuminated only by the moon, stars, and the lighthouse, I began to softly sing the song I had written for her; Flower of My Life. All the while I was singing, she held my arm tightly and put her head on my shoulder. When I finished, I began to sing Tall Trees in Georgia; the song brought to mind when she heard the chiming of her clock. To my surprise and much to my elation, she sang with me. Soon, we sat looking at the moonlit sky in silence. Finally, she looked at me and whispered that I was everything in her life. It overwhelmed me to hear it, even if I knew I didn't deserve this kind of love. We kissed before I picked her up gently and carried her to a secluded area. There, we made love under the starry sky with the ocean waves breaking on the rocks. She resembled a beautiful princess riding a white horse with her hair blowing in the wind, as I looked up at her with my back on the rough and sandy ground. My excitement became more intense, as her bounce made her knees dig deeper in the sand. I held her hips tightly as she brought me to the very edge of ecstasy, and with agony on our faces, we erupted with sheer pleasure that could only be reached with the soulmate of our lives. There was a chill in the air, but it didn't matter. What mattered was us; together alone, and in love.

I took her to my place that night and we talked for most of the overnight hours. The hours past as swiftly as a batting of an eye. We fell asleep finally with not a care in the world.

On the Saturday evening of that same week, I returned to the church I had neglected for too long. The pastor acknowledged my presence and smiled. I knelt and prayed to give thanks for the happiness and fulfillment Sarah brought to my life. I also felt something in the pocket of my jacket and thought perhaps it was another little note from Sarah. When I retrieved it, I found it wasn't just a little note, but a letter on her signature purple paper. When I read it, it made me feel more alive and I made sure to keep this one safely in my wallet so as to never lose it. I again gave thanks for having her in my life, but also for the strength to bear whatever would come my way in the coming hours.

# Week 10

## ~The Meeting~

IT all happened on the tenth week of that semester; the meeting, the attack (both of them), the arrest, the hospital, everything. I sometimes have difficulty thinking about it, much less talking about it. I must keep reminding myself it's all in the past, but it doesn't really help matters. I still feel all that happened; all the pain, all the hurt, all the shame.

I was in the director's office promptly at 7:00am that Monday. It's always good to get bad news out of the way as early as possible. As I approached his door, I was brought back to my student days in high school, where bullying was rampant. Getting in trouble was easy and the perpetrators were usually sent to the assistant principal's office for discipline. The uneasy feeling in the pit of your stomach was all part of the experience. So it was, for me on that day.

Dr. Price, The Director of Graduate Studies, was there along with the Dean, and the Assistant Dean of Students. I was surprised to see just the three of them there, as I thought there would be a lot more people.

"Good morning." I said.

Dr. Price spoke first, "Good morning. You remember Dr. Harper and Dr. Willis?"

"Yes, of course." I said, as we all shook hands.

"Can I offer you any coffee or anything?" he asked.

"No thank you."

We both sat in very soft cushy chairs on both sides of his desk. There was also a sofa, where the Deans took their seat. His office was bright and cheery. The walls were covered with pictures of students in cafeterias and libraries with smiles on their faces, as though that's what college is all about; socializing and having a good time. It's effective advertisement. Likewise, there were beautifully displayed pictures of the NYU grounds and buildings with their welcoming signs. The window curtains were opened to let the sunshine in, and between the sunrays and the warmth of the room, it was quite cozy.

Dr. Price was a very affable man. He was short and had a great sense of humor about it. His colleagues at the administration level used to call him Little Frank, which he didn't mind at all, but had all the wittiness about him to return the sentiment to anyone who understood his humor. He was one to enjoy a good roast and could deliver the same. But on that day, he was understandably more serious.

"Well, I'll get right to the point, Ray. We've been made aware of some very disturbing allegations." Price said with genuine concern in his voice.

I simply looked at him and waited. I expected him to be the spokesperson in the room, but Dr. Willis, the Assistant Dean, was the one to break the news to me. Willis was one of those women who belongs in politics or perhaps with a cushy job in the Department of Education at the federal level. Her hair was obviously dyed to make herself appear younger, and her choice of attire had the same purpose. She wore her glasses on the tip of her nose in order to look at you above them in a condescending manner, as she spoke.

"One of your students came forward with some damaging allegations of your having a relationship with one of your students, and perhaps favoritism especially with grading." she said with a judgmental gaze. She waited for a response from me, which she never received. She continued, "We've also been told you assaulted one of your male students as well."

They all looked at my bandaged hand, but I kept looking at her and waited for more. Finally, my attention turned to the Dean. Dr. Harper was a good-looking man in his fifties, with a full head of gray hair and beard. He seemed the most passionate of all who were there. Given more pleasant circumstances, I think I might have liked him. I guess I might have looked at him for an understanding gesture, which never came.

"Are these allegations true?" Dr. Harper asked.

After looking at all three of them, in turn, I finally spoke. "I'm aware of the individual who came to you with these accusations." I said. "I know who it is. It's Sean Russell." No one replied. I went on, "He threatened to injure one of my students and has shown a tendency towards violence and bigotry. He has also plagiarized on his midterm exam. He plagiarized his paper, which is grounds for dismissal. I already talked to him about this and he wasn't happy about it. In fact, he got very angry with me. This may be the reason he's telling you these things. He really should be expelled. I didn't want to come forward with this information right away to give him a chance to site his work, but it hasn't happened yet."

At that, Price retorted, "He said you hit him in your classroom. Is this true?"

Not knowing what to say, as my injured hand was a dead giveaway, I just shook my head.

"There was a witness, Ray. What happened to your hand?" Price asked.

"Accident." I replied.

Willis took over from there. "We have very stringent policies concerning ethical violations in this university." she said. "We expect all students and especially faculty and staff to behave appropriately according to those policies. We cannot and will not tolerate any violations as such, specifically as it relates to inappropriate professor, student relationships." She studied me before continuing. "We also have a strict sexual harassment policy that conforms to state and federal law. No one in this university is above that law and everyone is expected to refrain from any inappropriate contact. Moreover, professor and student romantic relations are not allowed to avoid violating fairness in grading policies, as well as conflicts of interest." She looked at the others, then turned back to me to resume reading the riot act. "Violence is also against university rules. We have expelled students engaged in violence or actions leading to violence with another student or faculty member. Surely, you understand these things." She spoke as if she had stayed up all night to memorize the student handbook on rules and regulations.

I replied, "Yes, I do understand these things, but nothing's been proven. I certainly hope I'm not considered guilty based on the accusations of a disgruntled student."

Price and I looked at each other for a while, then he said, "I'm afraid we're going to have to proceed with an investigation into this, Ray." His look became more business-like. "As for the plagiarism allegation, I'm also suspending the recording of your students' midterm grades pending the outcome of the investigation. There'll be no expulsion for plagiarism at this time."

Next, there was a moment of silence from everyone. It was as though they were giving me a chance to admit my guilt right then and there. The silence wasn't awkward but seemed to give everyone an opportunity to reflect on everything that had been said. If I had had the nerve, I would have had a Harper Valley PTA moment with them all. What were *they* hiding? What ethical violations were *they* guilty of? What sexual thoughts did *they* have about our student body? It was then, I couldn't help but think about the irony of having a Harper Valley PTA moment with Dr. Harper sitting about six feet away from me. One thing I noticed, though, was the room was getting very warm; to the point where I could have taken my shirt off and wiped the beads of sweat off my face, which felt rather flush. After enough silence, Price looked around the room and asked, "Is there anything else anyone would like to add?"

Harper spoke, "Ray, you've been an invaluable asset to this university for many years. The students love you and so do your colleagues at all levels, and we don't want to lose you. I promise you there will be a fair investigation, and we will stand by you to the best of our ability as far as the law will allow. But until the investigation is finalized, we have no choice but to place you on administrative leave."

If I could have run, I would have. If I were six years old, I would have run to my mother crying. But I was fifty-four and grown men don't cry in front of their colleagues. They don't run from trouble. They confront it head on and address whatever needs to be addressed. They solve whatever problem needs to be solved. They face the truth and banish the lies. They accept accountability for their actions and forgive others for theirs. But at that moment, if I could have run, I would have.

Just then, I got that tightness in my chest again. Only this wasn't just a tightness, as it had been before. This felt like someone threw a cinder block at my chest and my breathing was next to impossible. I don't remember much that happened after that sensation, but I do remember being on the floor in pain, looking up at the ceiling, and hearing someone shout, "Call 911!"

# ~Hospital Stay~

I woke up in a hospital bed. I later found out I was in the critical care unit at Tisch Hospital, where I had seen my father alive for the last time. I couldn't move, as my hands were restrained. Breathing seemed effortless, thanks to a ventilator my breathing tube was connected to. Aside from the breathing tube, I also had a feeding tube, so there was no way to talk. There were chest tubes, a catheter, an arterial line to monitor blood pressure I imagined, and of course an IV tube. I felt as though I was a dying patient, and must have looked exactly like my father did, weeks before. From what I could tell, it was dark outside. I didn't know if it was still Monday, or if enough time had elapsed to find myself into the next day. I don't remember much more than that for the simple reason of being heavily sedated, but I do remember feeling like I was dying.

I should have heeded the warning signs days before when it first happened. At the first sign of tightness in my chest, I should have been more careful or at the very least, followed up with my primary care physician. As fate would have it, I needed coronary bypass surgery to take care of a blockage. I wondered why it wasn't detected when I went to the emergency room the week before. All the more reason to follow up on it, I thought. It turns out, I was very lucky. After recovering from the successful procedure, the doctor told me I was fortunate to have been in the company of someone who knew CPR when it happened. I knew all who were in Dr. Price's room with me were certified to administer CPR, but I wondered who might have been the one to save my life. One of them, and possibly all three saved me. How terrible to think that moments earlier, I hated each and every one of them; regardless of their affability and apparent soft-spoken compassion, I hated them.

I was moved out of the critical care unit in the afternoon on the following day, but I couldn't possibly tell you what day that was. It was a day of drinking clear liquids and trying to tolerate small portions of solid food. Every once in a while, they helped me sit up on the side of my bed, where I would begin breathing and coughing exercises. I was told it was to reduce the likelihood of complications in the lungs. Since the tubes were taken out, I was able to talk a little with a great deal of effort. I asked if anyone came to see me or if anyone called to alert my family. The good people taking care of me didn't know any of those details but said they would find out for me.

Finally, someone who worked with social services in the hospital came to see me. She was a short woman with a soothing voice and a smile to match. I thought she would be the perfect soulmate for Dr. Price.

"Hi, my name is Celia. I'm with social services. How you feeling?"

I adjusted the bed a little to raise my head. "Not bad, considering." I replied.

"That's good. I'm here to help you make arrangements for post-hospital care. Depending on how you feel and how fast you get stronger, we can determine if you go directly home with a visiting nurse, or an aftercare facility."

"Oh, okay. I don't know where my clothes are or any of my possessions, so I don't have my phone with me. Do you know if anyone was called; anyone in my family?

"Someone at the school said they didn't have an emergency number on file for you, but we can take care of that today. You got a name and number for us to call?"

Much for the same reason I didn't supply the university with an emergency number, I didn't have a number to give Celia. My sons were too far away to offer any possible help. Even Joey was most likely in Europe. I thought about giving Carolyn's number, but decided the best person to help me was Sarah. So, I gave Celia her number.

"Could you call as soon as possible?" I asked.

"And who should ask for?"

"Sarah." I replied.

She wrote the name and number down, as she spoke, "Okay, got it. By the way, don't expect to be released until tomorrow at the earliest. The usual stay after an operation like that is usually three to five days. The doctor'll decide."

"Oh, okay."

"I'll pop in and out once in a while to see how you're doing."

"Okay, thank you."

"No problem. You rest, now."

With that, she left the room. Nurses came in and out throughout the day to probe and poke around to make sure my vitals were still doing okay. But I was anxious to hear from Sarah. I wondered how she would take the news of my condition, and if the reality of our age difference might have sunk in to finally push her away. I became more and more impatient but remained cool. Finally, later in the day, Celia came back to tell me she couldn't contact her.

"Are you sure you wrote the right number?" I asked.

"Well, her voice mail said it was Sarah."

Still I wanted to make sure, so I looked at what she had written down and it was indeed Sarah's number. It was so unlike Sarah to not answer her phone.

"Do you have someone else I can call?" She asked. "We need to contact someone."

The only other contact person left was Carolyn. After I gave Celia the new number, she left right away to make the phone call and I waited, wondering why Sarah wouldn't answer. Celia came back moments later and told me Carolyn was on her way to see me and make arrangements to get me home. Carolyn was always a good woman. It's a shame we grew apart, really.

Within an hour of the phone call, Carolyn was in my hospital room looking after me. She made sure I had plenty of water or ginger ale and propped me up in bed when I started feeling uncomfortable. She stayed for hours and took care of necessities like health insurance information and such things. She made plans with Celia that would be acceptable for my recovery at home, and at times just watched T.V. with me. She also made the necessary phone calls to Joey and Derek, and I was able to talk to both of them. It was nice to hear their voices, but I didn't like the tone of devastation and urgency they had at hearing I had a heart attack. The last thing a parent wants to hear is panic in their children's voices, regardless of the reason. I assured them I was alright, receiving excellent care, and the prognosis was very good according to the doctor. I informed them I would be home within a couple of days and their mother would be taking care of me until I was fully recovered. They were happy to learn I wouldn't be alone for the next few weeks. Joey offered to come home, but I insisted he concentrate on his work. We also engaged in small talk, which I adored for a change. I thought it was nice to talk about nothing, much to the irony of my attitude preceding the heart attack. But such is life. Sometimes we change when we learn of the value of life.

The third day of my stay at the hospital, was the day I was discharged later that afternoon. The doctor was happy with my progress and I had gone to the bathroom without much effort. So, Carolyn would take me home and make arrangements to get my car from the school and bring that home as well. Also, I was to have a visiting nurse come every so often to take vital signs, and such. Before I left, though, Celia came in to say goodbye and good luck. She also asked if I had gotten in touch with Sarah. I told her I hadn't yet but thanked her for alerting Carolyn. We said our goodbyes and she left the room. A nurse soon entered with a wheelchair to wheel me into the lobby.

On our way out, Carolyn asked, "Who's Sarah?"

"Oh, just someone I know." I said, hesitantly.

She didn't push the issue, as I'm sure she didn't want to put me on the spot; especially not, following open heart surgery. But I was sure the subject would come up again.

We finally made it home and I was able to walk by myself, but very slowly. I had never run out of breath so easily before the operation. They had warned me it would take a few weeks to get my strength back, but I still had no idea it would take so much out of me to walk. Once in the house, Carolyn brought me to my room to lie down which I didn't object to, as fatigued as I was. Sarah's toiletries and clothes were all around for Carolyn to plainly see, but she didn't question it or mention it in any way. I think she was being very careful with me. After she was satisfied I was all settled in, she asked if it was alright for her to run some errands and arrange to get my car. I insisted I was fine, and she should carry on with what she needed to do. I was sure to thank her before she left, and she humbly said it was her pleasure to help.

Before I fell asleep, I thought about the meeting I had had at the school and wondered what the status was of the investigation; if it had begun at all. Was my face on the front page yet with an incriminating headline? I knew I would have to address this at some point in the near future. I also tried to reach Sarah again, but to no avail. I was too tired to worry about the investigation but fell asleep wondering about what happened to Sarah.

## ~Confession to Carolyn~

It might have been Thursday or Friday, I really didn't know since time was not such a priority for obvious reasons. I remember waking up and noticing Carolyn was lying on the sofa she had made up as a bed. I got up to go to the bathroom, and when I got out, she was awake and up to see how I was feeling.

"I feel pretty good today." I said. "Still weak but not as bad as the last couple of days."

"Good. Coffee?"

"Can I have that?" I asked.

"You can, according to those instructions you were given at the hospital, but I picked up some decaf just to be on the safe side."

"Okay then, coffee sounds great."

"I also picked up some vitamins and mineral supplements." she said, as she cleared the sofa so we could sit.

I sat while she puttered around doing this and that. Soon, we were both sitting, sipping, and talking.

"Thank you for being there for me, Carolyn."

"Oh, don't thank me. I'm just doing what I should do for a friend. You starting to feel better?"

"Yes, I am. Thanks."

She didn't bring it up. I was the one to initiate the conversation I knew had to happen sooner or later. I decided it was time.

"You must be wondering why there are women's clothes and things all around." I said.

"Ray, that's none of my business."

"No but I want to tell you anyway. It's something I've been keeping inside of me for weeks and I feel I should tell someone."

"Well if telling is so important, I'm all ears."

I told her everything from my first meeting with Sarah, to the last night we spent together, and everything in between. I shared how I felt; how I battled with right and wrong, good and bad, joy and sorrow. I told her of how being separated from Joey and Derek was tearing me apart. I told her of my dreams. I told her of my wayward online secrets that happened even when we were still married, and how by some outlandish coincidence, Sarah was the one I flirted with. I told her of Sean Russell and our confrontation; the lying, the cheating, the blackmail. But mainly, I emphasized how Sarah had made me a different man; a better man. She had opened my eyes to what's important in life. She just sat and listened; listened to all I had to say and get off my chest. When the weight was off my shoulders, she hugged me as tightly as she could, being careful not to hurt me.

"Why didn't you say something sooner?" she asked, while still holding me.

I didn't answer that. I regarded it as a rhetorical question because she knew the answer. She knew what I did was shameful and anyone in their right mind would have looked upon my situation with reproach. We just held each other tightly for a while, without saying another word.

Finally, I asked, "What day is it?"

"Friday."

"I need to find out some things."

"What?" she asked.

"I need to find out about the investigation. I want to know if it made the papers and how badly I've been disgraced."

"I haven't seen anything like that about you, Ray."

"And why haven't I heard anything from Sarah?"

"I'm sure everything will be fine."

"No, I need to find out what's going on."

"Well, you're in no condition to go out. Is there someone you can call?"

There was. It was still early afternoon and I knew Dr. Price would still be in his office. I looked at my phone and there were still no texts or messages from Sarah at all. Worried as I was, I tried to call her and got the same voicemail I'd been receiving since being admitted to the hospital. I then called Dr. Price at the school. He wasn't in his office, so I left a message for him to call me as soon as possible.

Waiting is a terrible thing. You know what you want to do, yet you can't because you're waiting on someone. You're depending on someone else who might otherwise not even care about the importance of their response. Granted, there are times when situations can't be helped and no one is at fault, but there are also people who simply refuse to do their job with diligence. I'm sure Price not being in his office, was justified though. But it still felt terrible to wait for answers, so I tried my best to keep my mind occupied to not think so much. He finally called in the late afternoon.

## ~A Fragile Heart~

I answered the phone. "Hello?"

"Hi Ray, it's Frank Price." As soon as I heard his name, I thought Little Frank, which I would otherwise find funny but not at that moment. "How you feeling?" he asked.

"Much better than when we met in your office."

"Yeah, you gave us quite a scare. I'm glad you're alright now."

"So, what's the status, Dr. Price?"

"Well, there's been quite a turn of events, Ray. I'm not sure where to start."

"What happened?"

His voice was solemn, "There was an attack on Sarah Goldman." he said. There was a moment of silence on both ends of the phone, then he followed up with, "I'm sorry."

Upon hearing the news, I struggled with thoughts bouncing from one emotion to another; denial, anguish, fear, and many more I couldn't describe. I felt like my fragile heart was at risk of being damaged further.

"Is she alright?" I asked, in a voice that must have sounded very fragile as well.

"Last I heard, she was in critical care with multiple injuries."

I wanted a full explanation of what had happened. I had many questions and wanted details but couldn't bring myself to articulate any of what I wanted to say or ask. All I could do was shake my head and say, "What…?" Nothing else came out.

He went on, "She was found unconscious Monday morning; right around the time you were transported to the hospital."

"Oh God." was all I could say.

"You okay, Ray?"

"Yes. Do they know who did this?"

"Yes. They were able to identify the assailant through DNA that was found at the scene."

"DNA?"

"She was raped, Ray."

My eyes reactively closed tight, as I imagined the horror she must have gone through. I began to choke up and cry. She's such a fragile thing, I thought. I could also hear from a distance in the back of my mind, something I had heard a few days back, *'She's a kike and I can't wait to get my hands on her.'*

"Do they know who did it?" I asked with rage, sure of the answer.

"It was Sean Russell." he replied.

Just then, I dropped the phone on the floor and held my head in my hands. Carolyn must have heard the commotion because she came running. She ran to me, as I tried to somehow contain myself, but couldn't. She then laid me down on the sofa and picked up the phone, identified herself to Dr. Price, and inquired what was going on. She spoke with him for a while, then asked if we could call back later, to which he agreed.

She turned to me, "Ray, are you alright?"

Still sobbing, I was able to nod. She held me as she spoke softly.

"My poor dear, I'm so sorry." She continued to hold and rock me until I was able to compose myself. I eventually sat up, and we talked for a while. When she was satisfied, I was calmer, she let me call Dr. Price back. He picked up right away.

"Dr. Price, did they catch the bastard?"

"They have him in custody."

"I hope they hang him." I cried out.

"Any idea why he would do that? I knew he had a rough exterior, but I never would have suspected him of doing such a thing."

"No, no idea. He hated certain people."

"Yeah, they're charging him with a hate crime, along with other obvious charges."

"Hate crime?" I asked.

"Yes, the word Jew was written on the ground next to her. Fortunately, he's off the streets now."

"Too late." I added.

"Listen Ray, in light of what's happened, the administration has decided to suspend any investigation concerning the allegations against you. They've never been made public formally, and we're going to keep it that way. Your job is waiting for you when you're able to return."

This was of little consolation, but it was nice to hear. I thought about what Sarah said was written on social media, but that was not an official announcement. Those were rumors as far as anyone was concerned.

"What about the witness? I asked.

"The police already investigated any evidence tied to the attack on Sarah. They contacted us and the record shows Sean attacked you and you had no choice but to defend yourself."

"Thank you." I said.

"Just get yourself better and let us know if you need anything; extra time, or whatever. We'll talk about the rest of the details at some other time."

"Where did they take Sarah?" I asked.

"She's at Tisch on First Avenue, where they took you Monday."

"Okay, thank you for everything, Dr. Price."

With that, we said goodbye and hung up, as I just sat there in contemplation.

I wanted to be alone for a while. Carolyn understood. She helped me back in my room, where I remained very pensive. I sat near the window and stared out at the open space, where the trees stood tall and provided shade and shelter for all God's creatures.

# Week 11

## ~Fires of Hell~

ON the eleventh week of my relationship with Sarah, I made arrangements to go see her at the hospital. I called Tisch to make sure she was there and able to receive visitors. I was told she was still in the critical care unit. With that, I was not happy, as I knew her condition was still very serious.

Carolyn had been a big help, and she was more than willing to take me to the hospital to see Sarah. In many ways, her stay at my house was much like it used to be before we drifted apart. She also mentioned I had mellowed quite a bit, comparing me to the way I was when we were happiest in our marriage. She said I had changed. She wasn't sure if it was the heart attack or something else, but she saw me as a much more understanding and compassionate man. I knew what she meant. I had noticed the gradual change in me, as my relationship with Sarah grew. I became a better man because of her and I would be indebted to her for the rest of my life. I knew the important things in life because of her. I knew of the priorities in my life, no longer being work and other insignificant things, but rather family and loved ones, the elderly and the

Natania's of the world; taking the time to smell the flowers, listening to the chickadees, being aware of all my senses and enjoying giving as well as receiving. These were the important things in my life, and by virtue of these new convictions, I became a better man.

We were nearing Sarah's room, when I saw two people walking out from it. One was a short man, whom I assumed must have been her father. He had a black hat and sported a long beard, as well as recognizable Jewish attire including a prayer shawl, which I recognized as being a tallit. The one walking next to him was a shorter and much older woman who was supported with the aid of a walker. I noticed tears running down her cheeks. Her head was covered with a scarf, and the rest of her was covered with a long black dress. I excused myself as I approached them and introduced myself as Sarah's professor, while addressing the older woman.

"Excuse me but are you Sarah's grandmother?"

The man answered for her. "I'm Sarah's father and she is her grandmother."

I looked at her in awe, as she looked away from me. I wished right then and there I could have hugged her but didn't dare lest I violate any Jewish law.

"It's an honor to meet you both." I said.

Sarah's father nodded in acknowledgement, and they slowly proceeded on their way out. I suddenly felt so insignificant. How insignificant and lowly you feel when you meet a true survivor of horrors you never had to face. To realize this woman was so close to a horrible death and witnessed so many atrocities, was as humbling as any experience could ever be. I had survived a heart attack, but she had survived evil in its purest form;

scarred by the fires of hell. I looked back at them as they walked, wishing to stop them and talk with them all day. But that was a dream that would never come true. After a moment, I turned back toward Sarah's room and entered with Carolyn.

Sarah was lying in bed with all the necessary intrusive wires and tubes. Her head was bandaged to cover the multiple wounds inflicted by a crazed maniac with some kind of blunt object; perhaps a lead pipe or sharp rock, I imagined. She naturally looked frail with her eyes closed and not being able to speak or move. The beeping of the monitors seemed as ominous indicators of events yet to happen; good or bad. Again, I was humbled by what she went through; scarred by the fires of hell. As I looked at Sarah, I asked Carolyn if I could have a moment alone with her. Carolyn obliged and left the room.

I looked at her for the longest time before I approached. She didn't seem to be cognizant of my being there. Gone, were the smiles I had come to know. All there was left was a frail shell of the most beautiful soul I had ever met; one who would make such a difference in my life, as to change me from the person I was into a better person who understood the importance of happiness, sought in the most insignificant wonders of life. I walked closer to her bed and held her hand. She slowly opened her eyes a little, as I began to speak solemnly.

"Sarah...if there was anything I could have done to prevent this, I would have. I love you so much. I want you to know they caught Sean and he's being charged with a hate crime, so he'll be out of the picture for a long time. I can't wait until you're well again. We'll take some time for ourselves and go away again, like we did a couple of weeks ago. So, you take your time and get well because we have all the time in the world now. Every once in a while, I look at that picture I took of you next to our tree. It reminds me there's still goodness in the world; it's not all evil. It makes me think about how we met online to have a stupid virtual relationship, and then by some miracle, were brought together in real life to have a real relationship; to love one another for real. I thank God for that, every day. You've become my world and I can't bear to see you this way. So please, get better soon. I love you."

As I spoke, she never moved or reacted in any way. I thought perhaps it was the medication. I bent down and kissed her cheek lightly and began to sing. I sang ever so softly the song that had become so important to us; the song she was reminded of by the chiming of the clock; the song she had associated with our initial meeting that grew into a love relationship; "Tall Trees in Georgia". Her eyebrows raised a little and her eyes seemed to smile, as they had so many times before. As I sang, she looked into my eyes. Her eyes seemed to speak something her mouth could not; I love you, they seemed to say. But soon, her eyes began to close slowly.

I stopped abruptly as the beeping of the instruments ceased and began to emit a different sound; a sound that brought a slew of frenzied nurses and doctors into the room. They pushed me aside, as they worked desperately to revive her. I looked on helplessly as the sound of the instruments never changed. Her condition never changed. They continued to work on her until the very last moment of hope vanished and I, in turn, was scarred by the fires of hell. Soon, no matter how much or how long I would cry, she was gone.

## ~Beautiful Baby Girl~

In my grief, I felt terrible. Life couldn't have gotten any worse. But the day after Sarah's death, I received a phone call from Joey. He wasn't in Europe as I had thought. He was home in Seattle with his wife. She had just given birth to a beautiful baby girl named Sarah. The pictures he sent me showed how beautiful she was and how fragile. I told him to cherish every moment with her and protect her from the evils of the world, as there are many. They come in many forms and are sometimes unrecognizable and mistaken for good. There are also many things to learn in this world. Some of the most important and precious are learned from our relationships with others; our loved ones, our parents, and our children. One need not have a degree to be a teacher, as one need not be a student to learn.

# Present Day Continued

I remember those days like it was yesterday. It took me so long to get over the death of Sarah. I sometimes blame myself for not doing more to prevent it, but I have to trust there was a reason. After all, there's a reason for everything and everything happens for the greater good. But she will remain in my heart for the rest of my days on earth. At any rate, here I am now in the same nursing home I used to perform in. I've been in here since my stroke about three years ago. My room is small, but I don't need much room at my age. I don't mind being here, but I miss being independent as I used to be. I miss a lot of things. Every once in a while, someone will come in to entertain as I used to, but I don't think they're very good. Musicians are so critical of one another, I'll admit. But these so-called entertainers have a tendency to play old music just because the residents are old. And by the way, who wants to hear them do God Bless America, for crying out loud?

It turns out, Sean Russell got a life sentence for the murder of Sarah, among other charges. I sometimes feel guilty for wishing the worst for him, but I hope I'm forgiven for that. I'm sure the good Lord will see to it that justice is served in Heaven as on Earth.

I took an early retirement from teaching that year, even though the administration urged me to return. I didn't even go back to finish the academic year, in fact. I was quite tired after everything that had happened during that particular semester. Why risk a pending investigation, I thought? I think it was a wise decision on my part to call it quits. I was able to spend time with Carolyn, and occasionally, we even took a trip out West to see Joey and his new addition to the family. He's still doing well, and his family is growing, which I'm very thankful for. But I loved seeing their little Sarah growing. I began writing again in the abundant time I had. I wrote a few papers that were published, and my hope is it's done some good somewhere to someone.

Carolyn stayed with me, as I was recovering. She was supposed to stay until I was able to get around on my own again. But she stayed with me, as weeks turned into months and months into years. She said I had changed, and she grew quite fond of me again, like old times. It turns out we really got along as we did when we got married. We became good friends again, and our relationship eventually grew from there. We even became intimate again, but never got remarried. We remained that way until she died; natural causes, they told me; died in her sleep. I thank God for that, and I hope the good Lord takes me in the same way.

I haven't seen or heard from Derek since my stroke. He called me a little while after it happened to ask how I was, but that was the extent of it. I hope he's happy, but I'll probably never know. In any case, it's his life and I respect that. I only wish things had turned out differently with him. But who am I to judge?

Joey visits me once a year. Sometimes he'll try to come a couple times depending on his schedule with work, and of course, the family. When he comes, I'm usually able to talk him into taking me upstate. When we do go, I have him take me to the spot where Sarah and I had stopped; where the pine trees grow tall near the lovely stream. I have him wait for me at the stream where the horses drank so many years ago, as I walk to the tallest pine tree that became *our* tree; the one with the initials RS carved on it. When I'm there, I look out at the landscape and horizon to witness God's wonders. I sit on a large rock near our tree. This is the place I miss Sarah most, as I remain forever indebted to her for making me feel human. I make a ritual of taking out the last note she wrote me on her purple paper I had discovered while praying in church. I read it out loud as though she is there actually telling me in person. I read it slowly for the words to resound and be spoken in the way they should be:

*My dear love,*
*I can't begin to tell you what you mean to me and how you've changed my life. I love you dearly and will love you until the end of time. If I should be so blessed, I will always be with you until the end of our days and will cherish every moment. The time we spend together is not measurable by words or by earthly means, but rather by the spiritual bond God has intended for us. Thank you for loving me.*
*Love you always.*
*Sarah*

With misty eyes, I hold her photo next to her letter; the photo of her standing next to our tree. I look at it with love in my heart, and as best I can, begin to sing, *Tall trees in Georgia...they grow so high...they shade me so…*

The End

51188760R00176

Made in the USA
Middletown, DE
02 July 2019